HIGH PRAISE FOR ANNA DeSTEFANO!

"*Dark Legacy* combines Gothic overtones, secret government technology, a psychic heroine, a brilliant and charming hero, and a lightning-fast plot to create a sure winner."

—*New York Times* Bestselling Author Lori Handeland

"Anna DeStefano's remarkable stories of the healing power of love touch the heart with hope. One of the genre's rising stars . . ."

—Gayle Wilson, Two-Time RITA Award–winning Author

"This is what romance should be . . ."

—*RT Book Reviews*

NO WAY OUT

Maddie stared at Jarred as if she'd never seen him before.

"Sarah wants me to . . ."

"What?" he asked.

He'd held this woman. Kissed her. He'd helped her professionally every way he knew how. And he'd almost gotten shot for his troubles. Maddie Temple had him on the run from mad scientists, outside the bounds of local law enforcement, and hiding out in an overdecorated living room. All because of her twin sister's nightmares.

And that was when Jarred accepted reality, as he stared at the terror growing in Maddie's expression and promised himself he'd make it better somehow. If he had to go back to that morning and do it all over again, he'd still be right where he was—by Maddie's side every step of the way.

"You can trust me, Maddie. With anything. Tell me what Sarah's nightmares want you to do."

Maddie was clawing at the skin on her arms again. As if a part of her was trapped inside and trying to find a way out. "It's like we're . . . becoming each other."

Dark Legacy

ANNA DESTEFANO

LOVE SPELL NEW YORK CITY

To Andrew and Jimmy DeStefano
Wanting a "dream come true"
is the frailest of hope.
Your love taught me how to believe.

LOVE SPELL®

September 2009

Published by

Dorchester Publishing Co., Inc.
200 Madison Avenue
New York, NY 10016

Copyright © 2009 by Anna DeStefano

ISBN 10: 0-505-52819-3
ISBN 13: 978-0-505-52819-3
E-ISBN: 978-1-4285-0738-8

The name "Love Spell" and its logo are trademarks of Dorchester Publishing Co., Inc.

Printed in the United States of America.

10 9 8 7 6 5 4 3 2 1

Visit us online at www.dorchesterpub.com.

ACKNOWLEDGMENTS

There are so many people to thank for a journey that brings you to a place as wonderful as this. Too many to list, but here's to the good guys . . .

Many were there before . . . Georgia Romance Writers, from the very start; Anna Adams, who read my first rough pages and saw something worth writing a few more; critique partners—Lisa, Seressia, Tanya, Rachelle, Dorene, Missy, and Trish; everyone I served with on the GRW board—especially Emily, Traci, Maureen and Pam, who were my sanity even though they're laughing as they read this at the idea of me being sane. You're the strength that helped me begin.

Then dream became dubious aspiration . . . Michelle Grajkowski, agent and friend, you never told me I couldn't and you kept pushing until *Dark Legacy* was ready to find a home; Tanya Michaels, the sister I always wanted, you said this would happen and now a lifetime of free milk shakes are yours because you told me so; Bob Mayer, teacher, your weekend writing retreat smacked sense into my wanting to create something bigger, then it motivated me to make it happen. Without each of you, this novel and the series that follows never happens.

Until there was nothing left to do but work hard and believe, and even then I wasn't alone . . . Rita Herron, your encouragement while I pitched and waited was a lifeline; Patrice Michelle, you saw deeper when I was too immersed in story to find my way out; Lori Handeland, you took friendship and support to an unexpected place when you read and cheered and then lent your name to the party; Leah Hultenschmidt, editor and dreamer and coconspirator, you've made this wild ride possible and a blast from the first phone call—I'm so lucky it's your hand on the wheel.

Thank you all.

Dark Legacy

PROLOGUE

Gone.

Her father was gone. Dead. And Maddie Temple had felt every second of it.

She'd been across town studying with Keifer. Prepping for SATs—in the backseat of his VW Beetle. His hands in her bra, hers in his pants…sweet desperation and discovery and confusion, with just enough fear to make the bite of it sweeter. To make sure she was feeling her own need as much as his. Wanting him. Trusting him. Opening her mind and letting the world flood in, and her heart fill, and reason release.

No more barriers.

No more safe.

No more careful.

She'd been so close to finally knowing. To feeling normal, like other girls.

Then her mind had exploded.

She'd started to scream, and she'd kept screaming. She'd run from the car. From the shock on Keifer's face that confirmed she was a freak and she always would be. She'd raced through the rain and the dark, misty woods. Weaving, blind, toward nothing. Toward the sister whose unnatural link with Maddie was consuming everything.

Pain. Their father's pain. His shock and acceptance, both brutal and unfair. Every emotion he'd felt had rushed first through Sarah's mind, then Maddie's. Flashes of panic and denial. Silent screams that she'd heard from miles away. Overwhelming and obliterating and terrifying and endless. Then one final moment of blinding agony.

It had stopped so suddenly Maddie had stumbled to her knees, wind-shredded pines shifting overhead. She'd lost the drive-in burger Keifer had sprung for on their way to the mountain-rimmed lake that was a local favorite for parking. Emptiness had churned inside her. She'd been totally alone for the first time in her life. It had been excruciating.

It still was. After her mother's hysterical cell call, telling Maddie to get to the hospital any way she could. After Maddie's twenty-minute walk through the rain. After hours of waiting.

She'd been so sure tonight was the night. She'd been tired of hiding. Tired of being afraid of what would happen if someone saw her—really saw her. Her sister's mind had unraveled, but Maddie had been so sure she was free of it. She was finishing high school next fall, then heading for premed. She was going to have a life of her own. But it turned out all she'd really been was blind. Desperate, at sixteen, to feel something real. Something besides careful and cautious.

Now her father was dead, and her family was destroyed.

"He didn't suffer…" Maddie's mother sat beside her in the ER waiting room. Her posture—unnaturally straight—was denial personified.

Phyllis Temple's broken arm was in a cast. The gash in her forehead had required fifteen stitches. Her mild concussion was a concern, but she'd been thrown clear of the crash same as Sarah. Separated from the family car that had been pulverized, leaving Gerald Temple crushed within, to face the fire and the explosion alone.

"They said—" Phyllis swallowed. Her hand fussed with the bandage covering her sutures. She'd never been able to face life's shadows and failures. Every intrusion into the *happy* world she clung to was an assault on her mind. "The rescue crew said it was instantaneous. That he wouldn't have felt—"

"I know exactly what he felt!" Maddie shot to her feet. She paced across the too-bright waiting room. She clenched her fingers into fists. Rubbed her arms. Tried not to fall into the emptiness in her mind. Tried not to hate her mother and Sarah for being so weak, while Maddie had so far found a way to keep it together. "He… he…Daddy felt…"

"Don't, Maddie," her mother hissed. "You know I don't want to hear—"

"—the truth?"

"Maddie—"

"The truth is, Sarah's insane, and I—"

"You're fine!"

"Fine?" Maddie swallowed the memory of puking away panic and fear that hadn't been hers. "*Protect the secret at all costs*…Isn't that what you told us when we were kids? *Hide what you're feeling. No matter what. It's the only way*…Now Daddy's dead, and Sarah's somewhere in there"—Maddie motioned toward the doors leading to the trauma area—"unconscious, or worse. Out of her mind, after causing all this…And it's fine?"

"I never told you to hide anything." The guilt in Phyllis's expression said she knew she was lying.

They'd only been six, Maddie and Sarah, when they'd

found the crinkling, decaying piece of paper in the attic. And with it, a hand-drawn portrait of a woman, a relative, no one had ever talked about. A woman dressed in black with a scarf of some kind over her head, who'd stared at them from the picture. The writing on the paper had been hers, Maddie and Sarah had somehow known. A prophecy? A curse? Something about magical powers to be hidden until a pair of twins were born. Until a legacy could be released. A warning that both light and darkness would follow.

There'd been more. But Maddie and Sarah hadn't really understood what they were reading. Any more than they'd understood the strange things that seemed to always happen around them. Their mother had found them reading the paper. The picture and the prophecy were snatched away, disappearing forever. Within the week Phyllis had had her first full-on breakdown. When she'd recovered, she'd made Maddie and Sarah promise to keep what they'd found, everything they were feeling, a secret. No matter what.

The lies had snowballed from there.

"When is it going to stop, Mom? What else has to happen, before—"

"Tonight was an accident." Phyllis rushed to Maddie's side, grabbed her by the shoulder with her good arm, and shook Maddie with surprising strength. Her dark eyes flashed, crazed and dangerous—eerily like Sarah's. Then they cooled. "It has nothing to do with—"

"How long did it take?" Maddie pulled away. "How many years, until you could believe that all the other times were just accidents, too? Sarah, knowing what went on in the neighbors' houses. Both of us thinking we were crazy when we dreamed about the future—good things, bad things—and then watched our dreams come true. Sarah, changing other people's feelings. Weaseling out of one screwup after another because she could make people forget. Make them not care. We're not normal, Mom. Stop pretending we are! That anything is going to be okay. Sarah…We—"

"*You're* not Sarah." Phyllis's face was streaked with tears and blood. "You're not! You're fine. Sarah was always dangerous. Nothing seemed to help. Your father and I wanted to believe she would get better. The doctors gave us hope. Only there was nothing anyone could do to help her. But you're fine. It doesn't have to come true for you, too…"

"What doesn't have to come true? What are you so afraid of you wouldn't tell any of us, not even Daddy?"

Phyllis swallowed, her eyes too bright. Too large for her delicate face.

"He…He…" she stuttered. "Gerald loved you girls so much, we both did. And I let myself believe that that would be enough. But…but now he's gone. And Sarah, maybe she's gone, too. And it's all falling apart, and I can't…I can't take this. I…It's all my fault…Oh, God. Your father…Sarah…Where's the doctor! Why aren't they telling us anything? I can't lose Sarah, too. I can't lose you. I—"

Phyllis dropped her head into her hand, her legs crumbling. Maddie guided her to a chair. The scattered things her mother had said, and everything she hadn't, settled deep. The stupid curse would haunt Maddie for the rest of her life. It had something to do with Sarah's self-destruction. Phyllis's emotional frailty. Their father's death. All of it was tied together somehow.

But there would be no real answers. Not unless Maddie wanted to face the future alone. Phyllis needed her lies to survive. And Maddie needed her mother, her only remaining family.

"I'm not going anywhere," she heard herself promise.

The same promise she'd made to her twin, back before she and Sarah had learned to hate each other. When Sarah's mind had started becoming more and more fractured, while Maddie had somehow learned to turn off the noise—other people's voices and thoughts and feelings and pasts and futures, their hopes and dreams. "Whatever happens, I'll be here for you, Mom."

Sarah's head injuries were grave. She might never recover. Never again torture Maddie with the dark mysteries of their minds. Which was a relief, in a way. An unholy gift that Maddie's mind shouldn't be grasping hold of as if it were a lifeline. But what would life be like, without her twin's mania for a constant companion?

"She's going to make it." Phyllis rocked from side to side, her tears breaking Maddie's heart. "My baby. Sarah. It's not her fault. It's never been her fault. She has to make it. She just has to…"

"Mrs. Temple?" A man wearing rumpled scrubs rushed into the waiting area, reading a clipboard. "I'm looking for the Temple family?"

The doctor looked up. His frazzled expression said it was almost more than he could manage to focus on them instead of whatever was going on in the ER.

"How's my daughter?" Phyllis pushed out of the chair. "She was on my side of the car, not my husband's…not where the truck hit us. We were thrown clear and—"

"She struck her head against a tree." The doctor was absorbed in his chart again. "She was discovered unconscious at the scene?"

"Yes." Maddie had felt her twin's mind jerk from terror to stunned blackness, then to nothing at all. "She hasn't woken up since."

He nodded his head in agreement, reading statistics that were telling him what Maddie already knew. "We've stabilized her condition. The next forty-eight hours will be crucial. But I'm sorry. Even if we can keep her alive, the swelling to her brain could cause significant damage. If we can't reduce it quickly enough—"

"No!" Phyllis wailed.

Thank God, Maddie silently prayed, shame flooding her. Relief and shame, at the thought of being free of the damaged part of her. The sister who'd never had a chance to be right.

Maddie didn't want her twin to die. She didn't want to face alone the future and the daunting task of taking care of her mother. She didn't want to keep hiding what she was, what Sarah had become. But, God forgive Maddie, Sarah couldn't wake up. Ever. It was horrible. But it was the only way.

As long as her twin's mind slept—as long as whatever they'd been together stayed silent—Maddie might still have a chance to believe their mother's lies…

CHAPTER ONE

Ten Years Later...

"Die!"

The command echoed. A raven's wings spread. Bare tree limbs swayed.

The gun in her hand fired.

A scream ripped through the night.

"No!" Kayla Lawrence jerked awake to a room filled with shadow and silence and the dampness of a summer storm.

Her bedroom.

Another stinking nightmare.

She shivered, sitting up, her legs twisting in the sheets. She rubbed her hands down her arms, calming herself. Her head slid back to the pillow. She closed her eyes. The rustle of wings was still there.

...deeper than before...a humming...growing louder...closer...

...the sound of her car's engine, revving too high...

Her foot punched the gas pedal to the floor.

Acceleration ripped her from sleep.

"Shit!"

She yanked her foot back. Shook her head as her bullet-fast Mustang decelerated. She'd fallen asleep driving!

It was dark as death outside. What was she doing in her fucking car in the middle of the night?

Rain beat at the windshield. There were no wipers to clear her view. No headlights. Thankfully, no other cars in sight. She hit the brakes and swerved toward the side of the road. Stumbling into the warm rain, her silk nightshirt glued to her body, she rounded the back bumper and reached the grassy shoulder of a country highway.

Lightning flashed. Sheets of shiny black water rained down. She tilted her face toward the bare branches of the tree she'd stopped beside. The same one from her nightmares. She lifted a shaking hand to shove back her hair.

The next flash of light illuminated the gun she held before her face—an automatic, covered in blood.

"Die!"

A raven's wings spread. Bare tree limbs swayed.

The gun fired.

A scream ripped at the night . . .

"No!" Kayla lurched awake, in her bed once more.

A frantic glance to her window revealed a crystal clear winter night. No summer storm. No ghostly tree haunted by eerie specters with demonic, piercing eyes. She winced against a flash of lightning that wasn't there.

God, she was losing her mind.

No! They were just dreams. Twisted, increasingly bizarre. But they were just nightmares. Meaningless. They'd go away eventually. She rolled to her side, curling beneath warm flannel. She closed her eyes, refusing to let the ghosts win.

"Die!"

The malevolent command sent her scrambling, reaching for the bedside lamp. But the golden haze it cast only added to her panic. Her gaze traveled down the night-shirt that was soaked to her skin by the sickening sweat of fear. Down to the pistol she clutched in her left hand.

"Oh, God!" Her arm bent. The barrel dug into her temple.

Summer thunder rolled.

Raven wings spread.

A tree's ghastly limbs swayed.

"Die!"

CHAPTER TWO

Dr. Richard Metting rechecked every monitor. He listened to the information streaming across the intercom from the center operatives observing Kayla Lawrence's dream simulation. He accepted the reality that he'd failed to protect the woman lying on the exam table before him.

Not that he allowed his shock and surprise to register in his expression. Neither he nor Sarah Temple would make it out of Trinity Psychiatric Research Center alive if he didn't play the next few minutes right. Like the dispassionate scientist he'd been portraying for the last year. He nodded stiffly at a tech checking the leads to their research subject's heart monitor.

Sarah's pulse rate was up. Respiration choppy. Nothing they hadn't seen before. Nothing deviating too far from acceptable norms. Except Richard's test subject should be awake. And a handgun he hadn't designed to be part of the dream she'd projected into Kayla Lawrence had appeared in the other woman's nightstand drawer. Oh, and the still-unaware Lawrence was currently sleepwalking, trying to commit suicide with a weapon she wouldn't remember buying if she survived long enough to wake up.

He studied the young woman lying on the exam table.

The headset feeding Sarah sensory stimuli would play until his "Alpha" projector broke free of her shared dream with Lawrence. It emitted a seamless backdrop for tonight's storm variation, anchoring the reality Sarah's and Kayla's minds were locked into.

Using Dream Weaver techniques, Sarah linked with her host's unconscious mind. She utilized a set of symbols to implant a custom-designed dream that would be triggered later. Then she was supposed to retreat back into the collective unconsciousness—leaving enough echoes of nightmare to encourage her host's mind to forget she'd ever been there. The center's recon team tracked the host's actions after Lawrence woke, to isolate whether the embedded daydream was triggered on cue. And to make sure the host didn't become suspicious of the real origin of her behavior.

Except Sarah's work with Kayla Lawrence had never included the directive to purchase a weapon—not at this stage of testing. Not by Richard's design. And he'd never had this much difficulty disengaging Sarah from a shared dream.

Richard extracted the IV line from the shunt in Sarah's chest. He'd administered the recovery drug ten minutes ago. Standard protocol for aborting the REM state that nurtured the dream link. He stepped to the foot of the observation room's bed and pricked Sarah's arches with his probe. Nothing. No movement, except for her eyes darting from side to side behind their lids.

Damn it!

He'd infiltrated the center to stop this precise scenario from occurring. To be the one who brought Sarah Temple back from her coma, to discover what the other center scientists knew about psychically training the mind through dreams, and to limit their testing to experiments that caused no long-term harm. He was supposed to get Sarah out before Dream Weaver could be fully developed from her psychic gifts. Except he was no longer in exclusive control of her abilities. Maybe he never had been.

Sarah's hand jerked, then her arm. Involuntary muscle spasms. The heart monitor kicked into a tantrum. Her condition deteriorated into seizure. Alarms blared from every piece of equipment in the glass-enclosed cubicle. A crash team would descend in a matter of seconds.

"Alpha!"

Richard pulled her headset free. Gothic echoes of wind and lightning and a thunderstorm surrounded them. He fought the instinct to yell Sarah's name. To reach out to her, through the personal psychic link no one at the center knew he'd forged. He grabbed Sarah's hand, his body blocking the gesture from the camera recording over his shoulder.

His mouth at her ear, he whispered, "Come back to me, Sarah. Don't give in to this. Come back, so I can get you out of here."

CHAPTER THREE

...almost free...

Anger burned through Sarah, harsher than the fear. Jagged-edged, like the storm raging outside the Temple family car.

And her father's anger wasn't the worst of it. The farther they drove from the police station, the deeper his hopelessness grew. For the little girl he'd lost. The perfect daughter she'd never been.

"You're high again, aren't you?" he demanded from behind the wheel. "Your mother and I just sprung you from county lockup, and you're already high again."

There was no surprise in his voice. He sounded tired. He was giving up.

It was only a dream, some still-sane part of Sarah knew. A shadow dream she couldn't stop from happening over and over again. But believing this was real was the only blessing that remained. The only memory that was still her own. So she made her gaze lock with his in the rearview mirror. She took one more look, before—

"Holy shit!" Her father's attention jerked to the rain-soaked country road. His panic sliced into her.

Their car skidded across the center line. She screamed, just like a hundred times before. Held her breath. Prayed the tires would grab. But they spun faster instead, death racing toward them, more precious by the second. Because like an addict, Sarah was reaching for it now. For the grace that came only in this moment.

Her absolution.

Because a split second before the tanker truck pulverized the driver's side of their family's Chevy, her father's anger evaporated.

"Please, God, let my Sarah be okay. Make her okay again. Take care of my little girl."

The truth was agony when it no longer mattered. But Sarah's mind clung to her father's thoughts of unconditional love. He'd never really given up on her, not completely, even if he hadn't been able to say it.

Then she was ripped away. By her mother's shock. By the truck driver's curses. Her father's pain.

The agonizing jumble swallowed her. The psychic energy flared, beating at her, splitting her, until it became the metal-on-metal of impact. Then she was flying, breaking, shattering into the darkness. Reaching for her twin's mind . . . hating that Maddie had to be there . . . that Sarah couldn't stop herself from reaching for her sister, any more than she could stop the dream.

Sarah let the wind and the storm's anger surge through her. She pushed to her feet beneath the phantom branches of a looming oak. Her head splitting, her body broken, she fed on her mind's tenuous connection with her twin's. On the shared dream's power. She stumbled toward her father and the twisted, burning mess that no longer resembled their car.

He was still alive, his panic searing through her. And she would save him this time. She had to. They would both be free if she just made it before—

The explosion hurled her backward, slamming her into the tree's scarred trunk. Fire engulfed the Chevy, denying her *again. Then she was crawling through the mud. Pleading, when there was no one but her sister to hear.*

"Maddie ... help me ..." Sarah begged, needing the greedy flames to take her, too.

Before she and her demented dreams were responsible for someone else's death.

"God, please don't let me—"

CHAPTER FOUR

"—kill anyone else!" Maddie Temple cried, waking from a recurring nightmare of fire and destruction and loss. "Oh, God!"

She stumbled to the bathroom, consumed by ten-year-old memories that belonged to her coked-out twin. Memories, like the emotions Sarah had bombarded her with the night of the accident, that weren't Maddie's but wouldn't go away. She retched into the toilet, her father's desperation and shock and death still churning inside her.

Empty, her mind finally quiet, she collapsed against the side of the tub.

"Damn you, Sarah." And damn the guilt that heckled Maddie's revulsion for what her sister had become.

It hadn't been Sarah's fault that they'd always known things. Felt things they shouldn't. They hadn't dared let anyone see how much. Their mother would have been terrified. So Maddie and Sarah had turned to each other for support and comfort and control. But while Maddie's intuition had developed until she could sense enough of someone's pain to help them, Sarah's had escalated until she was experiencing everyone's everything.

Schizophrenia, one doctor had labeled it by the time they were ten. Bipolar disorder, another diagnosed at fifteen. By then, Sarah was self-medicating away the worst of her mania with drugs. She'd said it was like she *became* the person she was feeling through—a debilitating burden from which Maddie had tried her best to shield her twin.

Then at sixteen, Sarah had *become* their father, the night her reckless behavior put him on a collision course with a thunderstorm and a hydroplaning truck. The night Sarah had lost what was left of her mind and her toxic link to Maddie had been shattered.

Sarah had spent the last decade in a vegetative coma in a special-care facility over a thousand miles south of their Massachusetts hometown. After the accident, Maddie and Phyllis had moved to a sleepy Boston suburb to piece their fractured lives back together. As best they could, at least, while Phyllis's nerves grew so unpredictable she couldn't keep a job for more than a few months at a time. Which had left Maddie shouldering the responsibility for making the normal life they craved a reality.

She'd almost succeeded.

Then the dreams had come. Each more terrifying and vivid than the last. The emotions, as strong as the night of the accident. Just as clear. Just as horrifying. Every night of the last three months, Maddie became a teenage Sarah in the throes of the addiction Sarah had turned to in order to cope. She'd watched their father die, felt him die, over and over again—knowing it was her fault, Sarah's fault, as surely as if she'd put a gun to his head and pulled the trigger.

In the dream, Maddie saw it all, felt it all, became it all, right along with her twin. The images of the storm and the crash and Sarah's desperation to die waited for her every night. Each dream exactly the same—until tonight.

Tonight, the truck driver hadn't been shocked as Gerald Temple's car skidded toward him. Sarah—and through her, Maddie—had felt him waiting for the Chevy to cross the center line. Tonight, she'd seen the crash through the stranger's menacing gaze.

The truck driver had accelerated into the impact, taking dead aim for the car. His final thought echoing through Sarah's mind...

And Maddie's...

Die!

CHAPTER FIVE

"How could you not know someone else was programming her dream projections!" the raspy voice demanded over Richard's cell phone. "You're one of the Brotherhood's strongest psychics for God's sake."

Sarah was safely sedated. Her mind was back under Richard's control—at least as much under his control as it ever had been.

"If dreams were that easy to manipulate, the Trinity Center wouldn't have needed me so badly." Richard stepped deeper into the cover of the woods that ringed the center's property. It was dark, he hadn't breached any of the facility's perimeter sensors, and he was using the Brotherhood's secure satellite link. But Richard couldn't be too careful with his cover. Not now. "Sarah might not even be aware that someone besides me is guiding her Dream Weaver work."

"A project you fought to spearhead, because you insisted you were the only Watcher who could control the outcome."

"I was fighting for Sarah Temple and her legacy. I still am."

"Not much longer. Not if you can't control the risk the principle's becoming to—"

"The *principle*'s risk to anyone but herself has been contained."

"For now. The government won't be allowed to perfect a direct-strike psychic weapon. That was your guarantee to the Brotherhood. Your only choice now is to—"

"Get Sarah out, I know." Wind whipped the trees overhead, mimicking the sensory stimuli that had helped Richard map Sarah's dreams and build her psychic strength. But had he gotten her strong enough to face what came next?

"Extract her and all your dream research from center control," the voice spelled out unnecessarily. A mission didn't get more covert than this. If Richard failed, he failed alone. "We'll take the Temple woman in as long as you can control her. But if you can't get her and the footprints of your work out, with no ties to the Brotherhood, we'll be forced to contain the exposure. Everyone connected to Dream Weaver will be terminated, you included."

CHAPTER SIX

Maddie's breath misted in the frozen morning air. She'd been up for hours. It felt like she'd been standing there forever. Shivering in the hospital parking lot. Still not ready to go inside. Not ready to pretend for another day that her life wasn't falling apart.

Anger bubbled beneath the calm that people expected from Dr. Madeline Temple, ER trauma specialist. Her twin's anger and insanity had come only in the dreams at first. But echoes of Sarah owned more of Maddie's waking mind every day. No matter how hard Maddie fought, her comatose sister's demented memories kept taking more.

Or maybe it was Maddie's own mind. Maybe it was simply her turn. Like Sarah and her mother, this was her destiny. Maybe that was the prophecy Phyllis had been so terrified of. Maddie had managed to do some good with her life. It was time for the darkness to take the rest. Could it really be that simple? That hopeless?

She squared her shoulders against the ridiculous thought.

She was a grown woman, not a scared teenage girl. She didn't believe in curses and phantom prophecies. Besides, she had real problems to deal with. Problems like Dr. Jarred Keith, who'd become St. Christopher's chief of psychiatry less than a year ago. Notorious for keeping to himself, he'd surprised her by wanting to take their casual dates to a level she hadn't been ready for. He'd found the calm, sweet Maddie she'd been too charming to resist. She'd told him she needed to stay focused on her career. Then she'd stopped returning his calls. Ignored his repeated voice mails. Until last night.

Last night, Jarred hadn't left her a choice. He'd said he was sorry that it had come to this. He was *sorry*, but they'd find a way to clean up her mess of a life together.

Right.

Shrugging off a shiver, Maddie marched up the granite steps that led to the wall of windows fronting St. Christopher Memorial Hospital. *Focus on what's important. Forget about everything else.* She had a residency to save. After scraping and fighting for years to get where she was, she refused to let everything slip through her fingers. She wasn't losing herself now. She wasn't weak like her sister.

Maddie would handle Jarred Keith. Then she'd handle her nightmares, the shadows from her past, and her family's penchant for instability—alone. Whatever it took to not let the darkness win, the way it had with Sarah.

"There's something you're not telling me." Jarred was staring at Maddie from his expensive chair, behind his expensive desk.

Maddie stared back, swallowing the instinct to trust him. To invite him deeper into her messed-up life. Into her mind.

Expensive suited the man. But not as well as the warm, inviting clutter that softened the periphery of his office. His reputation with hospital staff bordered on hard-ass. But Maddie had always known better. Even if she hadn't, the sight before her would have confirmed what she'd felt the first day they'd met. The walls of Keith's office were covered with a hodgepodge of diplomas and civic awards. Small prints of impressionists' work. Those of modern realists. There was even a sampling of what looked like children's Crayola creations. His bookcases were filled floor to ceiling with volumes on varied topics. Fiction and nonfiction, aligned with less and less care the easier the titles were to reach.

Jarred's was an ordered but approachable mind. Intelligent but sensitive to subtlety and the value of indulging the imagination. Maddie had liked that about him—his logic and his no-bullshit approach to taking life as it came. The softness underneath the reserve he kept firmly in place for others. She'd liked it a lot. She'd felt drawn to him, first just a little. So little, she'd thought she was imagining the intensity of that instant connection. Just like she'd imagined all the other weird things that had started happening around the same time. But before she'd known it, Jarred had gotten inside. With each smile or his jokes or his gentle touch, and the way it all had eased the chaos brewing in her mind.

Not a good thing as it turned out. Not now that her job was on the line, and he had the final say. Not when she found herself wanting to reveal everything she didn't understand herself to a man who held the keys to her professional future.

"According to you and your bosses"—Maddie willed away her blank stare, settling for a smile that was closer to *You're imagining things* than *Help me!*—"there's plenty I haven't told Dr. Yates."

"I'm not Dr. Yates. And I don't like the hospital board putting me in the middle of this any more than you do."

"But here you are." And there his voice had been on

her machine last night, saying that her administration-mandated therapy sessions would be conducted in his office from now on. That accepting his help was her only shot at salvaging her future.

"You seem almost desperate to disengage this morning," he said. "If I didn't know you well enough to be worried, I'd be intrigued."

"Intrigued?" Actually, he was a smug son of a bitch, just like everyone had said. "Is that what shrinks are calling it now, when you stare at someone as if they're a juicy journal article you can't wait to write up?"

Before Sarah's nightmares began haunting Maddie, sparring with Jarred had been a guilty pleasure. First over a quick bite in the hospital cafeteria. Then when they ran into each other, grabbing coffee from one of the machines sprinkled about the building. Dr. Untouchable had finally admitted that he'd been inventing ways to accidentally hook up with her. They'd moved on to late-night or early-morning meals at a diner near her apartment, before or after one of Maddie's grueling ER shifts. Out of sight of any St. Chris staff who might find it gossipworthy to catch them together. Because just six months ago, the male-dominated realm of emergency medicine had been Maddie's playground. She'd finally made it. She was home free. No more worries.

Then Jarred had started to notice the bizarre things Maddie had hidden from everyone else. How she'd found herself eating food she hated but didn't remember ordering. She'd say something out of character—something rude and hostile like Sarah used to say. But when Jarred commented on it, Maddie wouldn't remember whatever had shocked him.

"So," he said, "you made things difficult with Matt Yates because he was treating you like just another patient. Well, you're *not* just another patient to me, Maddie"—he leaned forward—"but you're not giving me anything to work with, either."

"Maybe I'm trying to keep you on your toes." She took her own stab at smug. "We can't have such an important doctor wasting his time."

"Is that what I'll be doing? Is that what I was doing every time I tried to get the most intriguing woman I've ever met to open up about what was bothering her?"

Jarred flashed his Harrison Ford, circa *Raiders of the Lost Ark*, smirk.

For a moment, Maddie forgot how to breathe.

"Do your bosses know how inappropriate this arrangement is?" she countered.

"Do you want me to remove myself from the situation? Because if Yates had had his way, that call last night would have been your termination notice. Not me sticking my neck out to give you one more chance."

"Don't tell me you're pissed because I'm not thanking you for this!"

"Something's changed"—Jarred did that head-cocking thing shrinks do when they think they have all the answers—"since the last time we spoke. When was that, three weeks ago? Things have gotten even worse, and I remember offering to admit you to psych back then."

"I had a long night. Nothing new."

"Yates said you haven't been sleeping at all."

"Like I said, nothing new."

"Are the dreams that bad?"

"Who said anything about dreams?" Sarah's rebellious, eat-shit smile spread across Maddie's face. Maddie coughed, covering her twin's sass with the back of her hand.

"Okay." Jarred steepled his fingers in front of him, elbows resting on his desk. "Nightmares, then. Fantasies. Whatever's going on in your head while you're staring at the ceiling all night. Can the bullshit, Temple. I've read Yates's files. Not that I needed to. When we met, you were the most professional, best-liked resident on staff. What's been messing with you so badly the last few months that you have to be supervised when you see patients? Why wouldn't you talk to me about it back when I would have helped you prevent all of this?"

It wasn't the question that jerked Maddie straighter in her chair. It was the way the warmth in Jarred's voice washed over her. How the worry in his gaze felt too good, deep inside where she secretly needed him. Craved him, like an addict who couldn't resist the seductive pull of something she knew would destroy her. The man saw her—really saw her. And his undivided attention was as dangerous as it was warm…comforting…flooding her mind…

Making her skin crawl!

Because sometimes, it was like she could read Jarred back—the way Sarah had been able to feel people toward the end. Not just with intuition or empathy or a little brush of minds. But all out becoming the person's feelings. Taking them in. Making them herself, and her them. Sometimes it had felt like Jarred was in Maddie's mind, sharing his secrets while he dug for hers.

These days, everyone at St. Chris was happy to keep her freak show at a distance. But Super Shrink wanted in. So much for bluffing her way through this session the way she had with Yates.

"If my career is over," she challenged, "just man up and say it, then leave me the hell alone."

Eight years of college packed into six, most of it while Maddie was still a teenager. Her internship. Two years of residency. The only identity that would ever fit. It couldn't really be gone.

Jarred smoothed the rumpled end of his tie.

"It doesn't have to be." He flipped open a file—a red one. Yates's had always been blue. "Tell me about your twin."

Maddie was out of her chair and halfway to the door before she realized she'd moved. She reached for the doorknob.

"I wouldn't do that if I were you." Jarred's warning and a flash of last night's nightmare froze her in place. "The people who pay my salary want my diagnosis to jive with Yates's. And they want it soon. I've stalled them by not letting on how much I already know about what's happening to you. I argued that you were at the top of your med-school class. You aced your boards, years before most doctors finish their coursework. You're a diagnostic prodigy. Innately gifted beyond your colleagues' ability to comprehend. You deserve one final chance. But you're falling apart emotionally, Dr. Temple. You've become a threat to your patients. You've lost all ability to focus in the ER. So, you can drown in denial and keep fighting alone and fail. Or, you can accept my help figuring out what's really going on. Which is it going to be?"

Maddie saw a malevolent raven in her mind. Her father's car exploding. An evil tree swaying. She imagined her fingers around the raven's throat, squeezing until she was free of the darkness. Really free.

Die! Sarah's voice demanded. *He has to die!*

Jarred wheezed.

Maddie spun back as he fought to inhale. He stared at her, as if he didn't want to believe what was happening, or that she had anything to do with it. Through the shadows fogging her mind, she reached for what was left of who she'd dreamed she could be. She forced herself to focus on Jarred's warmth, not the bitter cold of Sarah's insanity.

White light, instead of darkness, had become Maddie's mantra the last few months.

Calm.

Healing.

Maddie was a healer.

"You have no business digging up information about my sister." Maddie shoved the last of Sarah's fury away.

"On the contrary." Jarred swallowed. Inhaled. Shook the confusion from his eyes. Cleared the rasp from his voice. "It is now officially my business. All of it. Whatever it takes to put your mind back together, even if it means ignoring my personal feelings for you. You're splitting from reality with increasing frequency, Maddie, and you're refusing to deal with it."

"So you're going to deal with it for me?"

"I wondered if there was a family history of dissociative behavior," he said. "Imagine my surprise to find you aren't the only child that your personnel records say you are. Your twin was involved in an accident as a teenager. Your father was killed as a result? There are records of her previous arrests for drug possession. Increasingly altered behavior. If Sarah was having psychological difficulties similar to—"

"She has nothing to do with me." The doorknob dug into Maddie's back. She crossed her arms and refused to feel trapped. Refused to let her mind see her hunky psychiatrist and his cozy office bursting into flames while she ran screaming from her twin's nightmares. "Sa... Sarah's problems, whatever they were, have been gone from my life for years."

With a slow blink, Jarred set the red file aside.

"Is avoiding your family history and the twin no one knows you have worth sacrificing your career for?" he asked.

A silly family prophecy, her mother had called what Maddie and Sarah had found. A bunch of nonsense written by a long-dead aunt who was burned at the stake during Salem's witch trials. The women in their family were overly sensitive to their surroundings, that's all. Overly aware of emotions and how they affected the world. Of what people were feeling. *A bunch of nonsense, really... Forget what you saw. Promise me you'll forget all of it...*

Except it was inside Maddie now. The darkness trickling out, no matter how hard she resisted. Phyllis had lost her husband and one of her daughters. She'd been slowly losing touch with reality since Maddie was a child. Sarah had gone completely insane. And now Maddie's mind was slipping...

"My sister's gone," she repeated, the sound of a storming wind roaring through her mind. She turned and got the stupid door to open. "Sarah has nothing to do with my world now, and you're damn straight I'll do whatever it takes to keep it that way."

Temple was losing it.

Jarred watched Maddie from across the frantic ER and wished Yates's report to the hospital board had been wrong. But wishing in Jarred's line of work did as much good as bashing your head against a wall and hoping it wouldn't hurt. When a nurse brushed past Maddie and the waif-thin resident bit her lip to hold herself together, his jaw clenched.

She's a liability the hospital can't carry any longer, the administration had concluded. And on paper they were right. But that hadn't stopped Jarred from battling into this mess on Maddie's behalf, even though he had nothing to offer professionally beyond what Yates had done. Nothing but months of watching Maddie's every move, while telling himself that a casual relationship was all he wanted. It was all he'd wanted with any woman since his marriage ended.

Jarred realized he was rubbing the sore throat he'd had since their session and stopped. *More than casual* wasn't something he'd done well since he was a child—hence his divorce from a woman he still considered a good friend. And Maddie had made it abundantly clear for months that whatever they'd started during their few dates was off. Period. Just when she'd clearly needed the kind of professional help he could give her.

Coincidence? The scientist in Jarred didn't believe in coincidences. Maddie looked utterly exhausted. Three months ago she'd reluctantly admitted to having strange dreams. Nightmares she wouldn't discuss. She'd even told him a time or two, before she stopped talking to him altogether, that unexplained things were happening. To the point that he'd wondered if sleep deprivation was messing with her short-term memory. After that, she'd shut Jarred out of whatever was troubling her. Right before she was put on an administrative plan that required weekly analysis of her condition.

He should have walked away and been glad to have dodged a bullet.

But Jarred hadn't known how to let go. Not of Maddie or the way being with her, even with her growing problems, had made him feel. Like he could breathe deeper. Relax into who he was. It had been the same, even during their disastrous meeting that morning.

She's the most magnificent thing I've ever seen.

Caramel brown hair. Pale skin. Petite. All curves and intelligence and inner fire. She was a vulnerable pocket Venus he couldn't tear his gaze away from. The compulsion to be near her, to talk with her and hear her voice in return, never let up. Watching her work was a turn-on all its own. Maddie Temple, all twenty-six years of her, was the purest healer he'd ever known.

Pain spread across her face while she fought to diagnose her patient. Jarred's own heart beat faster.

"He's bleeding out..." she whispered. She cleared her throat. Glared behind her. Found no one there. "Get a surgical consult over here!"

Everyone but Jarred ignored the striking picture she made working over the groaning man. She smoothed shaking fingers across her unconscious patient's forehead. Jarred's skin tingled in the same spot. ER staff swarmed around him, immersed in saving the rest of the family of four that had been cut from the aftermath of SUV-vs.-semi. Naturally, the semi had won. The mother and children were most critical. The father, triaged as stable, was the least of everyone's concern.

Everyone but Maddie.

Jarred had officially blocked off twenty minutes for a fresh glimpse of Temple's dysfunctional interaction with the trauma staff. He'd blown that estimate an hour ago. Noticeably freaked by the crisis rocking at full tilt around her, Maddie had stuck by the father's side. Her connection to the man seemed to grow with each gentle touch. Another nurse bumped into Maddie on the way to fetch type-specific platelets for the smaller of the two little girls. Maddie ignored the contact this time. She said something near her patient's ear. The father's agitation quieted. Jarred edged closer, needing to hear. The man's next groan sent Temple's right hand to his belly, palpitating. The fingers of her left aligned with pressure points on the man's face.

Jarred sensed her attention draw inward. He could feel her next shudder. When she swayed, he reached to pull her away from the patient, her distress becoming his own.

"I need a surgical consult," she yelled. "Now!"

Dr. Britton shoved past Jarred.

"Temple?" The ER attending sighed. "What the hell are you doing? This patient's stable, and I need you—"

"He's bleeding out," Maddie insisted.

"Listen, you little nutcase." Britton's scowl was understandable. For months, Maddie hadn't been up for diagnosing a hangnail, let alone an advanced MVA trauma. "Yell at me in my ER again, and I'll—"

"You'll what, Doctor?" Jarred didn't remember edging between them, but he and Britton were nose to nose.

Maddie was shaking behind him. No longer absorbed in her patient, she was falling apart. Shielding her from her boss's impatience wouldn't fly for long, but it felt right to Jarred.

Too right.

"Fuck off, Keith." Britton squared off. "I have three patients crashing because this asshole decided to have one too many beers with his lunch. I don't need you and wonder kid here"—he nodded to where Maddie was cowering behind Jarred—"demanding that I hold her hand while she hides in the corner."

"Then leave the hand-holding to me, and do your job. This *asshole* has internal injuries."

"Really?" Britton—six-five, lab coat and khakis covered in blood—squinted over Jarred's shoulder. "Another feeling of yours, Temple? And your diagnosis is based on what this time, voodoo? Your patient's alcohol haze saved

his sorry hide. Too bad I can't say the same for his family.
I don't have the time for this."

Britton pivoted to leave.

"What about a lawsuit?" Jarred challenged. "You got
time for that? Because that's what's coming when it turns
out you've let a man die instead of treating his injuries."

For reasons Jarred didn't have time to analyze, he
knew Maddie was right. He'd just watched her diagnose
a patient with nothing more than touch and intuition,
but he was certain her instincts were dead-on.

"Fine." Britton dragged Maddie to the injured man's
side. "What?" he demanded. "He's bleeding out where?"

Maddie's arm twisted in his grasp. Her complexion
paled to paper white.

"Let her go," Jarred said from her other side, careful
not to touch her.

She'd found a tenuous balance while focused on the
father, but her composure was shattering. She gasped,
struggling against Britton's hold. She'd be black and
blue.

The air around them seemed to thicken. The skin
along Jarred's arms and neck prickled as her agitation
grew. Just like during their session that morning when
the once mild-mannered intern's anger had boiled over
because he'd confronted her with the existence of a twin
she pretended she didn't have.

What the fuck was going on?

"Dr. Britton!" Jarred warned. "Let her go, now!"

Pain swamped Maddie from Britton's grip. Then he was
pulled away, and Jarred was there…God…hovering…
too close…the world around them flushing violent
red. Destroying the healing white she'd found in her
patient.

It had never been this bad before. The shaking and confusion after she read a patient's condition. The darkness closing in—the way it did in her twin's demented nightmares. Only now, Jarred's fear for her was part of the mix. His shock flaming through her mind, then her body. And Britton's anger, harsh and confusing and impossible to shut out.

She shouldn't be able to feel either of them. Not on her own. That only happened to Sarah.

This was wrong.

Not her.

Not possible…None of this should be possible.

Jarred and Britton were still arguing. Their words, their thoughts, made no sense through the frigid nightmare Maddie was slipping into. Maddie's fingers grazed her patient's arm. Warmth shot through the contact, softening the jagged chill and anchoring her to here and now. Then her relief sparked to agony. She gasped in a moment of blinding clarity.

Jarred jerked at her side as if he'd felt it, too. He turned shocked eyes toward her.

"What the hell was that?"

"He's bleeding from his spleen," she croaked, needing him to believe her. "Please…"

Jarred blinked down at her. His expression shifted from surprise to a touch of awe.

He grabbed the lapels of Britton's lab coat and hauled the man closer to the exam table. "Don't just stand there," he insisted.

Pain was swamping Maddie. Her patient's pain. A father's staggering flood of confusion and desperation. Growing weaker by the second.

My wife and daughters. Save them!

"Get off me!" Britton fought Jarred's hold.

My fault... The patient's head shook side to side. Death called to Maddie from his injuries. Menacing. Triumphant....*all my fault. Let me go*...

Let him go... Sarah's voice taunted. *You're too chicken to help him. Coward. Go ahead. Let the man die. Give up on being a doctor. Just like you gave up on being my sister*...

"No!"

Maddie snatched up the portable ultrasound. She shouldered in front of both men and prepped the patient's abdomen with gel. Explored for all of five seconds before she had it.

"There!"

The distorted image on the monitor shimmered as white misted the edges of her vision. The lesion along the man's spleen was a deadly shadow. A fatal rupture if it wasn't treated immediately. An injury there was no denying Maddie had felt, then seen with her mind. Long before the diagnostic equipment had revealed it to the men standing beside her.

"Shit!" Britton knocked her aside. "Bellamy," he yelled to the doctor who'd triaged the father. "Get your butt over here!"

The senior resident was laboring over the ten-year-old girl whose heart had stopped at point of impact. He and other staff poured into the tiny alcove. Maddie stumbled away, shivering, while the father's stats dropped. Alarms sounded. There was a shout for plasma. Orders for IVs. Adrenaline. The fight was on.

The trauma team's determination to cheat death whipped at Maddie. In the hallway outside, her hands covering her ears, she tried to block out her patient's silent pleas and the memory of her own father begging for Sarah's salvation.

People's thoughts. Their feelings. Their everything. From before. From now. Things that were still to come. Angry. Dark. Freezing dark. Building. Spinning inside her, until she clutched her stomach.

The reality of what she'd just done sunk in. The insanity of it. How was any of this possible? Her patient's injuries had...talked to her. Her *patient* had talked to her, and his mind was still screaming. Fury and fear and pleading she couldn't ignore. Just like Sarah hadn't been able to.

"Oh, my God!"

She would have collapsed, but Jarred's hands were there to support her.

"Get away from me." Nausea burned the back of her throat. Sarah's demented laughter seared the frazzled corners of Maddie's mind. "I...I'm going to be sick."

CHAPTER SEVEN

"You're making a mistake if you think another program lead could have achieved better results," Richard said to the scientists assembled for a center directors meeting.

It was the bluff of Richard's life.

Clearly, another psychic was manipulating Sarah's mind. Running shadow simulations. Possibly piggybacking them onto Richard's. Likely someone sitting around the conference table. Richard settled deeper into his chair and focused on not looking as if he were attempting to read everyone there. Not that he expected to discover much from a mind strong enough to challenge his control over Sarah.

"Kayla Lawrence's dream responses," he continued, "were on target until—"

"—until her mind regained control from Alpha, and she nearly blew her head off in her sleep." Chansley Whittiker's pointed, ratlike nose was flushed at the tip. "With a dream-planted weapon there are no records of you designing into our prototype's programming. You've insisted on projecting nonlethal dream symbols. You've preached keeping a clean dichotomy between your alpha testing work, and the weapons programming our client wants at beta stage."

"Controlling the host's responses is difficult enough

when Sarah's embedding everyday objects and tasks into Lawrence's subconscious," Richard explained. First, tasks like Sarah directing Kayla Lawrence to take a different way to work each day. To eat red meat for lunch when Lawrence was a diehard vegetarian. Then increasingly disturbing variations to test the limits of the host's mind. But nothing homicidal or suicidal. "Adding violent variations would—"

"Result in the disaster we observed last night?" Whittiker demanded. "With each failed simulation, you come dangerously close to exposing this center's work. You chose Kayla Lawrence from the list of hosts our client provided. You've maintained a stranglehold on overseeing Alpha's psychic and physical conditioning since you brought her out of her coma. You've given us one excuse after another for the side effects of Dream Weaver's infiltration into her psyche. All while you've been allowed free rein. But Sarah Temple's condition is deteriorating to the point that she'll be of no use to us soon. And a Beta field test is still nowhere in sight."

"Short-term paralysis." Tad Ruebens ran a finger down the report in front of him. He was the palest man Richard had ever known, including his gray hair and gray beard, even the piercing cruelty of his gray eyes. "Brain bleeds. Seizures. You've been cleared to use drug therapy…sleep deprivation…whatever it takes to maintain a subconscious link with the host, control the dream environment, embed programming, and trigger daydream behavior to test the boundaries of Lawrence's impressionability."

And to allow Richard unlimited access to Sarah's mind, so he could secure her trust and secretly train her for what her life would soon become. Defense tactics, escape strategies, weapons skills—whatever Sarah might need when the time came for her to escape the center and join the Watchers. To help them prevent the kind of evil abomination Dream Weaver would be.

"This board was fine with the side effects until now." Richard tempered his challenge with an indifference that threatened to choke him. Projecting confidence was his only means of protecting Sarah until the time was right to get her out of there. "You approved the physical conditioning and rehabilitation I recommended to keep her body strong, so her mind could grow stronger. You've trusted me to get to the bottom of every other glitch the program has encountered. What, precisely, is the nature of your concern now?"

He had to know how much the center's directors knew, while he scrutinized each of the other scientists to determine who had invaded Sarah's mind and sent his testing into this latest tailspin.

Ruebens pressed a button at his elbow. The other scientists at the table—buttoned down in their dress shirts and strangled within an inch of their lives by their neatly knotted ties—shifted in their seats. A 3-D image flickered to life above the table, generated from recessed projectors built into the floor and ceiling at each corner of the room. Its holographic result was equally clear from every chair. With the flip of another switch, video of Sarah's latest simulation began playing. Without audio the images seemed canned. Like B-movie actors going through the motions. Mad scientist. Subject. Just another day at work.

Then all hell broke loose.

Tension replaced Richard's clinical observation of his monitors as he fought to save a year of Trinity's top secret work, as well as his own responsibilities to the Brotherhood. Frantic movements masked fingers that had been shaking for the first time in his life. He bent closer to his subject. Whispered something. It looked like he was begging, when he should have been dispassionately summoning help.

Ruebens paused the projection on the image of the back of Richard's head, his expression and his words obscured by the camera angle.

Come back to me...Don't do this...

"We have a deadline, Dr. Metting." Whittiker and the other directors frowned at the reminder that the country's elite scientists were being held to a Department of Defense timetable. "Continued project funding depends on completion of a successful Beta field simulation. Our client wants proof that any psychic weapon we produce will be under strict control. And so far Alpha clearly is not. You've had some success, but last night was another setback. How did Alpha's dream programming direct the host to purchase a weapon? Kayla Lawrence is terrified of violence. That's what makes her an ideal test subject. And why would Alpha trigger a suicide attempt? How do you suggest we tackle these questions with the DOD?"

"I suggest you explain what I've been telling you in each of my weekly reports." Richard processed the heightened emotions filling the room. Detected a seething source of darkness. Hatred. But he was unable to pinpoint its source. "That Dream Weaver is nowhere close to Beta-test ready."

"That simple explanation isn't going to fly anymore." Whittiker glared through the lenses of wire-rimmed glasses as antiquated as his comfort level with Richard's psychic talents and the cutting-edge parapsychological research the center was peddling to the highest bidder. "Your credentials in the field of dream research are impeccable. Your marginal success has bought you this cen-

ter's leniency. But you've had over a year. And I've once
again spent the day trying to explain your theories, and
your failures, to a client who likes to keep things simple.
After last night's debacle, the simple fact is that the government's demanding to know what obstacles remain to
executing a field test—one that includes the kind of
weapons handling Lawrence displayed last night."

"Before I can answer that, I'll need more time with
both Alpha and Kayla Lawrence, once Alpha's recovered enough to project her next simulation."

"And to give you that time, what do you suggest my
latest excuse be? That Lawrence's impending breakdown
is threatening to expose us all? Or should I discuss that
your alpha prototype's escalating brain injuries are causing yet another postponement?" He pointed his index
finger into the image hovering above their heads. A
zoom parameter zeroed in tighter. "Or perhaps I should
chat with them about a lead scientist who's presenting
signs of significant boundary issues with his test subject?"

Richard took his time studying the 3-D image. Cleared
his mind. Analyzed. Reverted to battle tactics and narrowed his focus to only what had to be done next. The
Brotherhood wouldn't wait much longer. He had to es-
calate Sarah's recovery period and produce a successful
shared-dream result that would satisfy the center long
enough for him to prepare Sarah for their escape.

He reached for the hologram, grabbed the transparent
corner nearest him, and rotated the image to reveal what
he'd embedded just hours before—an altered frontal
view of his reaction to Sarah damn near dying on his
exam table. Instead of panicked, his gaze in the video
was that of a scientist determined not to lose a valuable
asset. He flicked several buttons at his elbow, reactivat-

ing the recording and engaging the audio he'd digitally spliced into it.

"Reset, Alpha," his image commanded with detached calm. "Target release, and reset to zero. Reset. Now!"

Sarah's agitation quieted. All body activity ceased, including the rapid eye movement of the dream state required to sustain her link to the host. At that exact moment, thousands of miles away, Kayla Lawrence had woken in hysterics from her psychotic nightmare. She'd been seconds away from blowing her head off with a very real handgun. Exactly the kind of untraceable, violent behavior a secret sector of the U.S. government was looking for in a weapon. A psychic weapon Richard had promised the Brotherhood, and Sarah Temple, that he wouldn't allow to become a reality.

"Return the subject to her observation suite," his image ordered the crash team that rushed into the simulation room. In the video, he turned from his misfiring test subject and her now-quiet monitors and began typing his observations into a workstation. "Prep for her next sim."

Richard paused the recording. He was once more scanning the other minds in the room, and once again discovering nothing he didn't already know. And at the moment, it didn't matter who had pushed his testing to this breaking point. He had to get Sarah Temple out of the center alive. Then he had to find a way to neutralize whoever had trespassed into her unstable mind and escalated the violence of Sarah's shared dreams.

"I suggest you tell the DOD," he said with the same calm he'd overlaid into the recording, "that removing me as the lead will set their testing back months." Denying them the proof they needed that Dream Weaver was precise enough to target any mind, anywhere—embedding homicidal dreams and then triggering waking action toward whatever target was chosen, no matter how out of character the behavior was for the host. "There isn't another scientist at this table, in the entire world, who can guarantee them a successful Beta field test. Like it or not, I'm the only shot they've got."

CHAPTER EIGHT

"Okay." Jarred was freezing his ass off in the dark parking lot beside Maddie's apartment building. "Now what?"

Now, you start the car and drive back to the hospital and work on the patient files breeding like rabbits on your desk...

Except he wouldn't be able to work tonight, any more than he had all afternoon. His mind refused to focus on anything but the devastation on Maddie's face when she'd run from the ER. Something inside her had broken, no matter how amazing she'd been with her patient. She'd fought for that man's life with nothing more than instinct. A patient who would have bled out without her diagnosis. But saving that father had destroyed her.

Jarred had tried to hold her, the way he'd tried to draw her closer for months. Months longer than he'd fought to hold on to his ex when she'd asked for a divorce. When something was over, it was over for Jarred. Like when his parents died, and at nine he'd had to find a way to get on with his life. Looking back and regretting what couldn't be changed was a waste of time.

Except there he was lurking outside Maddie's apartment, needing to be sure she was okay. Knowing she wasn't. He should be firing the car's engine and peeling rubber out of the lot. But *he* wasn't okay, either. Not without Maddie. His concentration was for shit. His mind was fixated on seeing her again, being near her again. Because something had broken inside him, too, when she'd torn herself from his grasp.

He was a leader in the field of psychiatric care. Rule number one in his world was not basing his own well-being on that of a patient's. But he couldn't detach from Maddie's spiraling hold on reality. He couldn't see a way out, or through, except helping her. Being with her. Fighting alongside her until they figured out what the hell was going on.

"The accident?" Phyllis's voice trembled on the other end of the phone line. "Maddie, why are you asking about that night... It was so long ago. Why look back now?"

"Because..." Maddie clenched her portable tighter and paced across her living room. *Because I can't ask you about Sarah's madness, or what you've been afraid of all our lives, or about a long-dead aunt's ramblings and whether they might not have been so nonsensical after all.* "Because... I need to know what you remember. What happened before we all got to the hospital. Did the other driver make a statement? Do you—"

"I don't remember anything, Maddie!"

The unnatural shrill in Phyllis's voice stopped Maddie's pacing.

"That's just it, Mom." Her fear and confusion surged into white-hot anger. "You never remember anything. Every time something scares you, you conveniently check out until your mind blanks on the details that might actually help me deal with what's going on!"

"Help you deal..." Fear rattled Phyllis's words, until they sounded as if they were coming from a stranger. "Maddie, nothing's going on. I'm fine. Everything's been fine for a long time. Why now? Why would you think I—"

"Me, Mom. Everything's not fine with me!" Though Maddie had been doing a bang-up job pretending otherwise. At least with Phyllis.

Perfect little Maddie . . . her mind whispered. *You've still got everyone snowed . . .*

"Sarah?" she asked out loud.

"What?" was Phyllis's breathy response. "What does your sister have to do with this?"

How did Maddie tell her? About the nightmares and the mess she'd made in the ER that morning. Or the patronizing voice in her head that sounded like her sister but was clearly Maddie's own sanity splintering even further. Or . . . how she knew that Jarred was walking up to her apartment just then . . . arguing with himself that he shouldn't be there, but he couldn't turn away . . .

The doorbell rang.

Maddie jumped, squealing.

"Honey?" her mother asked.

Chickenshit, the voice taunted. Sarah's voice.

"Damn it!" Maddie cursed, sick and tired of all of it.

"Honey, you're scaring me."

"Hold on a second." Maddie had originally planned to drive to her mother's place to talk about the night of the accident and whether the police had questioned the driver of the truck. But she'd never made it more than a few feet from her couch. "Let me get rid of whoever's at the door, then I'll try to explain."

Explain what? the voice wanted to know. *That there's an asshole on your porch, and you don't have the guts to tell him to piss off any more than you have the guts to confront your mother in person.*

Maddie jerked the door open.

"Piss off," she spat at the asshole on her porch.

"What!" Phyllis Temple gasped over the phone.

"Not you, Mom." Maddie muffled the receiver against her chest. Fought for control. *Get out of my head, Sarah. Just*—"Get out!"

Jarred Keith crossed his arms and leaned against her doorjamb instead—one foot over the threshold.

"Leave, Dr. Keith," she croaked. "You have no right to—"

"To know what the hell happened to *me* the two times I was with you today?" He sounded as pissed as she felt. "Or to finish my report about you for the hospital administration?"

Black brows lifted above icy blue eyes, skimming shaggy hair that would have looked unkempt on a less-imposing man. But on Jarred, the slightly ruffled effect was just more of the same. Dark, dangerous, and… alarmingly comforting to Maddie. The same comfort his touch had become after she'd been sick all over herself, and him, in the ER. And it was that touch that she'd run from.

"Leave, Dr. Keith," she managed to repeat.

"After your episode in the ER this morning, you're suspended from the hospital until I complete my evaluation. I would think—"

"I saved that man's life."

"Then you had a breakdown in front of everyone. Not exactly a confidence-instilling moment."

Maddie swallowed the compulsion to scream one of her sister's more creative curses. Jarred was right. Smug but right. She'd headed into the hospital that morning so sure she could keep herself together. That today was a fresh start. The same load of crap she'd told herself every other morning.

Then she'd freaked during her psych appointment. Shrieked at Britton, after pushing him around in front of the staff. Fled while her patient coded. Thrown up all over her shrink—her ex, almost-boyfriend—while she felt more and more of her twin's madness becoming her own.

She *was* a nutcase. Her entire family was a cautionary tale she'd never outrun. One Jarred already knew too much about. And there he was, signing up for more. Maddie shot him a look that suggested she wasn't the only one who needed professional help. Then she lifted the phone to her ear.

"...something wrong?" Phyllis Temple was babbling. "Are you okay?"

"Everything's fine."

Maddie's visitor stepped past her. A wave of warmth and worry curled around her. She backed away, holding up a finger to ward the man off. He stood his ground, his gaze understanding of all things.

Her body and her mind clamored to get closer. To let him see more of the parts of her she'd kept hidden for so long. Maddie didn't fall for men this way. She didn't let herself lean on anyone, not the way she wanted to crawl into Jarred's arms every time they breathed the same air. She couldn't risk that kind of honesty. Staying safe— staying separate—was the only way she'd managed the success she had.

"Mom, I'm going to call you back," she said into the phone.

"Who's there with you?"

"Someone from work."

"Someone asking about your sister? It's been years since you've looked back, honey. You've got enough to worry about at the hospital. Your whole future's ahead of you. Why—"

"I need answers, Mom."

"Why now? What's wrong?"

Wrong?

Maddie's gaze tracked Jarred as he helped himself to a tour of her apartment—something she'd never allowed when they were dating. His long-legged, making-himself-at-home stroll came to an abrupt halt beside the couch piled high with blankets and pillows. Her oasis when she couldn't sleep at night. Which had been every night since the nightmares had started.

"I'll call you back," she insisted. "Really, I have to go."

"But your father—"

"Mom—"

"It was an accident, sweetie. Your sister—"

"Mom—"

"Sarah was already lost. It wasn't her fault, but your father was so worried, and she was high again and—"

"Mom!" Maddie shouted, losing patience with her mother's rambling, because Phyllis still hadn't said anything more than she ever did. "If you won't tell me the truth about Sarah, I can't do this right now." Jarred turned to watch her come unglued. Her fingers clenched in the hair she'd been tugging at her neck. "I'll call you later."

"Honey, please—"

Maddie punched the phone off.

Perfect Maddie . . . the voice mocked.

"Get out," she snarled at the voice and her unwanted guest.

"You're a lot feistier now." Jarred smiled, not seeming to mind. "Rude, even."

Actually, Maddie wasn't rude. Ever. She didn't think of people as assholes, and she didn't scream at her mother. Sarah was the unpredictable, disrespectful twin. She'd never cared who saw the crazy inside her. Or maybe she'd just been too far gone to hide it by the time Maddie had been old enough to really notice. And Maddie had convinced herself that the same thing wouldn't happen to her. That if she just tried hard enough, let herself buy her mother's warped view of the world and shoved down all the questions and the confusion of the past, she could have this wonderful life that was dying before her eyes.

Maddie didn't bother wiping at her tears. "Look, I know today was a disaster. I'll e-mail the chief of staff my resignation in the morning. Consider yourself off the hook."

She was at the door. The door Jarred had left open, as if he'd sensed she'd feel safer that way. She yanked it wider. Stared at the floor. Waited for him to catch a clue. Jarred walked closer, but stopped in front of her instead of leaving. She could feel him staring. Wondering. Leaning in.

She flinched away.

Whimpered.

Relax...

The word, in Jarred's voice this time, echoed through her mind.

"So, it's not just when you touch a patient?" he said out loud.

She left him and the door behind.

"Get out!" Her body was shaking. She couldn't fall apart like this in front of him.

"If being around other people is this difficult, how do you handle the ER?"

His voice was so soothing, brushing across her frazzled nerves. Where had soothing come from? She wanted smug back. She *needed* smug back.

"You want to tell me what happened with that patient

today?" he pressed. "Don't bother saying it was nothing, because I felt it, too. At least some of it. Like I felt your anger during our appointment when I tried to make you talk about your twin. Even if you don't want to analyze what's happening to you, I do. Whatever this is, I'm a part of it now. Accept that and—"

He paused when she stumbled farther out of reach. Away from the instinct to trust him. To let this dangerous, tempting man even further in. To scream her confusion and keep on screaming until something, anything made sense.

"Okay." He slowly followed her across the room. "Let's talk about tomorrow, then."

The hallway bathroom was just behind her. The kitchen to her right, and beyond it the side door of her corner, ground-floor apartment. She'd left the dead bolt off. If she ran fast enough—

"Where will you go?" he asked, as if he knew what she was thinking.

Don't run from me, Maddie, his thoughts pleaded. Thoughts that she shouldn't be able to feel so clearly—not without Sarah there to fuel the kind of emotional connection Maddie had never achieved on her own.

"Stop doing that," she begged.

"Doing what?"

She sprinted for the back door. Hard hands yanked her to a halt from behind. Jarred's breath brushed her cheek. Needs from long ago, from when she'd been sixteen and still let herself need, rushed back.

No more barriers.

No more safe.

No more careful.

"Talk to me, Temple," Jarred insisted.

Trust me just this once, was his unspoken plea.

"No!" Maddie lifted a fist to her pounding head. Pressed her other hand to her churning stomach. It was too much. All of it, too much. His thoughts. Her patient's. Sarah's…

None of them should be in her head.

"You're making yourself sick." He steered her toward the couch and let her slide down until she crumpled into her snowy-white blankets and pillows. "Just like at the hospital this morning when I thought you were going to beat Britton to a pulp, which I personally would have enjoyed watching. But then you almost passed out in the hallway."

"*You're* making me sick."

Jarred and the thought of what it must have been like for her twin to go through this their entire childhood. Always open. No way out. The panic attacks and the constant fear. It had driven Sarah over the edge. Maddie panted. Swallowed. Pulled the blanket to her chin. She was so cold.

"You're…" She had no idea what to say next.

"How am I making you sick?" Jarred planted his hands on his hips, just above the age-worn jeans he always wore beneath his lab coat. "I'm offering a friend the courtesy of my best professional advice. But you seem convinced there's nothing I can do to help you."

There was nothing anyone could do, Maddie finally accepted. The nightmares were going to win. The guilt and the pain. The confusion. Feeling and knowing things she shouldn't. Other people's things. The same darkness Sarah had fallen into—the sister no one at St. Chris but this man knew about. Because Maddie had had been so determined to believe that there was no legacy of gifts the women in her family couldn't control. No spiraling need to—

Die!

"Don't." Jarred pried Maddie's left hand away from her other wrist.

Her nails had been scratching. Scraping. The bloody slashes on her skin oozed sullenly. Maddie flinched, horrified by what she'd done, and by the terrifying calm that came with the pain. The craving inside for more.

Jarred let her go, taking his heat with him. When he knelt in front of the couch, his eyes were an infinite crystal blue. Confused. Worried. Kind. Saying, *Trust me, Maddie*...

"I can feel it, too." His voice was a whisper now. "I don't know what it is, but I can feel it, and it's getting stronger. I don't understand, but..." He studied her abused wrist. Pulled out a clean handkerchief and covered the scrapes, pressing gently. Maddie was too drained to resist. Too stunned by the peace seeping into her from Jarred's touch.

I can feel it, too... his voice whispered through her mind.

When she could only stare, he sighed.

"I want to know how you do it," he said out loud. "How you do whatever you did for that man this morning. I saw it, I *felt* it. But a part of me still can't believe it. Let me help you deal with whatever this is, Maddie. Screw your job at St. Chris and what the administration thinks. I'll figure out some way to deal with them. To buy you more time. But you have to stop insisting that you can fix this...whatever this is...yourself. You're the most instinctive healer I've ever met, and you're on the edge of a complete breakdown that's about to take away everything you've worked for. Is that what you want? Do you want to be locked up for the rest of your life, just like Sarah?"

CHAPTER NINE

"Die!"

The command echoed through the night. Not the Raven's voice. The darkness had never been about the Raven. Sarah could feel him fighting to stop it. To stop her. But the dream's control belonged to neither of them.

The command to kill was too powerful. Impossible to deny no matter how strong her mind had become. And it was all the Raven's fault. He'd promised she'd never be here. She'd never become what they wanted her to be.

Sarah fought the drugs and the simulation protocol. The shadows. The dark impulse to kill. She wasn't doing this. She wasn't Death. It was just a dream that she should be able to stop, the same way she had last time. But this time she couldn't halt the inevitable. She'd never be able to, without...

Maddie...

Sarah's mind reached for her last resort. For her twin's emotional balance. The opposite of the weak, uncontrollable destruction that Sarah was becoming. But even though Maddie's mind was there, on the fringes of the dream, she was closed off now. Resisting Sarah's call. Determined not to let her in ever again.

So, like a good little girl, Sarah triggered Kayla Lawrence's death. Choking on useless tears, soundlessly screaming, she

*painted her host's dream world with a nightmare programmed
by a psychotic master. Then she was trapped, no way out,
watching the dream unfold. A lucid nightmare, because her
host was awake now. Daydreaming.*

Like a captive, horrified conductor, Sarah watched Kayla
reach into the bedside table drawer. Remove the gun she'd
thought she'd thrown away after waking from last night's
simulation. Check to ensure it was loaded. Smile in satisfac-
tion. Peace. Relief. Seductive emotions that had been planted
to give the host a false sense of safety, once everything was
in place.

But Kayla was cringing now, aware that something was
wrong . . . straining to regain control from the dream. Failing.
Because Sarah's mind was dutifully pushing the nightmare
toward its predesigned end . . .

The Raven screamed in denial. His wings spread.

Bare tree limbs swayed.

The gun fired.

A scream ripped through the night.

"No!"

Sarah bolted from her prone position. Upright. Blind.
The tug of tubes and embedded wires bit into her arms.
Her chest. Her face and scalp.

"Daddy!"

She'd killed him. Her father had been dead forever.
But in her shadow dreams she killed him again. Over
and over. And this time, she'd taken another life, too.

"Oh, God," she sobbed. She'd killed him. She'd killed
Kayla. She was Death now, just like they wanted.

"Damn it, take her down!" demanded the voice that
had refused to let her go.

Sarah's Raven.

The voice that had called into her darkness and pulled
her mind back. Then he'd made her dream. Told her it

was the only way. Her only chance to live again. He'd promised to teach her. Train her. Give her the strength she'd never had before. Make sure she stayed free of the darkness forever.

"What the hell..." He was muttering. But she couldn't focus on the words. "...doing awake!"

His voice wasn't echoing through her mind, she realized. He was above her this time, beyond the nightmare. She recoiled. Panicked. Grasped for the clarity that came only with her simulations. But her host was gone. The gentle spirit the Raven had taught her to link with. Kayla was dead. There was nothing out there for Sarah to immerse herself in. Nothing to see, to feel, that wasn't her own mind or the Raven's. And she'd never trust him again.

No host. No Maddie. No dreams. Because...

God! I'm awake!

Sarah fought against the arms forcing her down.

"Secure her leads," the Raven commanded. "Reset audio stimuli."

Her ears were covered.

The sound of wind and storm and haunted rustling returned. Weakness stole through her veins as the drugs took hold. But their pull was weaker than before. Or was she growing stronger? Was that even possible? She'd been dreaming for so long. Forever. Believing it would free her. Believing the Raven. Performing on command. Meanwhile, she'd been trained to kill, too. To become Death.

She shuddered, nightmarish screams haunting her.

"Reset, Alpha," the Raven whispered into her ear. Into her mind. Her programming lured her into a resting state, and in her mind she saw the Raven spread his black wings. She heard the wind howling through rustling, skeletal branches.

"Reset to zero," he insisted.

Zero—Dream protocol complete.

Time to rest, until the Raven was ready for her to dream again. Maybe another dream of death. A dream she would find a way to control next time. Because for a moment just now, she'd been beyond anyone's reach. And whatever it took, she would find her way back to that place.

They called her Alpha. The beginning of their plans. But one day very soon, she would be the end. Even if she had to disappear back into the darkness to make sure the nightmares stopped. But this time she wouldn't be going alone.

This time, Death would be taking the Raven with her.

CHAPTER TEN

Do you want to be locked up for the rest of your life, just like Sarah?

Jarred joined Maddie on the couch as his question visibly shook her. He was holding his breath, he realized. Willing Maddie to try. To keep fighting whatever was consuming her.

The serenity of her apartment finally registered. Muted colors of pure white and soothing blues surrounded them. Every edge was softened by pillows or billowing fabric. A full moon shined its ethereal light through opaque sheers. This place was more than Maddie's home. Her apartment was a protective cocoon for a battered healer. Somewhere to recharge after the day's fighting was done. This was Maddie's sanctuary. At least it had been at one time. She looked anything but tranquil now.

"Your sister was sixteen when she had her first psychotic break." He eyed Maddie's reaction to him picking up where their conversation had left off in that morning's session. "She'd likely been bipolar for years before that. Increasingly altered, according to the records I read. The tendency to disassociate is hereditary, Maddie, but—"

"Hereditary?" She shrank into the cushions. Then in

a rush, she was in his face, grabbing fists full of his sweater. "A tendency to dissociate? Is that really the best you've got, *Doctor*!"

She pushed him away, stronger than she appeared. Then she stumbled to her feet. When she tried to run, she tripped over the blanket. Jarred caught her before she hit the floor. He broke her fall with his body, then rolled her to her back.

"Stop it, or you'll—"

"Hurt myself?" Her nails dug into his forearms. "Hurt you?"

"Like Sarah hurt people?"

The startled fear on Maddie's face sliced into his heart. "Please," she begged. "Don't. I—"

"Like your sister hurt you and your family?" he continued, hating the pain he was piling on top of the landslide of emotions she was already enduring.

"St…Stop it." Tears trickled down her cheek. A violent shiver roamed her body.

"I can't help you, if you won't tell me how this started. I'm betting the two of you were close, before your twin's condition spiraled out of control. Now you seem to almost hate her."

The archived news articles he'd dug up when he should have been plowing through paperwork hadn't revealed much about Sarah beyond what her medical records told him. But he'd learned more than enough about what had happened to Maddie's family, to understand why the instant attraction between the two of them had spooked her. Of course letting anyone close again would seem threatening, after losing her sister and her father that way.

"You didn't just see what happened when Sarah began to lose herself," he pressed. He couldn't believe he was entertaining such an outlandish explanation. But somehow he knew he was right. "You...felt what happened to your twin, didn't you? Like you felt that patient's injuries this morning."

Maddie's fingers slid from his arms. Her body fell slack as she withdrew into that mind he wanted—needed—to understand.

"Somehow," he added, "you survived what happened to your family. You thrived. Excelled, after a trauma that should have devastated you. But something happened along the way. At some point over the last year, you stopped being able to deal with people and their feelings. With the patients and doctors constantly streaming in and out of the ER. And..." It was difficult to believe. "...No matter how much you've resisted my help or Yates's, I think you've known what's been happening since it started. Because...you felt the same thing happen before—to Sarah."

He let Maddie slide from beneath him.

"I c-c-can't do this." She trembled as she stood. Instead of bolting for the door again she slowly headed for the kitchen, her expression a devastating blank. "I tried. I thought I could take the control back. Focus. Get better so I could get back to work...But I can't. I...need...I need to..."

Jarred could hear her teeth chattering. But nothing showed on her face when she turned toward him. That degree of internalization could rip a mind apart.

"Stop trying to handle this on your own." He reached his feet, too, but he didn't shadow her this time. He'd already pushed too hard. Too much. *Be her doctor, man. Keep her safe. Nothing else matters right now.* "Whatever condition you and your twin share, it's better to face it than keep hiding. Once we're sure what we're dealing with, we can figure out a solution."

"We?"

"Together," he promised.

Jarred had no business promising her anything—not when it was clear that his involvement was part of what was terrifying Maddie. He should leave and transfer her case to another doctor who would monitor and manage it more professionally. He'd almost convinced himself to do just that, screw his selfish compulsion to keep this woman close, when Maddie drew a revolver from the drawer of the cabinet she'd stopped beside.

Fuck!

"Temple…" He breathed her name calmly, while he mentally kicked his own ass for not hospitalizing her when he'd had the chance. "What the hell are you doing?"

"I don't want to…" She stared at the gun, gone from him.

He felt it, as if she were someone else, *somewhere* else, and the nightmarish image before him was just a dream. She didn't see him slide closer as she lifted the deadly monster. Turned it. Pointed it at her head.

"I can't m-make it s-s-stop," she said. "I-I have to—"

He grabbed her hand and pulled the gun away from her head.

"No!" She fought him.

"Drop it!" He yanked her arm down. Pried her fingers back until he could rip the weapon away. "You're smarter than this, Maddie. You're a fighter. You battled for that father's life today. What the hell are you doing trying to throw yours away!"

"Like you care." Her voice was deeper. Not her own. "Like any of you fuckers care. Just let me die, before—"

He shoved her away and opened the revolver's chamber. The goddamned thing was full. The safety was off.

He dumped the bullets into his palm and flung the gun across the room.

"Oh, I care," he snapped, terrified for her. "For some reason, I've gotten myself attached to a woman with a death wish who keeps a loaded gun in her house. Which makes me more of a head case than you are, I suppose. Because here I am. Still. Convinced I can help you."

"I…" Clarity returned to Maddie's expression. Tears surged. She was back, the Maddie he knew, staring at the gun that had landed near the window sheers. "I've never seen that before in my life…"

Her gaze begged Jarred to believe her.

And for some inexplicable reason, he did. Just like he'd accepted every other crazy thing that had happened that day. The question was, what did he do next? Call an ambulance? Commit her to an indefinite psych hold, the way he would anyone else? But he couldn't abandon her that way. Not Maddie.

He *was* certifiable.

"How did the gun get into your kitchen?" he asked.

"I…I have no idea…" She scraped her nails up and down her arms.

He drew her hands to her side.

"Just let you die," he repeated, "before *what?*"

Maddie putting a gun to her head hadn't been a cry for help. There'd been determination in her eyes. Conviction. And he was certain she hadn't been aware of what she was doing.

"I…I don't…remember," she answered.

"You don't remember what?"

She jerked and focused on him as if she'd just realized whom she was talking to.

"Let me help you." He rubbed his thumb over the back of her hand, trying to soothe his own panic and fear as much as hers. "Technically, I have an obligation to admit you for observation. You just tried to kill yourself. But returning to the hospital's not the answer for you, is it? Not tonight. Not any night until we can find a way to keep what other people are feeling from hurting you." He might as well put it all on the line. The impossible, implausible thoughts that had been rambling around his mind since Maddie left the hospital. "That's what happened in the ER, wasn't it? When you got sick after diagnosing your patient and dealing with Britton's outburst. All of it…gets inside you somehow."

A small nod was her only response.

"But…Being around me doesn't hurt as much, right?" He relaxed a bit after her next reluctant nod. "Then let me help take care of you until we know more. Or are you trying to wind up in a padded cell next to your sister's across town?"

"Across town?" Loneliness and pain and hatred and guilt. Maddie's eyes filled with each emotion, one after the other, then all at once. Her confusion swirled around them, drawing him closer. "Sarah's hundreds of miles from here," she insisted, "in a long-term care facility in Georgia."

Jarred lifted an eyebrow, remembering the tense conversation he'd interrupted between Maddie and her mother. Maddie had been asking for information about a twin she'd assured him she wanted nothing to do with.

"According to the records I accessed over the hospital's medical link, Sarah Lynn Temple was committed to Trinity Psychiatric Research Center after suffering an irrecoverable mental breakdown. For the last ten years, your sister's been cared for just a few miles from here."

CHAPTER ELEVEN

Kayla Lawrence was dead.

Richard had used every safeguard he'd programmed into Sarah's dream conditioning. He'd stayed connected with her mind throughout the simulation this time. But he hadn't been able to stop the shadow dream from taking over. He hadn't stopped some perverted bastard from using Sarah to kill a woman whose mind she'd known intimately for months.

How could this have happened?

Richard terminated the com link to the center surveillance team watching Lawrence's apartment. The police were on scene. The suicide case was already all but closed. No suspicious circumstances for local authorities to investigate. It was a tragic tale about a seemingly content, middle-aged woman ending her life with no explanation.

No family to demand further investigation. No significant other who needed to understand the unexplainable. Viable hosts had been chosen for Dream Weaver based initially on their loner status. Richard had selected Lawrence from the government's list. And now she was dead. Sarah had killed the woman with the dream-projection skills Richard had taught her.

She'd never forgive him.

He'd never forgive himself.

He snapped his laptop closed and paced to Sarah's recovery room bed, shoving his hands into the pockets of his scrubs. He reached for her mind, knowing there would be nothing but silence there. It took her two full days to recover from a typical simulation. He'd rushed her into another projection this time. Now, after Kayla Lawrence's death…

Sarah had been so horrified, her mind had broken through her meds and the paralysis that came with deep sleep. She'd woken up screaming, semiconscious, fighting him and everyone else in the room before he'd taken her under again. Would her mind recover from this intact? Would she be able to link with him or anyone else again? Trust him again?

Video cameras were recording his every move, providing panoramic footage of every nuance of Alpha's emotional and physical state. Details he'd used to isolate the stimuli and suppressive routines needed to target Sarah's dream work. Images that, if he wasn't careful, would now destroy their chance to escape.

Tonight…Sarah would be nowhere near ready, and she would likely fight him when he brought her around. But their only chance to get out would be tonight.

"So." He gazed down at the one variable in his deep-cover mission that no one would ever fully control—Sarah herself. "It's time."

He chose his words carefully.

Performed for the cameras.

"It's all or nothing now." He caught faint movement beneath Sarah's eyelids.

She was dreaming. On her own. Beyond Dream Weaver protocol and Richard's safeguards—safeguards that had failed them both. Recovery meds seeped into her bloodstream through the shunt in her chest, regulating her comatose state. The recovery period between simulations was on nuclear countdown. Richard's team would be working up to the last minute—preparing a new host's background report, presumably for Sarah to use to return to her Dream Weaver work.

Not that the center's directors were going to let that happen under Richard's leadership. And he wouldn't be waiting for his replacement to be named. He pulled the cotton blanket higher, covering Sarah's body from the chin down. He'd reduced the potency of the pharmaceutical cocktail that kept her mind in its recovery state. He only hoped that would bring her around enough to follow him out of the center, while still keeping her under his psychic control. If not, he would most likely become the Dream Weaver program's second casualty.

"Get ready, Alpha," he said. "All hell's about to break loose."

CHAPTER TWELVE

"How long have you been lying to me!" Maddie shouldered Phyllis aside and continued into her mother's foyer. "It's all been a lie from the start, hasn't it?"

Jarred followed and kept Phyllis from stumbling into the oak-paneled wall. Damn him for insisting on coming with Maddie. Damn herself, for needing him right where he was—by her side. And for thinking *damn* so much.

"Please—" Maddie said to her psychiatrist-turned-suicide watchdog. "You have to go."

She was coming unglued. And having Jarred there to see it—she couldn't bear that.

"You're in no shape—" he argued.

"To drive, I know." Any minute, she was going to start begging him to stay. "Thank you for getting me here safely. But this is between me and my..."

She couldn't say it. She fought to meet the gaze of the *mother* who'd written Sarah off and made it so easy for Maddie to do the same. The woman who'd taught both her girls to believe the lies that had destroyed them all. Phyllis eyed Jarred, then took a hesitant step toward Maddie.

"Honey, I don't know what's going on—"

"Where are Sarah's records?" Maddie moved out of reach. She backed into the hall table. A vase, a cluster of happy family photos, crashed to the floor.

"Wh-What?" Phyllis stepped around the mess, her guilt turning Maddie's stomach. "Why? For God's sake, what does all this have to do with your sister?"

Maddie risked a glance at Jarred, wishing she could feel something of him in her mind still. But all that was there now was her mother's regret and self-loathing. Then Sarah's snort of disbelief.

Are you actually buying this act! the voice demanded.

She's sick, Maddie argued. *She's been too sick to face any of this for years.*

Maddie heard herself defending Phyllis—to nobody—and headed into the den. She'd find proof of Sarah's commitment to that research center. She'd use the paperwork to force her mother to finally tell her the truth.

"I know you have them somewhere." She didn't look back, but she could feel Phyllis follow. "You never throw anything away." She yanked open the credenza's bottom drawer and rifled through the hanging file folders. "I can't believe I never looked…" Her thumb slid across the edge of a folder. The heavy card stock sliced into her skin. "Shit!"

She sucked the cut into her mouth. Ignored the insane laughter chuckling through her mind.

What a baby, Sarah's voice heckled.

"Let me see." Phyllis tried to examine Maddie's hand.

"Don't touch me, bitch!" Maddie flinched at the memory of her twin saying the exact same words. They were the last things Maddie had heard Sarah yell at their mother.

Pain and shock flooded color into Phyllis's pale cheeks. "I don't know what's going on or who this man is, but you're bleeding all over yourself. I have some Band-Aids in the bathroom, and—"

"I'll get them," Jarred offered.

"I don't want a Band-Aid!" Maddie's explosion stopped him in his tracks.

There was a sea of soothing calm waiting for her in his mind. It was calling to her now, the same way it had that morning, tempting her. Maddie wanted to crawl inside Jarred and hide until everything and everyone else went away. *Trust me, Maddie...I can feel it, too...* But she didn't dare. She closed her eyes, trying to trap the impulse. Hold it back.

Keep the secret, no matter what...

"Maddie," her mother prodded. "Your thumb. I—"

"Do you think I give a fuck about my thumb!" Maddie cringed as more laughter accompanied her words. Sarah's laughter. Laughter only Maddie could hear.

"What's gotten into you?" Phyllis's hand rose to her throat.

"Could it be the same thing that got into Sarah?" Maddie could taste her mother's weakness now, the same weakness that had assigned Maddie the emotional role of parent for a decade. "You remember Sarah, don't you? The daughter languishing in a coma at a psychiatric care facility so specialized, there's only one of its kind in the country. A hospital too far away to visit, or so your excuses went. My excuses."

The ugly truth was that Maddie had been relieved to let her twin go when she and Phyllis had moved away from their mountain home in Lenox. She'd never been able to bring herself to face Sarah's rehab hospital. Phyllis had been adamant that leaving her twin at peace, with experts to care for her, was the best thing for all of them. And Maddie had drunk her assurances down. Except—

"She's been here all this time, hasn't she?" Maddie's glare dared her mother to keep lying. "We didn't move to Boston to start over near my college, and then stay for my job. We moved so you could be near her, while you let me pretend she didn't exist."

"Who?"

"Sarah! You wanted to be close to her. No matter what happened to Daddy, or what you said afterward. But…" Maddie dove back into the files, leaving a smear of blood on the first folder she grabbed. "…but you didn't want me near her. Why? Because you were afraid something like this might happen if we were ever together again?"

"Some…Something like what?"

Maddie ripped folders from the drawer, yanking them open, then flinging them to the carpet.

"Mr.…." her mother asked.

"Keith," Jarred answered. "Dr. Keith. I'm a friend of your daughter's at St. Chris."

Maddie snorted.

Friend.

Unwelcome images cavorted through her mind. Flashes from their dates. From that morning and what little she could remember of the last hour. Jarred's anger when he'd wrestled the gun away. The gentleness of his touch…his thoughts…even then. The sting of his concern, wrapping around her while he'd pushed her to confront what she'd never wanted to know.

"What's going on?" Phyllis's tone achieved the pitch reserved for when she was truly scared. Crazy scared. "Would someone please tell me what's going on?"

"Maddie's been having a difficult time," Jarred began. "And…"

Leaving him to his doctorspeak, Maddie dug until she found a folder hidden at the bottom of the drawer. The tab wasn't typed like all the rest. *Trinity* had been handwritten instead, in Phyllis's loopy script. She pulled it free and confronted the woman she'd believed was the one person on earth she could trust unconditionally.

"What have you done?" She threw the folder at Phyllis and ignored the roaring in her ears. Roaring that sounded too much like her twin's haunted summer storm. Like the truth hurtling toward Maddie on a raven's wings.

"I…" Phyllis tried pulling her into a hug. She began to cry when Maddie shoved her away. "You have to understand. I wanted to protect you and Sarah both, but—"

"Protect us from what? From knowing that we're insane, all of us? Ten years after the accident, and Sarah's still a vegetable. You can barely leave the house on your own. I'm turning into a raving lunatic. Whatever your secrets have accomplished, they haven't protected any of us from a damn thing."

Maddie looked from the fragile woman standing before her to Jarred's frown, then back. She could remember the bite of the pistol against her temple. The pistol she hadn't bought. Hadn't put in that drawer. And hadn't been able to let go of without Jarred's help.

"Protect Sarah and me from what?" she repeated. "The…curse you didn't want us to know about when we were kids?"

"What?" Phyllis eyed Jarred as if he'd grown three heads. "I don't know what you're talking about."

"Don't worry about Dr. Do-good." Maddie jerked her head toward Jarred. "He already knows more about our family than I do. He's the one who found out where Sarah was. He already thinks what happened to her might have something to do with what's happening to me."

Phyllis rubbed her hands over the sleeves of her conservative oxford shirt. Then down the front of the khakis that had been her uniform for as long as Maddie could remember.

"Mom!" Maddie shrieked.

"What…What does your doctor think he knows?" Phyllis asked.

Jarred stepped closer. Pulled Maddie's hand from where it was scratching her already-abused wrist.

"Ms. Temple—"

"Honey!" Phyllis rushed closer, her hands shaking as she reached for Maddie. She gasped at the angry welts on Maddie's inner arm. "What have you done to yourself? That's…that's exactly what…"

"Is this something your other daughter used to do?" Jarred asked.

Maddie flinched away from her mother, but closer to Jarred. She hated that a part of her needed him standing between her and Phyllis. Filling her with enough of his presence that there was no hint of Sarah now. No drive to hurt herself or someone else. He pressed some tissues he'd found into her hand, then pressed both against her wrist.

He was always pressing. Closer and closer. His touch. His…thoughts…

You can do this, Temple. You can face anything. Trust me…

Another nod of assurance followed, and Maddie felt her own tears start up again. He really was there, in her mind. Then his gaze slid back to her mother.

"How bad did Sarah's cutting become before her final breakdown?" he asked.

"Cutting?" Phyllis's gaze dropped to Maddie's wrist.

"It's an altered form of coping for children and teens who can't process the pain and emotion they're enduring." Jarred stepped closer to Phyllis, blocking her from Maddie's view. "It can become a lifelong compulsion, if not halted soon enough. But it's very rare for it to present itself for the first time in adulthood the way it has with Maddie. Every time she's forced to confront her memories of Sarah, as a matter of fact. There's often an emotional connection between twins that isn't clearly understood. There are likely other parts of Sarah's childhood behavior that might be blending with Maddie's worldview, even after ten years."

"What struggles?" Phyllis tried to get closer to Maddie. Jarred blocked her with his body.

"It's better if you talk with me for now," he warned.

Then he tensed—Maddie's first clue that she'd laid a hand on his back, near his shoulder blade.

"This is between me and my daughter," Phyllis challenged.

"Which daughter?" Maddie managed to stay. "The one you abandoned, or the one you convinced that she wouldn't end up in a loony bin herself. God, Mom!" Maddie buried her face against Jarred's back. Her arms snaked around his waist until she could clasp her hands across his belly, giving in completely to her need to keep him close. "Why not just let me go, too, when you did Sarah? Why put us through all this? Why pretend I'm any different, if you knew it was hopeless from the start!"

Jarred turned to Maddie. "It's not hopeless," he insisted.

"You *are* different, honey." But there was defeat in Phyllis's voice. "You're doing so well. And you're going to keep doing well. That's why…That's why I've let them study Sarah for so long. I thought—"

"Study her?" Maddie shoved Jarred away. She found herself backing Phyllis against the wall. "You turned my twin over to a research facility, because you thought, what? That they'd find a cure? That they could fix me, fix what's wrong with us? Whatever's wrong with our entire family. You sacrificed her so—"

"There's…there's nothing wrong with our family."

"Really? Then why are you shaking, Mom? Like everything I say, every horrible thing I'm thinking, hurts you—physically hurts you. Why did Sarah and I have to hide all those years exactly how much we knew and felt about everyone else, so no one would know we were there, somehow, in their minds? Why have I been avoiding you for months, so I wouldn't upset you more? Why do I feel like if I let myself explode right now, I might take both of you and this entire house with me!"

Sarah's laughter was back, as if Maddie's twin was enjoying the show.

"You have to calm down," Phyllis insisted. "You're talking like—"

"A crazy person?" Maddie's glance to Jarred challenged him to deny that's exactly what he saw.

Phyllis stumbled to a nearby chair, the fear and fight draining out of her. Until her expression was the kind of blank page Maddie had seen too many times.

"It is crazy…" Phyllis mumbled through her tears. "It's not true. It can't be true…It was just a stupid piece of paper. A family myth. Witch trials and public executions…because someone hundreds of years ago thought she could read people's emotions and make them do whatever she wanted…it's crazy…"

"A myth?" Jarred asked as Phyllis's rambling petered off. "Reading…"

"People's…feelings," Maddie finished, childhood secrets bubbling up until they found the crack that Jarred had become in her control. "Sarah and I have always… felt more than we should…"

"There's a fix…" Her mother was rocking now. Forward and back, her arms wrapped around herself like a child. "There has to be a fix…The doctor said they'd try to help Sarah. Then, if you needed it, they could help you, too."

"Help with what?" Jarred demanded. When Maddie

could only stare at her mother, he knelt in front of Phyllis. "Help your daughters with what?"

Phyllis swallowed, her head shaking, her gray-green eyes vague. Glassy. She was gone, the same way she'd left Maddie in the hospital ER ten years ago. The way Phyllis was always gone whenever knowing the awful truth about their family had mattered most. "I did it all for Maddie. For Maddie and Sarah…Sarah was asleep. Gerald was dead. Then the scientist at the research center said he might be able to find some way to stop…the legacy. And I couldn't lose Maddie, too. It…it's crazy. It can't be true. It just can't be."

Phyllis couldn't help Maddie. She'd never been able to. Maddie was on her own, same as always, finding the answers she needed. And without her mother's help, Sarah and the Trinity Psychiatric Research Center were Maddie's last hope.

CHAPTER THIRTEEN

"Your mother thinks all this has something to do with one of your ancestors being persecuted in the witch trials?" Jarred followed Maddie out of her mother's house.

He tripped over the uneven brick sidewalk and glanced back through the open front door. Phyllis was no doubt still sobbing in the den, unaware that they'd left.

"Did you hear something?" Jarred asked.

"Something?" Maddie stopped beside his car. Dug into her purse for her phone. "You mean like a menacing bird swooping down on us, only it's not really there?"

"What?"

"Sorry." She shrugged, pressing SEND. "Must just be me."

He grabbed the phone and flipped it shut, disconnecting the call.

"What the hell's going on, Temple?"

"What the hell are you doing talking to a patient like that?" She figured sarcasm was preferable to pitching another nutty. "You're losing your edge. Your professional boundaries. Get in your car and head back to your sane life before you lose even more."

Maddie grabbed for her phone, missed, and her fingers brushed the back of Jarred's hand. The shock of the contact rattled her already-misfiring brain. A rush of confusion. Jarred's confusion. His determination to stay with her. To earn her trust.

Her palm smacked his chest. His cheek. "Wake up and get the hell away from me. Before—"

He caught her next slap midswing. Grabbed her shoulders. Shoved her against his car.

"I'm awake, damn it! Enough to know that what your mother just said makes her more of a candidate for a psych hold than you are. Except—" His body brushed against hers. His eyes closed. "—I believe more of it than I should. And I've felt enough today to wonder if the parts that I don't believe might be true, too. And I can't help feeling…"

When he opened his eyes, Maddie was lost. Falling into all that soothing blue. He wasn't judging. Or blaming. Or moving away. He wasn't letting her go despite her rigid refusal to lean into his touch.

"Please." Things inside her began to soften and flow the way they did whenever he was near. But survival instincts clamored for her to run. To stay safe. Even though there was clearly no safe anymore.

"I can feel it, too," he said.

He'd said that before, at her apartment. She hadn't believed him then. She still didn't. She couldn't.

"You… You can't be…"

"Feeling what you do?"

He stepped away from her body, but not her mind. Not the place he was making for himself in her heart.

"I…" She watched her hand reach for his cheek. A weak, needy gesture.

You big baby! her twin's voice jeered.

Maddie curled her fingers into a ball.

"Damn it!" She dropped her fist to her side. "I'm not doing this."

He grabbed her hand back. Kissed her fingers one at a time until they opened.

"How long have you been hearing the voice in your head?" he asked—then he caught her reflexive jerk away. He pulled her against his chest. Her fingers clenched in his sweater. "I can…feel when it's there, Maddie. When you're not yourself. I have no idea what that means. But after what your mother said…"

"The…legacy." Maddie struggled to get the word out. To get away. "The stupid legacy. Lies. Always another lie, another excuse, until I don't know what's real. Except I can feel…hear…see things that aren't me!" He wouldn't let her go. *I'm here,* his voice said in her mind. Then she was holding on. Curling close. Needing him to tell her it was real. That she was real. "She…My mother won't admit it. Sarah's gone. My father's gone. And she still won't—"

"I believe you." He tucked Maddie's head beneath his chin.

And it was just that simple, that horrible, being believed. Having someone accept that she was lost and scary and freakishly messed up. Someone still willing to hold her, to kiss the crown of her head and be a buffer between her and her mother's broken mind. Maddie's tears left soundless trails down her cheeks, wetting Jarred's shirt. Staining him with the proof that she was broken, too.

"It's real, Maddie." His breath was warm against her hair. "You have to accept that, or—"

"Accept?" She inched away, as far as she could with the car behind her. She wiped her eyes and her nose on the soft suede of her coat sleeve. A hiccup followed. A laugh, misting the frigid air between them. Broken giggling. Tangible proof that her mind was slipping away.

And Jarred was her witness to it, while something in his gaze was breaking, too. The part that had still thought he could help her.

Which brought them full circle to what she'd intended to make crystal clear that morning. That she was in this nightmare alone, and he could go to hell for making her want it to be any different.

"Good-bye, Jarred." She grabbed her phone, edged around him, and headed toward the street. She redialed the car service she used sometimes for trips into Boston.

The click of Jarred opening his car to leave was the loneliest sound she'd ever heard. But it was the right thing. For him most of all.

"I programmed the Trinity Center's address into my GPS," he called out. "Just before I brought up the directions to your apartment. I'm heading there next, with or without you."

Maddie stood at the curb, her back turned. But she could still feel his concern. His warmth. His presence in her mind. Wrapping around her. Calming the chaos and pushing back against the angry residue of Sarah's brittle thoughts.

Maddie turned back.

"Need a ride, or should I just wait for you there?" His arched brow was a casual, flirtatious castoff. As if she'd simply been walking by and they'd never moved past the easy connection that had been so natural the first months they'd dated.

No baggage. No dark secrets. Just two minds, two souls that fit better than anything she'd ever known.

No more barriers.

No more safe.

No more careful.

Maddie jumped at the sound of her phone flipping shut.

"Tell me you're not ready for this." Jarred stared out his windshield at the Trinity Psychiatric Research Center. "And we'll come back in the morning."

"No," insisted the terrified woman sitting beside him.

He'd never seen Maddie look truly scared before. Her eyes narrowed as she looked at the imposing brick building looming above the parking lot. Her head tilted to the side, her hair shadowing her features.

"Screw this." She shoved her door open and pushed out of the car.

So much for scared.

"Slow down." Jarred jogged to catch up with her. "There's no rush."

Except he'd felt it, too, since leaving Phyllis Temple's house. Since before that. The pull of this place. The conviction that the answers were here. That they'd always been here with Maddie's twin.

He caught Maddie's elbow just outside the center.

"Sarah's in a coma."

"No"—Maddie's head jerked side to side—"she's not."

"Don't get me wrong. I hope she's better. I hope they know how to help you here, but—"

Maddie pulled free, but he caught her chin. Turned her head until he could see her eyes. Flat. Dilated. Drained of the life usually simmering there.

"I think they're killing Sarah here," she whispered.

Jarred nodded, accepting her truth as his own. He turned her loose. "Then let's go see what we can do."

Maddie pushed through the glass doors leading inside. He followed. It was either keep up or get his head bashed in when the door swung back toward him. No one was stopping Maddie in her current state. Which didn't bode well for the bookish receptionist posted behind the entryway's partition. It was a stark, contemporary reception area. Gray walls devoid of artwork. One severely stylish black chair to sit on. No cushion. No houseplants. No magazines. A NO LOITERING sign would have been redundant.

"Do you have an appointment?" asked the bun-wearing fiftysomething woman behind the half-open partition.

Maddie sucked in a deep breath, held it for several seconds, then silently exhaled. Admirable restraint, considering the day she'd had. Jarred was on adrenaline overload.

"I'm here to see my sister."

"And your appointment time would be…" The skeptical receptionist ran a bony finger down the schedule in front of her.

"We don't have an appointment." Jarred eased between Maddie's clenched fists and the partition that wouldn't protect a rhinoceros from her next explosion. "But if there's a doctor we could speak with—"

"*I'm* a fucking doctor." Maddie's nails dug into his arm.

Agitation wasn't the right word for what he was sensing in her. It was as if something dark and hateful had been taking over the closer they got to the center. Something less *Maddie.*

She marched toward the glass door leading past reception. When she tried to open it and it wouldn't budge, she yanked the thing harder, shaking the frame.

"If someone doesn't let me see my sister soon, I'm going to—"

"What do you think you're doing!" All ballsy exasperation, the receptionist pressed a button and released the door's locking mechanism.

Maddie pulled it open, but the receptionist had planted herself in Maddie's path, her finger raised.

"I'm afraid you're going to have to leave," the woman insisted. "This is a private clinic. We have strict visitation policies. Whoever you are, whoever told you could just—"

"I'm Madeline Temple, and you people are doing God knows what with my sister somewhere in this place."

Maddie looked ready to rip the woman's finger off. She flinched when Jarred grabbed her arm. The air tightened around them, her fury coiling like back draft ready to engulf whatever was in its path.

"I'm going to see her," she said to the receptionist. "I'm going to speak with her doctors. Tonight. Or someone here is going to..."

Die!

The threat came out as a growl, directly in Jarred's ear. Or had it been a menacing whisper in his mind? He'd heard that tone before. Twice, in fact. Each time Maddie had lost herself that day.

"Temple?" The receptionist's condescension dissolved. "You're a..."

The woman's hand rose to her throat. She choked. A wave of crimson spread across her washed-out complexion.

Jarred rubbed his own fingers against his neck, remembering that morning when he'd pissed Maddie off, only to find himself unable to breathe.

Die! Maddie's mind whispered again.

"You're..." the receptionist croaked. "I can't..."

"Stop it!" Jarred spun Maddie around.

He yanked her away from the other woman.

"What are you…" he started. "You're not…"

The dull-eyed woman standing before him couldn't be attacking a stranger. Maddie couldn't be able to choke people with her mind. That sort of thing only happened in sci-fi novels and overhyped TV thrillers.

"Jarred?" The Maddie he knew was coming back. She started trembling. "Help me. I can't stop her. I can't…"

"Can't stop who?"

"I can't breathe!" the receptionist gasped. "I can't breathe…Make her stop!"

"Maddie?" Jarred shook her, hard. Harder! "Let me help you, before—"

Die! Maddie yelled, only this time he was certain that her lips hadn't moved. And her eyes had gone flat again.

"Maddie?"

"Help me," the receptionist begged.

Let go, now! Jarred sent the command with his mind. *This isn't you, Temple. You don't hurt people, you help them. Don't do this!*

Maddie flinched. Her body relaxed. Her gaze misted with confusion. He looked over his shoulder to see the receptionist choke once more, her eyes bulging. Then her hand dropped from her neck, and she bent over, taking in several wheezing breaths.

Jarred's body grew numb.

He hadn't been imagining it all day. He really had been there in Maddie's mind. Or she'd been in his. One, two…three times now. And this time he'd intentionally tried to reach her.

I can feel…hear…see things that aren't me, she'd said at her mother's.

"Jarred?" She swayed in his grasp. "What…What happened?"

"You...went away."

Whatever she'd just become had been someone else. He was certain of it. Whoever had attacked the terrified receptionist still standing between them and the inner workings of the center, it hadn't been Maddie.

"Away?" Maddie leaned closer, surprising him not just with her unguarded acceptance of his touch. But with how much *he* wanted her closer. He wanted her thoughts whispering inside his head again. He needed to know he had his gentle healer back, instead of whatever she became when she was raging and wanting to tear the world apart.

"You went away," he said as gently as he could. "Like at your mom's earlier. It was the same thing that happened when you were with Phyllis. And when we were at your place, and you—"

"And I wanted to die..." Maddie shied out of reach, and it was like a part of Jarred was ripped away. "No. I wanted to kill. What's happening to me?"

"I...I'll go find a doctor..." The receptionist backed away, the way someone would from a feral animal. She scurried down the hall, around the corner and out of sight.

Jarred motioned Maddie to follow. She hesitated, her fear of doing what they both knew she had to do ripping at him. Then her spine straightened. She slowly stepped over the threshold and into the center.

"Let's move"—he couldn't stop his hand from caressing the small of her back, slight pressure that urged her to pick up the pace—"before Nurse Ratchet comes back with reinforcements."

"Where should we start?"

Jarred skidded to a stop at the simplicity of her question. "Wait here a second."

He headed back to the reception desk and found a center phone list, complete with a diagram of the building's floor plan on the back. Nice touch. He carried the laminated sheet back to Maddie. Turned it so the floor plan was faceup.

"What?" She frowned at his expectant look.

"Where do you think we'll find your sister?"

"What!" She glanced down at the sheet.

"You're connected to her. Somehow. Some way. That's what happened with that receptionist when she said you couldn't see your sister. It's what's been drawing you here for months, right?"

Sarah or something that was happening to Sarah was destroying Maddie. Jarred kissed Maddie's hand and placed it on the floor plan.

"Focus on your sister." He had no idea what he was saying, but it felt right, all of it. Touching Maddie again. Feeling her accept his help. Telling her to keep searching for the truth instead of shrinking back into her mother's denial.

"Where's Sarah?" he urged.

When Maddie's haunted eyes fluttered shut, he felt her...pulling inward again. She inhaled, and her consciousness seemed to spread out as she released the breath. She did it again. He caught the rhythm and followed, his touch still on her hand. He wanted her to know she wasn't alone. Or maybe he was the one who needed reassurance.

Maddie's body went rigid. And then it happened. Jarred felt the nightmare fill her mind this time. The horror Maddie must have been facing for months now, but she'd been too terrified to admit the truth to anyone. Not to her mother. Not to Yates. Not to him. Only this time it was happening to Jarred, too.

There was complete darkness, even though his eyes were wide-open. Rain and wind whipped around them. Their hands were locked in a death grip, while the world around them emptied of everything except the sound of their breathing. Flames flickered to life, along with the distant sound of screaming. The stench of hope burning to cinders. Then came a rustling that sounded like…wings. A menacing shadow descended, causing Jarred to look up to the branches of a leafless tree looming overhead.

Into the unforgiving eyes of a sinister bird he somehow knew was a raven.

The dream's stark surroundings swirled into sharper focus and then into a kaleidoscope of disbelief. Was this really Maddie's mind? Her imagination? Or was it… Sarah's?

This place.

It was Sarah's mind they'd fallen into.

He tipped Maddie's face with his finger, so he could see what her nightmare was telling him. That her sister had been…haunting her somehow. Pulling Maddie into a vortex of insanity that he'd led her back to tonight. The eyes that met Jarred's were dark gray, not Maddie's misty green. They filled with hate, as a woman who looked like Maddie but wasn't backed away and raised a gun to his chest.

"Sarah?" he asked, clinging to the knowledge that they were still in the nightmare.

Die! Maddie's twin screamed in his mind, clicking off the safety on the semiautomatic she held in the dream.

A dream where Sarah was suddenly hell-bent on killing him.

CHAPTER FOURTEEN

"Alpha . . ." the Raven demanded. "Engage, Alpha. Now!"

"Where . . ."

Sarah was lost in gray. A nightmare, misting between two worlds. One, where she stood aiming a gun at a man she'd never met. The other, where she was running for her life. Escaping the center with her Raven.

Where . . .

"Where am I?"

"You've memorized the center blueprints. Follow our escape sequence. Engage!"

Sarah's body shook in his grasp. His fingers bit into her arms as he lifted and carried her around the next corner. It was the Raven. In her dream. In her simulation. No. This wasn't just a simulation . . . And he wasn't just the Raven . . . He was the voice once again. The voice that had rescued her from the darkness . . .

"Escape sequence. Engage!"

The dream of the other world and the other man spun, then snapped away completely. But Sarah still held the gun. She was dropped to her feet. The Raven and his warm, familiar voice dragged her down another hallway. It all felt so real, this world. The floor was solid beneath her . . .

"Wake up, Alpha." The Raven pulled her along. "Come on, Sarah. You hate me after what happened to Kayla. Don't *think I don't know it. Use that hate and get your butt mov-ing. Your sister's blown my plans to get you out of here under the radar. The center's on alert. They'll know you've es-caped. There's no time. You'll never get your chance to make me pay for Kayla if you don't engage. Damn it, get us out of here."*

Her sister...

Maddie was here. Nearby. Standing with a man Sarah had never met, her mind locked with Sarah's through a dream link. In the dream, Maddie was holding the same gun as Sarah. Wearing the same killing smile Sarah wanted on her face as she confronted her Raven...

"Die!" Sarah tried to scream, but her voice was too hoarse. Too weak. Barely a whisper.

A real whisper...

Because she was awake.

She was really awake!

"That's it." The Raven's eyes were blacker than the hell he'd made of her mind. Piercing. Determined. He pulled her around another corner. Down another endless hallway. "That's it, Sarah. Stay with me. There's an as-sault rifle in your hand. The safety's off. All exits are locked and guarded. You're in decent physical shape. But you're weak from the recovery meds. This is a cluster-fuck, but we can still make it. Engage! Run the odds. What's our best escape route?"

Our?

She followed the Raven. Clung to him when she wanted to despise him. She winced at the unrelenting glare of the overhead lights. The echo of their footsteps thundered through her head. And over that came the racket of others approaching, their thoughts and feelings flooding her mind.

"We're being tracked..." she mumbled.

"Where? How many?"

"From...the right...No! The left. Five men. Six. They're..."

"How many? Focus, Sarah." The Raven barreled them through a heavy door that banged into her as it closed. Down a flight of stairs. Down a stairwell. "Feel the gun in your hand. Be ready to use it. Keep moving. How many are coming, Alpha?"

"Six," she reported, relinquishing control to her training. To her mentor, who she could remember had stitched up the shunt in her chest and the port for her feeding tube. He'd been gentle. Concerned. Taking care of her. Not an avenging Raven at all.

"Behind us now," she muttered through her confusion. "At the door."

The stairwell door burst open. Gunshots rained down, except bullets didn't blast around them. Instead, several wicked-looking darts lodged in the wall mere inches away.

"Under here!" He dragged her beneath the last flight of stairs while she opened fire.

Through countless dream sequences, linked to the Raven's mind, she'd learned battle tactics and weapons handling. Daily, grueling physical therapy had rebuilt her muscle tone and kept her body taut. She was primed to be a killing machine, but she made sure each bullet missed its target—just enough to preserve life instead of destroying it.

"Focus, Alpha." The Raven fired a gun she hadn't noticed before. "Find us a way out!"

Focus?

A demented laugh escaped her control. Then her arms gave out. Her rifle clattered to the ground. She let the pain and the darkness and the death and the hate pour into her mind, wanting it to be over. The Raven's feelings and the men trying to catch them and the others cowering in their offices in fear and...

Your sister's here...

The sister Sarah had been forced to link her mind with whether she'd wanted to or not.

"Maddie's really here?"

Sarah could feel her now. Closer than before. And Maddie was losing her mind.

Sarah had always needed Maddie's balance. Her peace. Maddie had been Sarah's light before the darkness had taken over. Before Maddie began to despise her. Before she'd been glad to be rid of Sarah. Now Maddie's mind was falling apart, as she dreamed of killing a man the way Sarah longed to kill the Raven. Served her right, the self-righteous bitch.

"Reload." The Raven shoved a fresh clip into Sarah's hand.

She went through the motions without thought, fed by training simulations and her fury at her twin's betrayal. She opened fire, following the Raven's orders—for now—while her mind dug for the link with her sister. The connection that was strengthening Sarah. Returning to her the control that could finally end the nightmares.

"Fuck you, Madeline Grace Temple!" Sarah yelled.

She would be free. Her sister could deal with the fallout. It was Maddie's turn to be the center's lab rat.

CHAPTER FIFTEEN

Richard reached into his go-bag for the last of the clips he'd packed.

His hastily prepared escape plan had turned into a what-not-to-do scenario the Brotherhood would relish telling for years. Assuming he and Sarah actually made it out of the center alive. Sarah had advanced from mumbling incoherently while she stumbled along at his side, to cursing her sister at the top of her lungs. So far, they'd held off the security guards at the top of the stairwell. Thank God security was shooting tranquilizers instead of bullets. But Sarah was far from stable. It was like having a misfiring bomb sputtering to life next to him.

Still, she hadn't taken a single life. She'd held off their pursuers with precision and more stamina than should have been possible. But every soul bearing down on them was still intact. Impossible to believe. Inconvenient as hell, since their numbers were growing. But amazing all the same.

"The exit route, Alpha. Find one that's not being guarded. Get us out of—"

"My name's—" She grabbed him by the throat, finding lethal pressure points.

Richard tried to swallow. Tried to speak. Tried to keep his vision from fading to nothing as blood flow was cut off at his carotid artery. Then Sarah's grip loosened. Gasping for air, he stared as her ebony irises became ringed with a glittering green. Her twin's eye color.

"Sarah?" he wheezed out. "They're going to trap us in this stairwell if you don't snap out of it. Use your link to Maddie if you need it. Be pissed at her or at me or whatever it takes. But keep your focus here, just like in our simulations. My simulations. Listen to my voice. Escape sequence. Map us a way out."

Sarah jerked. Her hand tightened around his throat, then dropped. Her breathing calmed. Her eyes cooled to the pools of gray he knew he could control.

That a girl.

Then the ground-floor exit door crashed open. Sarah had the security team neutralized immediately, firing above their heads and forcing them to retreat. When the door slammed shut again, her gaze locked on Richard's. She was waiting for his next command, but he could feel her mind flowing beyond his. Toward her twin. Merging all too easily with a consciousness he hadn't programmed her to touch.

"What do you sense?" he asked, shrugging off the implications. Now wasn't the time to dig for Sarah's shadow-dream programming and who'd implanted it. "Where are the security teams moving?"

"Two more groups are coming." She didn't react as Richard reloaded his weapon and shot an arc of cover fire toward their friends overhead. "There's one unguarded route left, but there's a low probability of success."

"Low is better than dead. Engage, Alpha. Get us the hell out of here."

CHAPTER SIXTEEN

"Temple!" a warm voice shouted from inside Maddie's nightmare.

Another of Sarah's nightmares. Storm and winds and a swaying forest with a Raven circling overhead. Only this time Maddie was holding an automatic weapon.

"Wake up!" the voice insisted. "Put the gun down. This isn't you. You're a healer."

But her twin was a killer. And the Raven was at Sarah's side somewhere nearby. Pushing her to shoot. To run. Demanding every shred of sanity she had left. And Sarah was dragging Maddie along with her.

The Raven had to—

"Die!" Maddie screamed, ramming the rifle's muzzle into his chest.

Into Jarred's chest, where he stood in front of her in the dream.

Jarred . . .

Not the Raven . . .

His eyes widened. His gaze darkened with anger that she instinctively knew wasn't for her.

"It's this damn place." He cupped her cheek, his hand warm against her ice-cold skin. "Whatever they're doing to your sister here, it's affecting you. You're . . . feeling her. This isn't you, Maddie. Stay with me."

"Pull the trigger!" the Raven hissed through her mind. "Execute!"

But Jarred's warm presence wouldn't let her. As long as he was with her, there was no threat to eliminate.

Except her.

Maddie was the threat.

"You...You have to run," she said. "Get away from me..."

"I'm not going anywhere." Jarred's fingers found hers next to the gun's trigger. "I won't let this place get away with whatever they're doing to Sarah. But you have to wake up for me, sweetheart."

Sweetheart...

Maddie's finger twitched. He simply curled his hand around hers, trusting her with his life. It may have been only a dream, but his trust was real. Undeniable.

The Raven shrieked, suddenly looming above them in Sarah's nightmare. The bird dove, wings spread, talons bared.

Bare tree limbs swayed.

The gun in her hand fired.

"No!" Maddie's scream ripped through the night.

But the gun wasn't there anymore. And she was no longer cowering in a ghostly forest.

"I've got you." Jarred's voice shook, but he was strong and solid beside her. He'd wrapped his body around hers, where she lay in a terrified heap on the floor. "God. Is that...That's what you're seeing every night when you sleep?"

"Just a dream..." She tried to crawl away. The need to expel the emotion, the feelings that weren't hers, rose. Surged. "Let me go! It was just a dream..."

"I won't let them get away with this." Jarred cradled her head to his shoulder.

She covered her ears against lingering waves of nightmare.

Always another dream, Sarah's voice chanted.

Always alone…

Maddie wrenched away.

"It's okay." Jarred followed.

Her stomach rejected what little she'd eaten that day. He cursed and pulled her hair back.

"I can't take it anymore." She wiped the back of her hand across her mouth. "Get away from me before I hurt you. I don't want to, but she'll make me. She's going to—"

"You're back with me, Maddie. Sarah's not here. I've got you. You didn't hurt me. You're not going to. Whatever that was, it's over."

"That was Sarah. It was me. And it's never over… Always the same."

"No, it's not the same. This time, you weren't alone. I was there." Certainty rained down from his gaze. "Wherever your mind went, mine was there, too. Has that ever happened before?"

He'd been there.

He'd really been there.

"That was Sarah's nightmare?" he prodded. "The rain. That bird. It was a raven, right? Telling her to run. Forcing her to fight people she didn't know. Those were the ramblings of a madwoman. It wasn't you."

Maddie flinched at his brutal description of her sister.

Jarred rested his forehead against hers. "I'm sorry. I know she's your twin, and you still care about her no matter what's happened. But Sarah's dreaming all this up and forcing it on you." He rocked, as if he couldn't quite believe what he was saying. "All these months, when you've been…losing yourself in her dreams, has any of it been anything but your sister's deranged fantasies?"

Maddie blinked. She let herself really hear what he was saying. Process what had just happened. See what was real.

"It's not just a fantasy," she said. "Someone...someone's designing Sarah's nightmares...Only they're real, somehow. It feels like someone's forcing her to do what she's doing. To kill. And tonight, she..." In the back of Maddie's mind, she sensed her twin still running for real...Hating for real...Shooting a real weapon at real people...Drawing on Maddie's control, the way Maddie had balanced Sarah's gifts when they were kids. Which meant a part of Maddie was trying to hurt people, too.

"Get away from me!" she begged, but she couldn't let go of Jarred's arm. "You have to..."

Run! the Raven hissed through her mind.

And Sarah was running. Fighting to be free. Running into the darkness and the rain. The thunder and gunshots...while her mind whispered that she had to kill the Raven.

"Wake up, Temple! Stay with me." Jarred's voice brought Maddie back to his side. She was in his arms still, on the carpeted floor of the reception area. "You have to fight this, damn it. Whatever it is...have to... with me..."

Maddie felt herself shaking. Her body, out of control. Her mind. Because Sarah was still there, deep inside. But she was leaving, too. Leaving Maddie to a world filled with fear and chaos, the way Maddie had abandoned her.

"Maddie?" Jarred eased her flailing body to the floor. "Maddie, stay with...Dammit...with me...! God, you're..."

Seizing.

She was having seizures.

Like Sarah's, when they were teenagers. When the emotions had raged. When there'd been nothing left of

Sarah's mind for the feelings to feed on, so they'd ravaged her body instead. No one had been able to help her. Now, no one could help Maddie.

Sarah's darkness was coming for her...

The nightmare...

The Raven...

"...the hell away from her!" Jarred's touch was yanked away. "Maddie!"

Footsteps pounded around them, while Maddie fought for consciousness. There were uniforms. Guns. Anger. Fear. She was feeling it all. She couldn't stop it. She couldn't escape. Cold hands locked onto her trembling body. The relentless waves of emotion filling her became a blinding search for release. Because a part of her was outside the center now...

...stumbling and running, with the Raven's blood dripping from her fingers.

She was looking back. She was Sarah, and she was free. Maddie was the one who was trapped. And that made Sarah smile and wave as she slowly shut her mind away and left Maddie to face the center alone.

"No!" Maddie's world spiraled back in focus. She was staring up from the reception floor, into the unforgiving eyes of a uniformed guard.

"Get the hell away from her," Jarred bellowed, still fighting to protect her. Two other men had him pinned to the wall. "Don't you fucking touch her. I'm her doctor, and—"

A gut punch doubled him over.

"Leave him alone!" Maddie demanded in her twin's nightmare voice.

She couldn't move, but she didn't have to. In the nightmares, Sarah had controlled people with her mind. And somehow Maddie could now, too. The receptionist. Jarred that morning. Maddie's patient. She'd been able to do things to all of them—through all of them—with her thoughts alone.

Jarred's guards dropped to their knees in agony the second Maddie thought of choking them. Then the man holding her began clawing at his throat. She rose to her feet. A bed of dry, crumbling leaves crackled beneath her. Like the ones beneath her sister's feet as Sarah stopped running to look back.

Maddie had never felt stronger. Freer. There was no weakness in her now. No fear. Only hate. Sarah's hate for the Raven.

And Maddie's, for the men trying to hurt Jarred. She wouldn't let them take him away from her, the way the storm and the truck had taken her father…

Jarred's guards were down. Maddie's eyes had gone dark. Her expression was a numb kind of blank that terrified him. There were security officers collapsing all over the hallway because of whatever Maddie was doing. If he could just get to her, maybe he could stop this. But he couldn't make his body move. She wouldn't let anyone move.

"Stay with me, Maddie. Don't do this. This isn't you."

"Of course it is." Her smile was the saddest thing he'd ever seen. The men who'd been holding Jarred rolled to their backs, their eyes open and staring blind, their chests straining for oxygen. Maddie admired her handiwork. "I can't let them take you away, too…I won't let them…They have to—"

No, they don't, Jarred argued with his mind. *I'm here. No one's taking me away from you.*

There were tears in her eyes now. She'd heard him. Good girl.

Let me get you out of here, he said, *before—*

"Ah!" A sharp pain bloomed in his upper arm. Buzzing

roared through his ears. Then the ground was rushing
toward him. He landed on his guards. A scream sliced
through him. Maddie's silent scream of rage as she
clutched the dart sticking out from her neck. Their
minds were still joined, and together their worlds misted
to a vision of a bird soaring down the hallway, transform-
ing into a flesh-and-blood man.

Raven! Maddie said in the dream. Sarah's Raven.

Jarred blinked the real world back into focus, only to
see the same man standing over him, blood oozing from
a gash in his forehead. He trained a very real semiautomatic on Jarred.

"Release my men, Ms. Temple," he ordered. "Or your
doctor friend dies."

CHAPTER SEVENTEEN

"No one inside this room but me," Richard instructed the security team guarding the holding suite.

He wiped at the blood trickling down the side of his head, trying to piece together the various ways his and Sarah's escape had gone completely to hell. Culminating with her bashing his head in with her gun and running on her own. Then he'd barely stopped Madeline Temple from either killing a center security team, or getting herself killed by them. Now Richard had her and her companion, both of them tranquilized, to deal with before he could disengage himself and his work from the center for good.

He applied his palm to the security scanner. Leaning in, he waited for the secondary system to verify his retinal imprint.

"But what if—" the security guard to his right muttered.

"No one!"

"But the directors—" The man was one of the guards Madeline had been strangling downstairs. He grabbed Richard's arm. "They've ordered the center locked down and the intruders isolated. The directors want to interrogate them themselves."

"Then by all means." Richard ripped his arm away.

"Escort the directors here personally—after you show them how well you've secured every last inch of this facility. That should take at least a half hour once they arrive, wouldn't you say? I'll have completed my examination of our guests by then, and you'll be free to personally introduce Madeline Temple to our illustrious board. She should be awake and thrilled to see you again."

The guard swallowed. Hard.

Weak little shit.

Richard pushed into the room. Recessed lighting blinked from dim to full, triggered by motion sensors. Dr. Keith and his *patient* were laid out on side-by-side, stainless steel tables. A fast-acting sedative had taken care of Keith downstairs. Richard hadn't been nearly as accommodating with Madeline. He'd custom designed her tranquilizer for her sister almost a year ago. For the weeks just after she'd emerged from her coma. Richard had later perfected his mind-control matrix to keep Sarah's psychic abilities muted when his mind wasn't there to guide hers. But a dose of the tranquilizer had always been available, just in case.

Richard ignored the center's unconscious guests and logged into the computer console on the opposite wall. Two minutes was all he needed to shut down the suite's video and audio recorders. Next, he reverted the unit to a discrete workstation that could no longer be accessed via the central network.

He needed time to think. To assess. To regroup and figure out how to convince the Brotherhood not to issue a termination order for Sarah or himself. Or her twin now.

He'd bluffed his way out of cooling his heels in his own holding cell. Barely. If Sarah hadn't attacked him, giving him grounds to say she'd been using him as cover all along, he wouldn't have made it this far. As it was, he was treading very precarious waters. And he was doing it with a concussion—blustering and ordering around the few center security guards not out tracking Sarah. He'd controlled where the intruders were secured. Now he needed a Plan B—since Madeline Temple's arrival had torched his A Game.

But why had Sarah's twin been there at all? The better question was, *who* had gotten her there. Her presence had helped Sarah find the psychic wherewithal to escape not just half the center's security, but Richard, too. Sarah had fallen into her twin's mind and harnessed the power of their connection as if she'd done it countless times before.

Damn it!

Someone else's dream programming had reconnected the Temple twins' minds. The same programming that had disrupted Sarah's recent dream simulations and triggered Kayla Lawrence's death.

He felt with his mind for increased activity in the hallway. So far, nothing. But his reprieve wouldn't last a second longer than it took the center's directors to review the surveillance tapes of Sarah's escape and the sketchy story he'd given security. Richard pulled a syringe from the lab coat the guard hadn't bothered patting down and administered a stimulant directly into a vein in Jarred Keith's arm. The Temple woman was on her own. Her mind would be in disarray once she was fully conscious. Lord knew what damage her link with Sarah was still doing. But Richard's primary concern at the moment was keeping the three of them alive.

A groan drew his attention to Keith's exam table. The other man's eyes were blinking.

"Rise and shine, Doctor."

Richard helped him sit.

"There's very little time for me to explain what's going on." Even if he could explain what he didn't fully understand himself. "Twenty minutes on the outside. There are forces working here that are beyond my control. It's crucial that you know our lives are in danger, and that—"

A low growl was Richard's only warning before Keith launched himself off the table. Richard sidestepped and stared with clinical fascination at the rumpled, moaning heap the other man had made on the floor.

"Admirable, Dr. Keith, considering the narcotic swamp I've made out of your nervous system. But save your strength for getting your patient out of here. Is anything I'm saying making a dent? Cough twice if you understand. Once if you don't."

The other doctor's hate-filled glare was a positive sign.

"Good." Richard waited for Keith to collect his thoughts.

"Who are you?" the man rasped. "Where are we?"

"I'm Richard Metting, Sarah Temple's doctor. And you're in the bowels of an underground, government-funded research facility that's doesn't exist on any blueprint ever drawn. Even though Trinity Center is the toast of Boston's nonprofit fundraising circles, you and your Ms. Temple have obviously already discerned that more goes on here than the pedestrian study of ailments of the mind."

"You mean like—" Keith tried to struggle to his feet, lost his balance, and landed back on his ass. He stayed there, still glaring. "—like the psychic testing of patients without the consent of family, like you've been doing to Sarah Temple?"

"Your instincts are good, Doctor, and to the point. But explaining what I've been doing here would take too long. You're just going to have to trust me to—"

"Trust you?"

"To give you the high points, yes." Metting sighed. "For instance, during my tenure here, I've discovered several features of this facility that few others know about. There's a labyrinth of hidden corridors leading from each of my research theaters, including this one. And the one behind that panel"—he pointed to the wall Keith had propped himself against—"will take us beyond the center's perimeter sensors. I would suggest we get as far away from here as we can, before Madeline regains full cognition."

CHAPTER EIGHTEEN

"We?" Jarred shook his head, certain he'd heard the other man wrong. "And when exactly will Maddie be awake, after *you* shot her full of God knows what?"

He made it to his feet this time. Then, a more difficult challenge, stumbled to Maddie's side so he could examine the puncture wound in her neck.

"Assuming she's as resilient as her sister," Metting said, "taking into account the adverse effects of whatever lucid dream she and Sarah were cycling through when Sarah escaped—"

"Lucid what?" Jarred's already-pounding head cramped a little tighter.

"—and given her tranquilizer's typical half-life, I'd say she'll be able to move in under an hour, but she'll be disoriented. You should expect some short-term memory loss, from the seizure more than my drug protocol."

"And exactly how did you know she had a seizure?"

"It's an expected side effect of a link as powerful as I suspect Madeline and Sarah share. Especially since Madeline's psychic endurance hasn't been strengthened to cope with separation." The other man checked his watch. "Her connection with her twin is going to be unstable until—"

"You mean the bipolar twin whose mind you've been exploiting?" Jarred felt like a damn idiot for hanging on the bastard's every word. But these were the answers that

Maddie needed, and he was getting them for her. Then he'd happily take Metting's head the rest of the way off.

"Technically, Sarah Temple's never suffered from a dissociative disorder." Metting grimaced. "But I suspect that the dream work of one of my colleagues is responsible for creating that very condition in both women now. Sarah's been resisting that unauthorized interference. I assume Madeline has, too. But the resulting conflict has taken a psychic toll. Add in the way the twins' psyches have been thrust into close proximity today, and each woman's individual consciousness will deteriorate further the longer they're kept apart."

"Forced? You're saying Maddie was driven to the brink of insanity, so she'd stumble into this circus!" By nightmares and voices her sister…sent her?

"By someone at this facility who—"

"By you!"

"No, by someone who didn't fully understand what they were doing. Bringing these women together, while their mental barriers have been weakened by whatever dream contact they've shared, will reap disastrous consequences I never would have initiated."

"Then who?" It was the only question Jarred could process. He ran a protective hand over Maddie's hair. "If all this wasn't your doing, then who?"

"I don't know yet." The other doctor's clinical expression slipped to something as close to fury as the soulless man likely got. "Someone else working on Dream Weaver."

"Dream Weaver?"

"A government weapons program. One that's been infiltrated by an inexperienced third party operating beyond my control. Whether she realizes it nor not, Madeline has been sloppily subjected to—"

"Oh, she knew. You've been driving a brilliant doctor insane for three months!"

"Three months? She's been having nightmares for three months?"

Jarred nodded; then he was in the other man's face. "How did you know about the nightmares?"

"Because projecting Sarah's dreams is my domain here. But it's become clear that someone else has been performing unauthorized experiments with both twins' psychic abilities."

"Experiments?" Jarred clutched Maddie's hand again.

"We don't have time for this." Metting's exasperation came complete with a sigh that was going to get his teeth knocked down his throat. "Your twin is psychic. My twin is psychic. Their minds are now joined, both inside and outside their dreams. Hence, the homicidal scene I walked in on in reception."

"That was..." Jarred dropped Maddie's hand. *His* twin?

"That was what?"

"I...I don't know."

"Exactly. What you need know is that as long as my patient's on the run without someone to control how she projects her psyche into the world, *your* patient will continue to be in as much danger as her twin."

"As opposed to the danger Maddie's in right now, from you?"

Metting sighed again and glanced toward the door. "If you really want to save your patient's sanity, you're going to have to trust me and do exactly as I say."

"You're insane!" Jarred's shout caused Maddie's head to jerk. "I don't trust a damn thing—"

"It's no coincidence, Dr. Keith, that these women's minds are connected again."

Jarred stiffened, his brain fully engaging for the first time. "How the fuck do you know my name?"

"I know a great deal, Dr. Jarred Mathew Keith. That

you found your way into psychiatry after surviving the loss of both your parents before the age of ten. That you and Madeline Temple have more in common than childhood tragedy. Not the least of which is your genius IQ that should already be stringing together the random details you've observed tonight and processing at least part of what's going on here. And I know," Richard added as Keith braced himself on the balls of his feet, "that you're contemplating taking another crack at beating me to a bloody pulp."

"It would be satisfying to try."

"Curb the impulse."

"You people have—"

"You have no idea who my people are or how critical it is that you and Madeline help me find Sarah."

"Help you?" Jarred's laugh burned on its way out.

"*I'm* the choice you have to make, Doctor. Between running blind or giving Madeline the only intervention that will save her and her twin."

"By bringing them under your control?"

"Better me than the bastard who wants to use them as psychic killing machines."

"You're the Raven, aren't you?" Jarred squinted. "In the nightmares Maddie keeps having with her twin. I saw a raven in Sarah's nightmare. And then you were there."

"You've..." It was Richard's turn to stare. "You've shared their lucid dreams?"

"Nightmares, Dr. Metting. Of an all-powerful Raven controlling Sarah. Making her do horrible things to people while she makes her sister watch, over and over again, until Maddie thinks she's the one doing them."

"And in these nightmares, I'm a—"

"You're the Raven, you maniacal bastard."

CHAPTER NINETEEN

Silence vibrated through the holding suite. Richard was too stunned to say anything. Sarah had projected him into her dreams—as a raven. And Jarred Keith had participated in the Temples' link.

Sarah's sister moaned—a woman whose face was so similar to her twin's that Richard felt the impact of it each time he looked at her. Footsteps approached the suite's locked door. Followed by impatient knocking. Then pounding.

"What's wrong with this scanner?" Ruebens bitched outside. "Get this door open, Dr. Metting. What the hell's going on? The directors are assembling, and they're demanding answers."

"What do these people…" Jarred Keith's tone was nonconfrontational for the first time since regaining consciousness. "What do you and the government want with Maddie? If you're trying to say that someone in this place has been—"

"—intentionally targeting Sarah's sister, to ensure that Madeline's unstable enough to require intervention, too? Ah. The light flickers dimly."

"Dr. Metting!" Ruebens pounded on the door. "This is unacceptable. Dr. Keith, the directors of this institution apologize for you being held against your will this way. I assure you the administration will get to the bottom of your deplorable treatment. And, of course, we'd be happy to help Dr. Temple in any way we can. Please, help me get this door open so I can straighten out this misunderstanding."

Keith's attention snapped to the suite's door, then back. Richard pressed the hidden mechanism to open their escape route. He waited. Keith picked up the woman he'd kept a hand on from almost the moment he'd regained consciousness.

"No one's hurting her again." Jarred hitched Maddie higher as he stepped to Richard's side. "Try it, and you're a dead man."

"Admirable, Dr. Keith, but naïve." Richard ushered him inside the tunnel. "Madeline and her sister are both going to hurt more. All we can do is contain the damage that's already been done and get them stronger. It will be quite some time before their minds are fully intact again and under their own control."

He flipped a switch to swing the floor-to-ceiling panel shut, secure it, and activate overhead lights. A flat-screen monitor flickered on. It revealed a split image of the now-empty room behind them, and of Ruebens and the guard attempting to override the suite's security outside. Ruebens typed away at the scanner's keypad, looking ready to rip the device free of its mounting.

"It's only a matter of time before they make it inside and discover the tunnel," Richard mused. "I have a car hidden in the woods at the end of the viaduct. Take your chances here, with them, or come with me."

Jarred set Maddie's feet on the ground. Her cheek came to rest on his shoulder. Her eyes were tracking back and forth behind their closed lids. She was dreaming. No doubt linked with her twin, who was outside somewhere, running while she was dreaming herself.

Richard headed down the corridor.

"Is this really where you want the woman you love to wake up," he asked, "while she's disoriented and terrified of the power growing inside her?" He slowed his pace once he heard the echo of the other man's footsteps following. "It's good to know your instincts are sharp enough not to trust the people who've been brainwashing Maddie's sister into—"

Richard's legs were kicked out from under him. His already-aching head struck a protruding chunk of granite on his way down. Keith's booted foot pressed across Richard's throat.

"*You've* been brainwashing Sarah." Keith leaned his weight into Richard's windpipe. "You're the one I don't trust."

"I'm—" Richard couldn't grind out more.

"Sarah hates her Raven. And so did Maddie when she turned on me, then on those guards. Both women wanted to kill you, and that's good enough for me."

"I've been trying to—" Richard grabbed Jarred's foot and shoved it away. He rolled to his side and tried to get his larynx to work again. "I've protected Sarah the best I could. You don't understand the circumstances surrounding—"

"You've protected her so well, you're driving her twin out of her mind!" Keith advanced, but the woman in his arms began to struggle against his hold.

"I had nothing to do with dragging Madeline into this," Richard argued. "But I'm the only person who can tell you how her mind is going to deteriorate. I'm the only one who can help her use her abilities to find her sister. And trust me, reuniting the two of them is the only way either will survive."

How could things have gotten so out of control so quickly?

Richard had been flying under the radar for too long. He'd become overconfident. He'd been too focused on one battle, on protecting one sister, without considering how the government bastards he'd thought he'd snowed might be planning to use the other. He tried to stand, but the tunnel was spinning around him like a fucking top.

"No time…" he gasped. "There's no time to debate this."

"You're right," Keith agreed. The other doctor frisked Richard's pockets. Snatched the Land Rover keys. "But it's you who's out of time. You deserve whatever those men back there do to you."

Keith shoved Richard back to the ground. He picked up Maddie. He'd made it several yards away by the time Richard pushed himself to his feet.

"Dream Weaver is a top-priority weapons program the government intended…intends…to implement on a global scale. This project will produce a successful field test, or the principles being studied will be terminated in a manner that guarantees no one will ever know what transpired at this facility."

Keith finally turned back.

"Terminated?" he asked. "Principles? I swear, I hear the words coming out of your mouth, but you're making as much sense as a bad espionage thriller."

"How's this for making sense, then? The woman in your arms won't survive the next forty-eight hours without her sister's help. Or mine."

"She's going to be fine." Keith started walking again. "I'm going to help her. Then I'm sending the authorities to deal with you and whatever you've done to her sister. That's what you're really afraid of."

"By the time anyone else steps foot in this place, my

existence and evidence of any work that's been done with Sarah Temple beyond caring for her chronic vegetative condition will be erased. The police will merely uncover proof that a paranoid, increasingly altered woman broke into the center and removed her unresponsive twin from the authorized care of her doctors."

Keith sneered over his shoulder. "There are cameras all over this place."

"Video and audio can be digitally manipulated in ways that would blow your mind, Dr. Keith." Richard fought to follow, leaning against the wall for support. "The center won't be found culpable for Sarah's abduction. And they won't stop looking for her or Madeline. Not after the trouble they went through to pull her into Sarah's programming."

"*You* dragged Maddie into this."

"Then why am I letting you go?"

"Because I just kicked the crap out of you." Keith hesitated, as if he was debating backtracking for another pass.

"Where do you plan to go?" Richard ignored the pain in his side and kept walking. "Home? Yours…hers? They'll find you. They'll most likely use local law enforcement to help them."

"Then we'll go to the police first, before you—"

"The government won't let you get anywhere near anyone who will put them at risk. They'll anticipate every possible move and stop you before you can make a report. These people will kill anyone—do whatever it takes—to secure the Dream Weaver outcome they need."

Keith kept walking.

Richard stopped, accepting that he'd never catch the man. Not like this. He pulled his cell phone from his pocket instead. He punched in a contact number—a number he'd given to only one other person.

"Dr. Keith," he rasped. "Catch!"

The other man turned and grabbed the phone out of the air.

"What's this for?" Keith asked.

"For when you realize that I'm right."

"That's never going to happen."

"I'm uniquely qualified to help these women. But I can't unless you convince Madeline to find her sister and bring her to me."

"That's *never* going to happen."

"Yes, it will. Because very soon, you're going to understand that I'm your only option. Just don't wait too long, or Madeline's mind will be too far gone to save. Just like her sister's will be if I can't find Sarah before she breaks from reality completely."

Someone wanted Sarah to kill. She was resisting. Running. But soon she'd have no chance of fighting her shadow programming. She would grow even more volatile. More dangerous to herself and others. Richard had to find her before it was too late, something he couldn't do without Madeline's help.

CHAPTER TWENTY

Sarah stumbled through the darkness.

Through the forest. Rain and wind and death flowed at her...around her...through her...

Where was her host? Where was the Raven, promising he'd keep her safe from the horrible things others wanted her to do?

"Can I help you?" someone asked.

Sarah whipped around and the world kept whipping. Swirling out of focus. There was no center now. No voice to bring her back or help her rest.

"Ma'am?" He was a blur standing by the monkey bars.

Monkey bars? There was a swing set, too. And a slide. A sandbox. She was in a park. A playground. No woods. No summer storm. She was freezing. She was alone.

She was awake.

"Ma'am?" The blur came toward her. Then whoever it was, was on the ground writhing in pain. Like the Raven had been when she'd hit him with her gun and run.

She'd wanted to kill him. She could have. She had been in control again, with Maddie so close. In the end, Sarah hadn't been able to.

But the command to kill was still inside her. Driving her. Screaming for her to be Death.

"No!" she cried.

The man at her feet groaned.

Then she was running again, her hands clawing at her ears. Digging for the dreams she'd run from. But she needed them now to make reality go away. To make everything that she'd done not real. Not her fault. Killing her father. Killing Kayla. Leaving Maddie to face whatever the Raven was doing now, because Sarah had abandoned her.

But it *was* Sarah's fault.

All of it.

She was *Death*. Nothing beyond demented nightmares. Beyond killing. There was no one to stop her now. No more coma protecting her. No more Raven guiding her. And no more Maddie reminding her of what she'd never have.

Sarah was finally free.

Stumbling through the darkness…

Through the forest…

Rain and wind and death flowing around her…

CHAPTER TWENTY-ONE

"...just a little bit farther, Temple," a voice whispered to Maddie.

Her feet were moving over leaves and tree limbs and roots and vines. The voice was close. But the nightmares were closer. Sarah's nightmares.

"I didn't...those men," Maddie said. "I tried to kill them, but it wasn't me. It was...Tell me it wasn't..."

"You weren't yourself," came the assurance she needed. "...still not...have to keep moving...car has to be around here...somewhere..." There was worry in the voice. Fear. "Just keep moving, Maddie."

She clawed at her ears. At the sounds of wind and rain that weren't really there. But it wouldn't go away. Neither would the heckling chant deep inside that she was Death...

"Stop it!" she shouted at no one.

"It's going to be okay."

Her arms were dragged to her side.

"But those men..." Her knees buckled against a vision of men on the ground, sprawled in agony. "I'm not... Sarah doesn't want to hurt them, but without the Raven—"

"He's not going to hurt you anymore," the voice said. It was Jarred keeping her on her feet. He was still there.

"The Raven won't ever hurt you again. Not once I find... God damn it! Where's his car?"

"Car?" Maddie fought to think. Why couldn't she think? "It hurts...Jarred?"

"I'm here. We're out of the center, and..."

The center?

"Oh, my God!" she gasped as the horrifying, confusing memories rushed back.

Security officers with guns had tried to stop her from seeing her sister. Maddie had been trying to kill them. While in her nightmare Sarah had shot her way out of the place, using Maddie to help her do it.

"Sarah..." she sputtered.

"She's made it out, too, I think. But—"

"Out?"

"He said she escaped, and that—"

"He?" Sarah had been in a vegetative state for nearly a decade. "Even...even if Sarah woke up, she wouldn't be able to walk...Who said she got out?"

"Metting. The prick said he was her doctor." Jarred held her against his side. He looked wildly around the woods they were walking through. Then he struck out in a new direction. "That's right, sweetheart. Keep walking. Keep talking to me. Metting's part of the nightmares you've been having. He and Sarah."

"Nightmares?" She and Jarred had come to the center because of Sarah's nightmares. The ones where she was killing people.

"Thank God." Jarred dug a remote from his pocket and pressed a button.

A green SUV parked behind a cluster of overgrowth blinked its lights through the night. Jarred helped her to the passenger side and opened the door.

"Whose car is this?" she asked.

"Dr. Metting's."

"Who?" He'd said that name before. "Who... What's going on?"

Flashes of what had happened before swirled together with images that felt like now, but none of it made sense.

"I think Metting is your sister's Raven," Jarred explained.

"Sarah's what?"

"Her doctor. He was very helpful, explaining how he's responsible for screwing up your life and your mind, then denying any of it was his fault. It was particularly kind of him to lend us his keys after I kicked the shit out of him for holding a gun to my head."

...your sister's Raven...

The Raven was coming!

"No!" Sarah screamed through Maddie's mind.

Maddie struck out, contacting with solid flesh. She was Sarah, and she was shaking and hating and running through the woods and fighting the compulsion to kill whatever crossed her path. She needed the Raven, but she hated him!

"Maddie?" He secured her arms behind her back. She kicked him. He pinned her to the side of the car, his hips slamming against hers, his thigh riding high between her legs.

"I'm going to kill you," Maddie spat in the Raven's face. She strained against his strength, the world oozing death and darkness around them. "You turned me into this, you freak. I'll kill you. You can't stop me!"

"Maddie! It's—"

"I won't let the dreams make me—"

"Temple! It's Jarred!" A hard hand shackled both her wrists. Then warm fingers cradled the side of her face. "The Raven's not here. Metting's still in the center, and I got you out. We have to leave before they realize we're gone. He said…Metting said you and Sarah would still be connected. That's what's happening. You have to fight her, Maddie. You have to…wake up for me. You're safe now."

Safe?

Run! Sarah insisted. *Don't trust the Raven…*

"Let me go!" Maddie struggled harder to get away. "I'll kill you if you don't let me—"

"Maddie, you have to listen to me." He gripped the back of her head, pulled her cheek to his, and spoke directly into her ear. "I'm Jarred, not the Raven. I don't blame you for being scared. But I need you to stop fighting and get in the car."

Her head shook from side to side. She was going to kill him. Bite him. Stop him from—

Their noses brushed.

Their lips.

Their breath mingled.

Stalled.

Their gazes locked in a moment of blinding connection that snapped Maddie back to herself.

"Jarred?" She couldn't breathe. She couldn't remember. What couldn't she remember? "Jarred, what… Where…where's Sarah?"

"Shh…It's okay. You're back with me. You're safe now." His mouth brushed hers with each word. His lips trembled while he spoke. His hand released her wrists and came up until he was cupping her face with a gentleness she couldn't bear.

"Don't," she pleaded. "I'll hurt you. I'm—"

"You're not hurting anyone. Look at me. Stay with me."

She did look then. And she lost herself in what she saw. What she felt. His concern. His thoughts and emotions reaching for her. His thumbs stroking her cheeks.

His body feeling more real to her than her own. His strength, calling to her on an elemental level she hadn't let herself feel since she was a teenager. When for one forgotten moment she'd dared to need another heart beating next to hers.

Maddie leaned into his touch, wanting to believe this was real. That Jarred wasn't a dream that would disappear with the next blink of her eyes. Their mouths were inches apart.

"Maddie?" Need vibrated on the sound of her name. "We can't—"

"Stay with me," she begged, tensing for rejection. *Please don't leave me.*

I'm here, was his unspoken answer.

The next touch of his lips, the next taste of him, was like coming home. Like forever. Jarred's kiss deepened, stunning her with how much more she wanted. Grounding her and giving her the control she needed to take more, and more. And then more. He was there. He was really there. Another dream? Maybe. But she wound her arms around him anyway. And she opened her mind, the way she'd been afraid to reach for any other man. If this was still a dream, she would gladly lose herself in it forever.

But flashes of nightmare were her reward for trusting. Because she was running again, like Sarah was running...

And this time Jarred was with her. While danger raced after them...Death chasing them, until it sounded like a raven, wings rustling, swooping closer...

"Jesus, God!" Jarred pulled away, still supporting Maddie against the car.

"I'm sorry," she sobbed.

Then she was running for real. She didn't get far before Jarred's strong arms wrapped around her waist and pulled her against his body, her back to his chest.

"Don't!" she cried. "Let me go, or I'll—"

"I'm here," he said. "*You're* here. And I'm not letting you go, no matter what that was."

"The Raven…" she whispered. "It was Sarah and her Raven and…"

Jarred's head nodded against hers. "I saw him, too, inside the center. And just now. I saw what he's been doing to you in Sarah's nightmare."

Images replayed in Maddie's mind. Of guns firing and screams and Sarah fighting the madness she was sucking Maddie into, then needing Maddie in the insanity so Sarah could survive it.

"It wasn't just a nightmare. It wasn't just Sarah." Maddie shivered. "In the center, I was killing—"

"No. You didn't kill any—"

"But I hurt them."

"You were trapped in some kind of vision…" Jarred's hold on her tightened. "This connection you have with Sarah. Just like a minute ago. You weren't yourself just now. And at the center, in your nightmare, when I saw—"

"*You* saw?" He'd said that before. Maddie shoved him away. Or at least she tried. "You didn't see anything."

Jarred guided her back to the vehicle. "We'll figure it out later."

"Figure out what?" That she was losing her mind? And maybe he was, too, if he thought he knew a damn thing about any of this. And now, he thought he could see…

He thought he could know…

"I need…" she stuttered. "I need my mom."

Someone already damaged, like Maddie. Anyone but Jarred.

"Later." He pushed her onto the seat. Protected her head as he swung her legs inside. Fastened her seat belt.

Maddie grabbed his arm when he would have pulled away. "My mother needs to get her ass over here with the police. She needs to demand—"

Sirens wailed in the distance.

"Whatever's going on here, I don't trust the cops to be able to do anything about it." Jarred's voice was low and reasoned and harder than she'd ever heard it. A wave of barely leashed violence assaulted her. "Metting said… He's been right about your condition so far, and he said not to trust the authorities. He's a bastard, but I believe him about this. It's not safe to talk to anyone. Not until we know more."

"What…What else did he say?" Maddie could remember a face, now. The Raven from her nightmares, walking toward her. A real man looming over her, looking bruised and battered and terrifying.

"That it's not a coincidence that Sarah's gotten well enough to fight her way out of whatever's going on in the center, while you've gotten sicker. That someone wanted you here with her."

Maddie cringed at the sound of more sirens. "Do you really believe—"

"I don't know what to believe." Jarred shut her door and rounded the front of the vehicle. He slipped behind the wheel and started the engine. "All I know is that I don't trust anybody but the two of us right now. Which means we're on our own figuring out what to do next."

Then he was driving the SUV like a demon. Careening down a rough trail, headlights off so no one would see them.

"We have to…" *We?* When had she stopped thinking of them as *her* and *him*? When had Jarred become the only thing keeping her from flying into a thousand pieces that would never go back together? "Where are we going?"

"Damned if I know." Jarred swerved to avoid a tree she didn't see until it whizzed by, scraping the paint on her door.

"My mother's?" she asked. "Maybe she can—"

"No."

"But she knows…" Maddie's rage for Phyllis surged from the betrayed part of her that was becoming more like Sarah by the second. "That bitch knows more than she's told me. She—"

"No." Jarred burst from the woods, tires squealing as they caught on the asphalt of a rural highway. "It's not safe there now. It's not safe anywhere. You can't go home again, Maddie, not until we're sure this is over. Neither of us can."

Jarred tried to focus past Metting's threats. Past the memory of Maddie clinging to him in the woods. Her desperate kisses. Her need for him, even while she'd tried to run. They had to talk, but he had to get her—and himself—calmed down first.

"Tell me everything that doctor said," Maddie demanded. She was more awake, but she was still altered. And her agitation was growing again. The unfamiliar environment wasn't helping.

He'd brought her to his ex-wife's apartment, the only place close he could think of that wouldn't be an immediate giveaway to whoever was chasing them. Once upon a time, it had been his apartment, too. He still had a key. He'd been watering Victoria's plants while she spent six months teaching in England. They couldn't stay there long, not if Metting's government conspiracy predictions where to be believed. But it was a chance to breathe. To try to swallow what had just happened.

Maddie wouldn't stay put on the couch. She'd been pacing on and off since they arrived. And when she wasn't, she kept picking up Victoria's knickknacks and studying them as if she should remember them somehow. Then she'd back away, as if terrified to try to remember anything at all.

"How much of Sarah do you still…feel?" he asked. It was a nonsensical question. But it was the only question that mattered. That, and: "Are you feeling them, because—"

"Because I'm just like her?" Maddie finished.

"Like her, how?"

"When she runs, I'm there. When she tries to hurt people, I'm there. When she k-killed that woman, I was—"

"What woman?" Jarred swallowed his instinctive denial. "How do you know your sister killed someone?"

Maddie blinked. "I don't know. But a part of me was there. Like she needed me there. Like I was killing—"

"You aren't Sarah."

But someone wanted her to be. Every outlandish thing Metting had said was ringing eerily true.

"Sarah needs me," Maddie argued. "She's always needed me. And now she's—"

"I don't think she's causing this. Not intentionally." Sarah was insane. Dangerous. But someone else was driving this runaway train Jarred had strapped himself to.

"Then who?" Maddie stared from across the room with those too-dark eyes. "Who's causing this? That Metting guy?"

"He says he was helping her." Jarred watched as Maddie began practically walking in place. She couldn't seem to stop her hands and feet from moving.

"Sarah's Raven was helping her?" Maddie's laugh was empty, except for the hate that flared inside her each time the man's name came up. "This is all his fault."

"Metting said it's a government testing program, and he was there to get Sarah out. That someone else was—"

"Testing!" Maddie was full-blown pissed now.

Jarred stepped closer as Maddie stared at a collection

of crystal paperweights Victoria kept on the mantel. Amethyst, smoky quartz, lapis, black agate, and several others that she'd found since their breakup. Some of them were wicked sharp where they came to a point.

"Metting said he was trying to escape Dream Weaver *with* your twin, so he could protect her. You were linked with Sarah. You tell me—what the hell was going on when we got to the center?"

"They…" Maddie's body stilled. "They were running…Sarah and the Raven were running together… He was…helping her…The bastard keeps telling her to trust him!"

Jarred winced as Maddie's fist clamped down on the sharpest of the crystals. It sliced through the pad of her forefinger, but she didn't seem to feel it. He snatched her hand away. And in that instant, everything that was Maddie rushed through him. Anger, then fear, then loneliness and anger, until he was deep enough to find the healing white that was truly her.

It was the white he focused on.

"How…" He couldn't stop himself from asking. "Tell me how you know what Sarah was doing. How could you have felt—"

"She needed…" Maddie shuddered in his grasp. "Sarah needs me when things go dark. And then I know… whatever she knows. And she takes whatever she wants. Then she leaves. Until she needs something again."

"She needs you in her dreams?" Jarred pushed.

"Before, it was dreams. But now she's awake, and she still needs me and she's hurting people, like…"

"Like?"

"Like she hurt my father."

Jarred watched as the woman he knew faded away, and her past crept closer.

"How did Sarah hurt your father?"

That night—her father's car accident—was a watershed moment for the Temple family. Whatever the twins had been before that night had changed forever in a single moment of blinding tragedy.

"She killed him…" Maddie pulled her hand away. She wrapped her arms around herself. "It was only a matter of time. She's—"

"That's what you see in your dreams? Sarah thinking she killed your father?"

"Yes. No. Maybe, but—"

"Metting said the center was experimenting with dreams, and that you've become part of it somehow. You can't trust anything you've seen with Sarah. Not at the center or in your nightmares. Your father's death was an accident."

"What if it wasn't?"

"Why would Sarah want to kill him?"

"Because she's a monster!" Maddie stalked away until the couch was between them. "Because I'm…we're… she's Death!"

Jarred didn't crowd her. "Why do you think she's Dea—"

"Because she told me!" He watched Maddie grab her head. Her hair. Pull as she listened to a world he couldn't see. "She's shown me…every night…"

"In your nightmares?" The dreams someone besides Metting had dragged Maddie into?

"They're Sarah's nightmares. She keeps having them, and she needs me there. It's like she wants to be back at the accident, or she doesn't have a choice, or she's trying to make it right somehow. So she keeps dragging me with her so she won't be alone, so she'll be strong enough to stop it. And when she can't, she starts blaming the driver of the truck and making it all his fault. So he'd be the one who had to—"

"What truck driver?"

"The bastard who aimed for our family's car and killed our father!"

Maddie's head came up. Her gaze swung from one end of the living room to the other. Then she stared at Jarred as if she'd never seen him before.

"She wants me to…"

"What?" he asked.

He'd held this woman. Kissed her. He'd helped her professionally every way he knew how. And he'd almost gotten himself shot for his troubles. Maddie Temple had him on the run from mad scientists, outside the bounds of local law enforcement, and hiding in his ex-wife's overdecorated living room. All because of her twin sister's nightmares.

And that was when Jarred accepted reality, as he stared at the terror growing in Maddie's expression and promised himself he'd make it better somehow. If he had to go back to that morning and do it all over again, he'd still be right where he was—by Maddie's side every step of the way.

"You can trust me, Maddie. With anything. Tell me what Sarah's nightmares want you to do."

"Sarah wants me…I think she wants to kill the truck driver."

"The driver that hit your family?"

"She actually thinks she remembers him aiming for the car." Maddie was clawing at the skin on her arms again. As if a part of her was trapped inside and trying to find a way out. "It's like we're…becoming each other."

"But they're just nightmares."

"And if they're not? Like when…when I want to shut someone up and I'm angry and they keep talking, and suddenly they're choking…and those guards…when they were hurting you, and then they were on the floor, and Sarah was making me—"

"You didn't hurt them, Maddie. Not really. Sarah didn't make you do anything." Mostly because Metting had arrived. Metting and his outlandish excuses for the research he'd been doing into whatever Maddie and Sarah were experiencing.

The parapsychological implications of what the man had said fell so far outside any traditional diagnosis Jarred had studied, he didn't want to believe them. But he could feel the conviction rolling off Maddie. The compulsion to face what neither of them wanted to.

"It's only a matter of time." She was staring at the cut on her finger. At her ravaged wrist. She rubbed at the blood trailing down her hand. "My entire family is cursed. My mother was so freaked about us, she turned Sarah over to be studied like a lab rat. To be turned into…"

Maddie looked up then, her glance begging Jarred for the truth.

"A government weapon," he finished for her. He brought her hand to his lips. Then he wrapped her finger in a tissue from the box Victoria kept by the couch. Maddie was bleeding inside, too, where he couldn't reach her. "Metting could just be covering his ass. But when he said the center wouldn't stop hunting for you both…It was hard not to believe him."

"Psychic weapons testing?" Maddie's hand turned in his. She was holding on instead of shying away. "You can't really believe that."

She was searching Jarred's face, maybe even his mind.

Jarred had no idea what she was capable of—Metting had been right about that, too. Which meant Jarred was shooting blind and probably fucking up royally.

Was finding Sarah really their only chance, like Metting said?

"You…" Maddie pulled back. "You're thinking I need to find my sister. Take her to the Raven, like he wants… You've been working with him all along… You're—"

"What?" Jarred tried to hold on to her, but she jerked away.

"…*help me convince Madeline to find her sister and bring her to me*…" Maddie mimicked, in an exact replica of Metting's voice. Verbatim what the man had said while she was still unconscious.

Jarred felt the hair rise on the back of his neck. She was reading his memories now?

"I wouldn't take either of you back to him," Jarred insisted.

"You want to use me to find Sarah." Maddie's entire body was shaking. "You're just like him!"

"I want you to have the truth about what's going on, and I can't give that to you on my own. You have to know what's inside your mind and Sarah's, or none of this is going to get better. That means you have to find her. Screw Metting and what he wants."

"I…I can't." Maddie backed into the couch and would have toppled over if Jarred hadn't caught her. "I don't want to know where Sarah is."

"She's your best chance to—"

"I won't look for her." Maddie stepped away. "I n-never should have gone to that place tonight. Now I'll never be free of her. I hate her. I won't—"

"You don't hate your sister."

"Don't I? She's still running. I can feel it, the same way

I can feel you when you touch me. Except she's not here. She's out there somewhere, insane and running for her life and hurting people still. And I can still feel her. I want her to keep running, so I'll never have to think about her again. Except, I can't think about anything else. She wants to kill the Raven. She wants me to wrap my hands around his neck and—" Maddie shuddered. She clenched her fists, and Jarred could feel invisible fingers closing around his throat. "—squeeze until the hate goes away. Like our father went away. Like Phyllis and I abandoned Sarah at that place, for those people to do whatever they wanted to her, as long as she never bothered us again…"

"Stop this!" Jarred backed Maddie into the wall. He took her hands and forced them around his throat. He stared into her beautiful green eyes and watched as another woman's darkness fought to take over. "This isn't you, Maddie. It's Sarah, trying to make you believe you deserve to—"

"To die!" She squeezed, her strength surprising them both. Her eyes widened as he fought for breath.

"You can stop this," he said against her grip. "Don't give in to your sister. You don't have to be afraid of finding her, Maddie. You're a healer, not a killer. You can stop this. You have to. Stop her now!"

"J…Jarred?" Maddie's eyes rolled upward. Her fingers loosened without letting go. "Jarred, I…I don't want to…"

"I'm here."

Her entire body began to convulse.

"Shit!"

He caught her when she would have fallen. Laid her down on the couch and held her arms against her side.

"Stay with me, sweetheart. Maddie!"

He'd pushed her into this. He'd been pushing her since that morning. And every move he made only created a bigger mess. He wiped at the blood trailing from her nose, then at his own unshed tears. He kissed her hair and found himself praying for the first time since he was a child.

"Hold on," he begged as her body convulsed. "Please!"

Damn it. Maddie was so certain she and Sarah were cursed. As if the dreams, their link, were innately evil. And he couldn't keep her with him long enough to tell him why she was so sure. He needed more answers, danger or not. He grappled in his pocket for the cell phone that bastard Metting had tossed him. He flipped it open and stared at the number on the display. The number Metting had punched in. Ignoring it, he dialed information.

"Give me the home of Phyllis Temple—Boston," he said as soon as the line connected. When he was switched to a recorded message, he selected automated dialing.

"Hold on." He curled Maddie's body tighter against him and listened to her mother's line ring.

CHAPTER TWENTY-TWO

"…needs to know what she's facing…getting worse."

Maddie felt the words more than she heard them. And she felt warm. Safe. It was a wonderful dream…

"…she can't talk right now…" the voice said. A man's urgent voice. "No, it didn't go well…Mrs. Temple, you don't understand. I have reason to believe that Sarah's no longer at the Trinity Center. She and Maddie are both in bad shape…"

Maddie felt the words get closer and the sentences longer and longer and the voice more like…Jarred's.

Mrs. Temple?

The Trinity Center?

Sarah?

The dreams. The government. Death.

Run!

A ghoulish flash of darkness and woods and hysterical fear jolted Maddie awake. She was chilled to the bone but still wrapped in warmth…in Jarred's arms.

"Mom?"

Jarred smiled. A reassuring turn of his lips that mocked the worry in his eyes.

"No, ma'am," he said into the phone. "She can't talk right now. But she needs answers if she's going to find her sister and figure out—"

Maddie yanked the phone away.

I'm not looking for Sarah!

Jarred's hand covered hers over the phone.

"Talk to your mother, Maddie. If there's anything she knows—"

"About Sarah?"

Jarred blinked. "Talk to her about you. Because..." He brushed her bangs from her face, while Phyllis's chatter continued on the other end of the phone. "Because I love you, and I can't stand to think of these people hurting you anymore. I don't know enough yet to stop them. Maybe your mother can remember something that will help us."

Us?

Love?

The government—the Raven—were after Sarah. They'd used Maddie's mind to do God knew what to her sister's. And Jarred loved her? He kissed her lips with a softness that brought tears to her eyes.

"Ask your mother if she agreed to the Trinity Center's dream experiments," he said. "Don't let Phyllis off the hook until she tells you exactly what the doctors at that facility were looking for."

He was being so careful with her. But Maddie could feel the barely leashed violence inside him. A determination to fight whatever this was. Whatever he had to do to help her. Maddie brought the phone to her ear. Her twin's voice whispered through her mind, trying to drown out what Phyllis was saying. Maddie shoved her confusion—Sarah's confusion—away.

"Mom—" Her voice shook. She felt her sister stumble somewhere. Fall...*Sarah's fingers were grasping at the dry leaves covering the ground...* "Mom, you have to tell me what's going on."

"How should I know? It's been hours since you stormed

out of here, and that doctor friend of yours is talking nonsense. You didn't really go to that place, did you? Why couldn't you leave things alone?"

Bitch! Sarah screamed in Maddie's mind...

Sarah was still running...nowhere to go...no safe place to hide. But she wasn't going to curl up and wait to be dragged back to those bastards she'd escaped from. She wasn't—

"—fucking killing anymore!" Maddie blurted into the phone.

"What!" Panic shredded Phyllis's question. "Honey, tell me you haven't—"

"Turned into Sarah?" Maddie's world flickered in and out of focus. Jarred slipped a supportive arm around her shoulder.

You ok? he mouthed, reaching for the phone.

When she shook her head *no* but wouldn't let him take the cell, he cuddled her closer. Comfort and concern and something deeper washed over her. Something she didn't dare let herself trust.

...because I love you... he'd said.

"Maddie." Her mom was begging now. "Please don't do this to yourself, like—"

"I'm already like Sarah." Maddie closed her eyes, accepting what her insane dreams had been trying to tell her all along.

"Honey—"

"For months now I've been like her, but I was afraid to tell you. Afraid for you. What are you afraid of, Mom? Me losing my mind, or you finally having to face the truth."

"Maddie, I didn't know—"

"Of course you didn't. You never have. You've always done whatever it took to hide from the one thing Sarah and I needed. For once, would you just be honest with me?"

"Where are you, Maddie? What's—?"

"Tell me about the voices. The ones Sarah couldn't stand. In her dreams. In her mind. The feelings, everywhere. All the time, whenever she was around other people. And then when she went to sleep, those same people were in her dreams. Now people are dying…because he wants them to…however he wants them to…"

"Maddie!"

"—because he told me to kill her and I didn't have a choice…or maybe I didn't really want a choice…" Somehow Maddie knew it was Sarah talking now, but she couldn't stop herself. No matter what Jarred thought, Sarah was the one in control. "I don't want to kill anyone. Sarah doesn't, not really. But now she…we don't have a choice—"

"Stop this!" Phyllis snapped, sounding like a mother for the first time in ten years. "Stop it now. I don't know what nonsense that Dr. Keith has been filling your head with. But if you need a therapist, we'll find someone to help you who won't—"

"I need an exorcist. Sarah's—"

"Sarah's in a coma. She's not—"

"She's not in my dreams? She's not in my head now, running from people she wants to kill? Is this what you had in mind when you turned that research center loose on my sister! Did you promise them two for the price of one?"

Maddie could feel Jarred's concern grow, and she couldn't take it. Not while Phyllis was denying everything, exactly the way Maddie had known she would. Maddie shoved him away. Sarah's hate pushed just a little closer.

"I…I did no such thing!" Phyllis sputtered. "Your father's insurance barely left us enough money to live off of, let alone deal with your sister's chronic condition."

"So you abandoned her to those monsters!" Monsters Maddie could see through flashes of Sarah's memories.

Wheeling Sarah in and out of rooms. Forcing her through dream simulations. Exercising her body, but keeping her mind numb until they needed her to dream. Secret simulations that never ended. Drugs and tubes and wires and dreams…Everything Jarred had said… the government weapons testing…all of it was true.

"I agreed to research trials that could possibly…" Phyllis's voice caught. "…improve Sarah's quality of life, when I couldn't afford to—"

"You let them experiment on her for money?"

"No! They were studying her brain activity. Her responses to stimuli. Whatever they could do to try and reach her and control…To help her. Help you. To understand—"

"Understand what, Mom! What does the government want with us?"

"The government? You're not making any sense, honey."

"Like Sarah wasn't making sense before the accident?"

"Maddie…" Her name came out as a sob, then Phyllis couldn't seem to stop crying. "Don't do this."

"You knew it was inevitable." Maddie took her first cleansing breath in months, the truth becoming an awful kind of freedom. "So you made a deal with the devil and gave Sarah away."

"This isn't supposed to be happening. The curse isn't real…"

"Tell me where the curse came from. What does it mean?"

"It's nothing…It's a myth. No one's taken it seriously for generations. That stupid paper, rambling about twins fulfilling our family destiny. I threw it away. I refuse to believe—"

"You believed, or you wouldn't have been so afraid our whole lives."

"It's *not* real."

"Well Sarah's nightmares are real, and I keep having them. Daddy's accident. Sarah running, thinking she's a killer and wanting to…to die…"

"Maddie, you can't let your sister—"

"She's sending them to me, Mom! I'm not *letting* her do anything!"

Maddie checked to make sure Jarred was listening. To make sure he heard just how unhinged her family was. If he didn't leave, she'd kill him eventually. She could feel it coming. Sarah's mania was building. Soon there'd be no stopping her.

"You need to calm down," Phyllis said. "Calm down and let me help you—"

"You want to help me? Tell me how she's using me, Mom. Tell me what's wrong with all of us, that my sister could use my mind and do all the things she's doing. And then you tell me it's not my fault, everything she's done. Everyone she's hurt."

"She's not doing anything, honey." Phyllis's unflinching denial was the final straw. "She's been asleep. And, besides. You're nothing like her."

"I *am* her." It was the healing part of Maddie that had always been the lie.

"Stop this now! Stop—"

"I…Sarah…we…" It was all flooding back, everything that had happened at the center. "We hurt people tonight. Together…"

Maddie had been there exactly when Sarah had needed her. Their minds had…linked. Until Maddie had wanted to stop those bastards at the center, the same as Sarah. She'd wanted to—

"Oh, my God!" She gripped the phone tighter. "*I did it. I killed people tonight!*"

"No." Jarred pulled the phone away. "You didn't kill anyone. I have no idea what Sarah's done, but you didn't kill anyone tonight. You couldn't, Maddie. That's not who you are. You were—"

A crash rattled over the phone.

"...Stay away from me!" Her mother shrieked as Maddie yanked the phone back to her ear. "You can't do this. You...Don't point that gun at me!"

"Mom?"

There was a rattle. The phone banged against something.

"Maddie!" Phyllis screamed. "Help me!"

The silence that followed was final. Empty. Then came Sarah's laughter. Menacing. Desperate. Hate, racing toward Maddie. Sarah's hate for their mother.

"Mom! Stay away from her. Can you hear me?"

Sarah heard. Maddie could feel her sister's smile. Hear her laughter. Because their mother was finally going to—

"*Die!*"

The command echoed. A raven's wings spread. Bare tree limbs swayed.

The gun in her hand fired.

Phyllis's scream ripped through the night.

"No!"

Jarred caught her as she crumpled to the floor. "Maddie?"

"Sarah," Maddie whispered. "My mother..."

The world was darkening around her. Only this time she welcomed the terrifying numbness.

"Sarah's...She's killed my mother..."

CHAPTER TWENTY-THREE

"Let us off here," Jarred said to the cabdriver.

They were still several sleepy, residential streets away from Phyllis Temple's house. Maddie roused herself enough to raise a questioning eyebrow. Jarred paid the driver, got them out of the cab and waited for the car to pull away before responding.

"No point in announcing our arrival," he explained, "when we don't know what we're walking into."

Maddie hadn't even been able to tell Jarred if what she'd heard over the phone was real. Her mother's screams and Maddie's conviction that Phyllis was dead could have been another of Sarah's demented dreams. But Maddie had gone ape-shit until he'd agreed to take her to the Temple house—regardless of Metting's warnings to steer clear of people and places she knew. She'd barely responded to anything Jarred had said since.

He pulled her into the shadows of a hedgerow fronting a federal-style, two-story home. Uncoordinated still but growing stronger, Maddie followed without comment.

"It's only a few more blocks," he assured her.

"I'm fine." The crisp night air had cleared more of the vagueness from her voice.

At the next corner he walked them between the two houses, then cut across an unfenced backyard.

"We have to be careful."

"Because of Sarah?" Maddie asked.

"I don't think she'd really hurt you."

"Yes, you do. She wants to destroy me. She killed my mother." It was unnerving, the complete lack of emotion in Maddie's voice or on her face, after she'd been so irate at Victoria's.

"You don't know that. You said yourself, the scream you heard sounded like your nightmares."

"Where Sarah kills someone—with a gun."

"But I didn't hear gunfire, and I was standing right beside you. The call disconnected before I took the phone."

"Because Sarah killed her!"

Maddie swayed. But she kept walking on her own, weaving toward her mother's house.

"This isn't your fault." Jarred followed close behind.

"Stop coddling me," she demanded.

"Stop insisting on taking responsibility for everything your sister does. You didn't know that Sarah—"

"I knew. I've known for months, and I was too afraid of what was happening to admit it. Because of that, my mother's—"

Jarred held up a hand, waiting until a car passed before he led her out of their shadowy shortcut and closer to the road. "Even if something has happened to Phyllis, you—"

Maddie stopped cold.

"What if she's still here?" she asked.

"Who, Sarah?"

"I can't feel…" Maddie tried to keep going. Tripped over a raised tree root and hit the ground hard.

Jarred crouched beside her, his body shielding hers from any cars that might pass by.

"I can't tell if Sarah's there or not." Maddie turned away. "I can only feel her when she wants me, too… when…"

"Have you ever attempted to reach Sarah's mind on your own? Have you ever tried to—"

Maddie flinched. Then her head rolled toward him,.

"Sarah…" she whispered, her pupils rapidly dilating.

She lurched to her feet and darted toward her mother's place.

"Maddie!" He took off after her. "Don't! We have to—"

She kicked into a sprint. Brushed into a tree. Kept barreling forward, blind and separate from him and about to burst around the next corner and into her mother's front yard.

"Maddie!" He turned up his own speed and grabbed her from behind.

They went down. His palm muffled her scream. Panic consumed them both as her emotional control shattered. They hit the ground and disappeared behind an cluster of azaleas. Branches scraped his cheek. He protected her body as best he could. Maddie's nails dug deep. Her fury deeper still. She squealed against his fingers. Her mind battered his. Her eyes darkened completely—to the gray he expected to see one day in Sarah's gaze. He pinned her to the ground.

"We're almost there," he said, ignoring the feel of her body squirming beneath him. "Stay with me. *Me*, Maddie, not Sarah. Don't let her take control. You can stop her."

She bit his fingers. He held firm.

"You can do this," he insisted. "You're almost there. Focus on helping your mother. Helping yourself. Hell, focus on helping Sarah, if that's what you need. But don't let the darkness win. Trust me, you're strong enough to stop it. We're out in the open. It's too dangerous for you to fall apart now. Stop it."

She continued to struggle, not hearing a word.

Trust me Maddie, he repeated in his thoughts. *Come back to me.*

Trust me . . .

Slowly quieting, she blinked up at him. The green began to edge out the gray in her eyes.

I . . . I do . . . her mind whispered back. *I'm here . . .*

He thought back, realized what had happened, and let his fingers slide away from her mouth.

"Okay," he said. "That was my fault. The next time you try to reach your sister's mind, we'll—"

"I didn't." Maddie shook her head. "I didn't try . . . That's impossible. I can't—"

"I think you did. And I never should have suggested it in the open like this. I'll be more careful. But your mind *did* reach for Sarah's, and not only that—you found her. She was here for a few seconds, because you wanted her to be." Maddie was still shaking her head, and he couldn't stop himself from kissing her. And then kissing her again. Whatever it took to get her believing in him. Believing in herself. "You're strong, Maddie. Look at how you're racing to your mother, no matter how afraid you are of what you'll find. You're scared, but whatever you have to face, you're strong enough to handle it. And if that means confronting Sarah—"

"No! I can't. She'll—"

"You can." Another kiss quieted her. A deeper kiss that felt like giving Maddie a piece of his soul, so she could see the amazing woman he did. "You can do anything, Madeline Temple. Now let's deal with your mother and whatever we can find at her house that will tell us more about Dr. Metting and his Center of Doom."

Maddie stared at Jarred's mouth, then into his gaze. He did everything he could to make sure all she found there was confidence—not the fear lurking behind his sarcasm. The fear that no matter what he did, he was going to get Maddie killed before all this was done.

"I want to use the back door." He kept things conversational as he got her to her feet. "Once we're sure it's safe, we'll go in through the kitchen and find your mom."

Maddie nodded slowly. He guided her around the back of the house, neither of them seeing or sensing anything out of the ordinary. It was another quiet night in the suburbs. No sirens or police lights flashing because the neighbors had heard a commotion or, worse, a gunshot.

Maddie leaned into him.

I'm here... her thoughts said. She hadn't responded when he'd said he loved her. But she was starting to believe in him. To let herself need him.

He stopped beneath an overbright moon, shining through an enormous oak that took up half the backyard. He gazed down at her.

"I'm here," she repeated out loud. "Me. Not Sarah."

She kissed him...sweetness and fragile courage and need reaching for him. And he kissed her back, praying he would be worthy of the trust she was placing in him.

"Of course it's you." For him, it would always be her. "Whatever we find in there, you weren't a part of it. Tell me you believe that. Thinking it's your fault will only make it easier for Sarah to come back. It's like she's waiting to take advantage when you're weakest. Don't let her."

Maddie was shaking in his arms, but her mind was calmer. She nodded her head, her lips clinging to his once more. She rested her head on his shoulder. The simple acceptance of it humbled him.

"You're not alone," he promised. "I'll be here, no matter what."

Madness. Insanity. Danger. Sinister government experiments. Nothing could tear Jarred away.

They watched Phyllis's house. When several minutes passed and Maddie had stopped shaking and there'd been no sound or movement from inside, he said, "Let's go."

Maddie clung to him as far as the patio door, which was slightly ajar. An eat-in kitchen was visible just inside.

"Stay here," she said to him.

Like hell.

Jarred threaded his fingers through hers. Then he stepped over the threshold first, placing his body between his fragile healer and whatever waited inside.

Maddie focused on Jarred's strong back as he led the way.

Horrible sounds still scrambled for control of her mind. Her mother's screams…The Raven's screams…Sarah's screams…Other people's screams…Then Jarred's voice saying he loved her, over and over again. Until she could hear him above all the rest.

Stay with me, Maddie…

And she had. Her mind was with him now, not with Sarah. And wherever Jarred was, was where Maddie wanted to stay.

The house was still around them. There was nothing to feel there. No one. She bumped into Jarred, only then realizing he'd stopped.

"You okay?" he asked.

Maddie's nod mustn't have been very convincing. He glanced at the death grip she had on his hand.

"Wait here." He pulled out a kitchen chair.

She headed for the dining room instead. Jarred had said she was stronger than she thought. Strong enough to see this through.

"Mom?" she called in a voice she barely recognized.

Jarred stayed only a step behind her.

Careful...

His warning wrapped around her. Warming her where she'd been cold since... since losing the connection she'd had with her twin as a teenager. A decade of cold. Whatever she and Sarah had been as children was now a twisted darkness that everything would sink into, until—

"Maddie?" Jarred asked.

Stay with me, sweetheart...

She realized she'd stopped with her hand on the half-open door to the dining room.

"I don't think there's anyone here," he said.

"I know there isn't. I can feel it."

In her mind, Maddie turned to Jarred and curled her body into his as she let go of the hope of seeing her mother again alive.

"You don't have to do this." He reached for her in reality. "I could—"

"Yes, I do." She inched away. "Whatever happened to Phyllis, I have to face it."

Whatever Sarah had done. Whatever evil Maddie had unleashed when she'd participated in her sister escaping from the center. It was time to stop hiding.

Help me, her mind begged Jarred's.

All right. His reassurance was rock solid. *Whatever you need.*

With Jarred's strength behind her, Maddie pushed open the door to the dining room. The hinge creaked. She tripped over the portable phone lying on the floor.

Jarred grabbed her, then picked up the unit, pressing several buttons and watching the display.

"What?" she asked. Something in his expression was scaring her.

"Don't worry about it right now. Let's see what else we can find."

Jarred glanced around the dining room, and only then did she have the courage to look more closely herself. At nothing, it turned out. There was nothing to see. No Phyllis. No sign of a struggle, except maybe the phone Jarred was still holding. But it could have simply fallen onto the floor.

Maddie slapped her palms to the dining room table.

Had she imagined the entire thing?

"Phyllis was here when I called," Jarred assured her. "I spoke with her first, remember? And she didn't just disappear into thin air."

"Mom!" Maddie ran into the family room. Silence welcomed her. Emptiness.

Sensing Jarred's strong presence behind her, she stumbled up the stairs and ran down the hall.

"Mom, it's Maddie. I need to talk to you. I need to know more about the center..."

She careened into her mother's bedroom, desperate to find the woman she'd sworn just hours before to hate forever. But Phyllis wasn't there. She wasn't anywhere upstairs. Maddie turned on every light in every room and checked each closet. Each bathroom. By the time she dragged herself back downstairs, she was exhausted and pissed again and more terrified than ever.

"I didn't imagine it," Maddie insisted. "I didn't!"

They made their way back to the dining room. Maddie wandered into the kitchen, feeling Jarred close behind her. She almost wished he hadn't come now.

Chickenshit! her twin's insanity shrieked. *If you don't want the asshole there, make him leave.*

Maddie's fingers grazed her mother's gourmet knife set, displayed in its fancy chopping block. Her hand clenched on the knife with the wicked serrated edge that Phyllis preferred above the others. It wasn't the largest in the bunch, but it could slice through anything, including Maddie's fingers on several occasions.

"You okay?" Jarred asked behind her.

Feeling separated from her body, Maddie slid the lethal blade from its home.

Die! the voice insisted.

Jarred's hands cupped her shoulders. His closeness surrounded her with a sense of peace. Of belonging. "You're not alone. I'm here."

Maddie blinked the knife and her twin's deadly intentions into focus. She spun toward Jarred and away from the counter. Took his hand and dragged him back to the dining room.

She tried to piece together which parts of the phone conversation with Phyllis had been real.

"You called my mother," she insisted.

"Yes," Jarred confirmed.

"And I talked to her after you did."

"Yes."

"And…" *And what?* she begged him with her eyes.

"You said you heard a gunshot?"

"I…" There was no evidence of a shooting anywhere. No blood or a stray hole in the wall or anything. "I…I don't know. I thought I did…I know I heard Phyllis scream…"

And Sarah had been laughing. But had Sarah been at the house, trying to kill their mother? Or had she been in Maddie's mind, preying on Maddie's and Phyllis's drama. Dreaming of haunted trees and birds of prey and that damn gun.

"She screamed," Maddie scraped out. "I know I heard my mother yell at someone who was in the house… Someone who surprised her. She told them to get out. They had a gun. She told them to put it down. And then she screamed…"

"But?" Jarred asked.

"How do I know what happened next was real?" Her mother had been terrified, but—"How could the gunshot *not* have been real, if the rest of it was?"

Jarred took another look around the room. He walked to the other side of the table where the folder that she'd found in her mother's files had been left. A piece of paper lay on top of it. A handwritten note. Joining him, Maddie picked up the paper with a shaking hand. Her vision refused to unblur long enough to process it.

Jarred didn't have the same problem. His expression grew murderous as he read.

"Whoever surprised your mother," he snapped, "I'd say your sister's off the hook."

Maddie sank into a dining room chair in relief. Jarred set the paper down before opening the folder. Maddie concentrated until the note shimmered into focus.

> Find Sarah. Bring her back to Trinity. Or Phyllis Temple dies.

Maddie's entire body began to shake.

Find Sarah…

…back to Trinity…

"I…I can't." Debilitating fear took over, laughing at Jarred's assurances that she was strong. Maddie was going to be the twin who killed Phyllis after all, because—"I can't go back there. I can't...I can't find Sarah...I won't. It's...it's that doctor. Metting? He did this. You said me bringing Sarah to him was exactly what he wanted. He wants us both back. Because he—"

"It wasn't Metting. If he was here, it's because your mother asked him to come. Which means she wouldn't have been surprised to see him. She wouldn't have screamed at him to leave."

Jarred was staring into the folder labeled TRINITY. The one with Maddie's blood smeared over the edge. He'd moved aside what looked like a standard hospital admission form—filled out and dated ten years ago. There was only one other thing in the folder, a single slip of paper with numbers scribbled on it in masculine, block handwriting. And in the same hand, the name *Dr. Richard Raventhall Metting*.

"What?" she asked.

Jarred looked closer, as if to be sure. He grabbed her mother's phone from the table and checked the display. Then he pulled the cell they'd been using from his pocket and pressed several buttons.

"What!" Maddie demanded.

"This is the last call Phyllis made." He showed Maddie the number he'd accessed on the portable. "And this is the number Metting put into his cell before giving it to me."

They matched.

"How did my mother know Sarah's doctor's private number?"

Jarred handed her the paper that had been inside the folder. It wasn't yellowed with age like the admissions form. It was newer. Much newer. And the same phone number—beside Metting's name—had been recorded on it.

"When he started working with your sister, he must have given Phyllis his contact information," Jarred said, "just in case."

"In case of what?" In case Phyllis's other daughter started losing her marbles, too? In case Sarah ever got away from him? In case he needed Phyllis to betray both of her twins one day, instead of settling for sacrificing only one of their lives? "Why would she have called him?"

"When Metting gave me the phone," Jarred bit out, the world around them fading from light to gray as Maddie's thoughts spiraled into confusion, "he said to call him when I was ready for help. When—" He gazed down at her, at the way she was scratching at her already-raw wrists. "—when I'd realized he was my only hope of saving you."

CHAPTER TWENTY-FOUR

Richard sat in the darkened car beside a darkened curb, beneath a gas lamp that would never again illuminate its quaint, suburban street.

Dr. Keith and his charge were being careful, euphemistically speaking. They'd used the backyard to enter the Temple home. But Richard had seen them approach, and he doubted he was the only one on their tail. He'd had a head start. He'd been tracking the GPS chip in the cell he'd given Keith from the moment Richard had reconnected with the Brotherhood. But every light in the house was on now. If the center didn't have the pair in their sights yet, it was only a matter of time. And Keith and Temple were just sitting there, waiting to be picked off.

They'd been inside for quite a while. Too long a while. Richard checked the digital display on his dash. One hour ago on the nose, Phyllis Temple had phoned him. Her call had clinched Richard's go-ahead from his elders to stay on the Temples' trails, with a sizable recon team supporting him. He had twenty-four hours to bring both twins under Brotherhood control, or the Temples' psychic legacy would go the way of others over the centuries. Other exceptionally gifted families with powers that could have insured the safety of generations to come, if they'd been brought under the Watchers' guidance. But they'd become too volatile. Perverted until they became a danger to the world around them. So they'd been forever silenced.

Richard had arrived at the Temple home in time to watch Phyllis be carried away, unresponsive, by three masked men. Richard's team had tracked the unmarked SUV she'd been tossed into as far as the interstate, before losing the vehicle after it caused a multicar pileup. Richard had stayed behind, sensing more visitors were en route. He'd hoped to isolate Sarah by staking out the empty house. Still, Madeline would do nicely. Assuming her psychiatrist watchdog was ready to accept the inevitable and invite Richard into his confidence.

So far, no joy. And they were running out of time. By Richard's estimate, given how long Sarah had been without the pharmaceutical cocktail that had masked the more homicidal aspects of her splintered personality, they had only hours before Sarah suffered a complete meltdown. Unmonitored and on her own, she'd self-destruct. And she'd take her twin and whoever else got in their way with her. Richard couldn't let that happen. The Brotherhood wouldn't let that happen.

But he still had a chance. The dream symbol Sarah had chosen for him had been a raven. And that meant everything. Most people saw the menacing black bird as an omen of death or evil. But in dream symbolism, a raven was also a bearer of magic. A messenger of change. A trickster that exposed the truth behind secrets and returned the dreamer to a state of healing and harmony—the very things Richard had first worked with Sarah to bring about. That's how she'd invited Richard into her nightmares.

Some part of Sarah still believed in him, beneath the

hate and pain he'd helped cause. Toxic emotions he'd have to cleanse from her mind once the Brotherhood had her back. Once he'd circumvented the survival and combat skills he'd taught her and found a way to save Sarah, her twin, and the future his shortsightedness had endangered.

None of which would happen if Madeline Temple didn't find a way to trust him first.

CHAPTER TWENTY-FIVE

Sarah was dying.

Down deep, where she was still pissed and running and fighting to hold on, a part of her accepted that she was lost and alone and dying.

She was Death.

The command echoed. A raven's wings spread. Bare tree limbs swayed.

The gun in her hand fired.

A scream ripped through the night.

"No!"

Sarah struggled to her feet, stumbled, and landed hard on the filthy floor of a rotting, vacant building she'd crawled through a broken window to get into. This was the tomb for that final sane part of her. This was where it would end.

Dark and empty. Nothing…closing around her, until she could see…

Until she could see her twin taking her place.

The good sister drowning in filth instead of Sarah. The healer killing everything she cared about. Killing, because it was who she'd been taught to be.

Why had Maddie been at the center? To laugh at Sarah, that's why. To laugh at Death, because Maddie had always been better. But Sarah had shown her. She'd used her. Just like when they were little. Then, just for fun, she'd pointed Maddie at those guards surrounding her and her doctor. She'd shown her twin what she really was. What they both were. And Maddie had started fighting. Trying to kill. Angry and drowning in the hate and the fear and the loneliness, just like Sarah. The good twin had been choking the life out of men she didn't know, while Sarah ran.

And it had felt amazing.

Better than anything in a long time.

Until Sarah had stumbled into the woods. Then even farther away. And now their link was nearly gone, abandoning Sarah to her demented memories and fractured dreams and her need for her Raven…

The command echoed. A raven's wings spread. Bare tree limbs swayed.

The gun in her hand fired.

A scream—

"No!"

The Raven wasn't there. Sarah had killed him. At least she'd tried. And when she couldn't, she'd run and left him Maddie's mind to pick apart. He was stalking Maddie now. Sarah could feel it. Just like she could feel the evil that had taken their mother. She'd felt them cart Phyllis away. She'd laughed while it happened, while Maddie had cried, until the darkness of it had choked off every thought. Every sound. Every sensation in Sarah's world. Until she was completely alone.

While Maddie had run through the night to help… then wandered through the house to help…then finally accepted that there was no help coming. Not for them. Not for the madness or the pain or the loneliness.

Except Maddie hadn't been alone. Sarah had sensed that, too, through their fading link. There'd been arms to hold the good twin. To guide her. A deep voice in the darkness, in her mind. A promise that Maddie would have help as she faced the truth. That she could survive it.

The way a deep, piercing voice had once promised Sarah the same things. The voice coming to her before the dreams, while she was still in a coma, freeing her and binding her to him. Helping her live. Chaining her to a world he'd soon teach her how to destroy.

Her Raven's voice.

The command echoed. A raven's wings spread. Bare tree limbs swayed.

The gun—

"No!" Sarah screamed into the empty night.

She hated the Raven.

Or was it that she needed him to see the evil inside her—her drive to be Death—so he could fix it somehow? Is that why she hadn't been able to kill him? Except, the Raven wasn't there now. And neither was Maddie.

Sarah would have no help.

The sane part of her knew she'd never survive now.

The command echoed. A raven's wings spread. Bare tree limbs—

"No!" It wouldn't go away. She had to make the dream go away. "Stop it!"

She crawled as far as she could before collapsing onto the floor. Collapsing into the truth.

The Raven had given her back her life. Now all she wanted was to die. Because he hadn't stopped the other creature in the dreams. The Wolf that fed on hate and had poured it into Sarah. Then the bastard had linked Sarah's mind with Maddie's. The good sister who despised Sarah and had abandoned her. Sarah hadn't wanted Maddie in her mind again, but the Wolf had insisted, or he'd take the Raven away.

So Sarah had done what she was told. She'd found Maddie's dreams. Then she'd learned to hate the Raven, even more than she hated her sister and the Wolf. Because it was the Raven she'd never survive without.

So, it was all Maddie's fault, really. Maddie and her happiness and her ability to love and her forgiveness for everyone, including their mother. Everyone but Sarah. Maddie who'd come to the center and given Sarah the strength she'd needed to break free of what she craved most.

Sarah's Raven.

The command echoed. A raven's wings spread. Bare tree limbs swayed.

The gun in her hand fired.

A scream ripped through the night.

"No!"

The darkness couldn't have Sarah. Not yet. She had to find her sister's mind. Sarah would use their link again. Let it strengthen her while it drained Maddie. Because Maddie had to pay.

Maddie's dreams.

What Maddie wanted most.

That's what had to—

Die!

CHAPTER TWENTY-SIX

Jarred had somehow gotten Maddie out of her mother's house.

He'd called another cab from Metting's cell, giving another phony name just in case. No way could they have gone back to Victoria's apartment or used Metting's car again. Not with the center and God knew who else after them. He'd had the cabby drive around aimlessly to be sure no one was following. Then he'd paid for the taxi with the last of the cash in his wallet, in front of a no-tell motel somewhere in the rural badlands between the suburbs and the fringes of Boston's industrial hub. He'd secured a ground-floor, street-adjacent room with the cash he'd lifted from his ex's hiding place in the cupboard above her refrigerator.

He walked to the bed and laid a near-catatonic Maddie on the cheap spread. Then he checked the room's single window, making sure it would open if they needed an alternative exit. He secured the insubstantial locks on the window and the door. Then he rechecked them both. He was officially freaking out.

Someone had kidnapped Maddie's mother. Someone not associated with Richard Metting. And whoever it was wanted to use Phyllis as bait to lure Sarah and Maddie back to the center, where they would likely—

Die!

Jarred spun around, half expecting to find Maddie standing behind him, her eyes crazed the way they became every time her sister's dementia returned. But she was curled in the fetal position on the bed, motionless except for her eyes darting back and forth behind their closed lids. Whatever was going on in that amazing mind of hers was a metaphysical puzzle that the scientist in Jarred had to solve. And whatever was going on in her heart…

Her heart was home to him now. The bond between them grew stronger every time it whispered through his mind. They had to find the sister who was terrorizing Maddie to the point of incapacitation. But even if they did reach Sarah and somehow got her well enough to help them, there was no way in hell Jarred was turning either woman over to the center. Or to Metting. Though the man seemed less of a threat now, because Jarred and Maddie had other, bigger, threats to contend with.

The entire situation was a clusterfuck. And Jarred's pushing Maddie to face her family secrets had accomplished exactly nothing. The insanity stalking her every move claimed more of her mind by the second. Just like Metting had said it would.

But Maddie finally trusted Jarred. She'd initiated their kiss beneath the looming tree in her mother's backyard. Her mind had begun to clear once she let herself focus on him. When she'd focused on them, rather than her sister's insanity. That connection was Jarred's only remaining weapon. Their bond would have to be strong enough to see Maddie through the next crisis.

Terrified of what that "next" challenge might be, Jarred crawled onto the bed beside Maddie, cradling her soft body against his. He breathed in the fresh scent of her until he no longer felt alone. His mind brushed hers, out of habit now. His fingers tunneled through the auburn fire of her hair. He rolled her to face him and tucked her in closer. He shouldn't be closing his eyes and letting his exhaustion settle deeper. He should stay alert and aware in case they'd been followed. But this was Maddie in his arms. His mind. His heart. And she was suddenly all he could feel.

There were no good answers to any of their questions. The threats to Maddie and her family kept growing. But with Maddie in his arms Jarred could almost believe his promises that they could face anything together. And as promises became thoughts of hope, his thoughts drifted toward dreams of Maddie. A place where there was no room for fear or failure as long as they were together. No room for anything but the light caress of her breathing against his neck. Her feminine moan of approval as his hands splayed across her back, following the line of her spine, until it dipped just above her hips…

A wash of soft, white peace seeped through him. The shadows of deepening sleep bloomed into gray, and then into the gentle promise of a dawn sky.

"Stay with me," his mind called. *"Come back to me, Maddie. Show me what you need."*

Jarred was floating just beyond her dreams. Then with a vibrant rush of color, his mind dove toward wherever Maddie was. Searching for what he'd lost. Finding himself welcome. Finding relief and joy, because he'd been gone too long, and he was needed more than he'd ever thought he could be. He was loved here. He was craved with the same all-encompassing passion that had been building inside him.

Maddie's lips fluttered against his skin as she filled him with images that were really feelings. Nothing had form wherever they were, but everything meant something amazing. Something uniquely Maddie. He saw a woman's view of the world, combined with a poet's dream of what each morning's new beginning could be. A healer's soul, creating hope from failure and faith from doubt. A lover's lost passion, firing streaks of crimson through a growing collage of sensation. Her hands clutched at his body. Her dream shifted to another plane, his consciousness and imagination her hostage for the ride.

In their dream, Maddie was free. They both were. She wasn't weak, and he wasn't protective. She wasn't broken, and he wasn't on the outside helplessly watching while she lost her mind. God no. He was with her. He was her. And she was him, and he was never letting her go. And he wasn't just dreaming, he realized...Their minds were linked, but he was also touching her body, holding her, making love to her, feeling Maddie respond with erotic abandon in...

Reality...

Jarred opened his eyes—half dreaming still, half awake. He rolled Maddie onto her back, pursuing now instead of passively following her lead.

No more barriers. No more safe. No more careful... her mind whispered, her thoughts giving his permission to take more. Give more. All of him. All of her. Everything. And then her eyes opened, too. They were dreamy and soft with sleep, but she was with him in this reality that was all theirs, too.

He cherished her soft body with his hands. The taut muscles beneath his touch trembled. Her legs quivered as he raised them to wrap around his hips. He angled her body closer. They were both splitting, who they'd been falling away so they could become something new. Something truly free.

They clung to each other. In their shared dream they

were on the soft grass of a country hill. The sun and the breeze and the smell of spring tempted them to reach for more.

"Don't hold back," Maddie whispered. "Don't…I don't want to be afraid anymore."

"I'm here." Jarred kissed a path down her neck, his hips rocking against the damp heat pooling between her denim-clad thighs. "No holding back."

His body rocketed to full arousal. He wanted to strip her clothes away. Bare her breasts to the warm sun. Drown in every inch of her until he was sated. Except he'd never have enough. He'd never want to stop. And she was just as ravenous—a woman who'd been running from him for months.

"Kiss me again," she breathed, the need in her voice demanding that his mouth return to hers.

"Yes."

And it wasn't a sweet kiss she offered. It was biting nips of her teeth. A wicked smile in response to his growl. Her tongue intertwining with his, inviting him to lose even more control because she knew she'd be safe with him. The wildness in her, the strength he'd know was there, wanted all of Jarred in this sunny place that pain and fear couldn't touch.

He deepened the kiss. His fingers plucked her nipples, his touch roughening until she purred with pleasure. She arched as his nails scraped down her waist, down the soft fabric of her sweater until he'd reached its hem. Her fingers met his there, and they both pulled the material up her body and over her head, baring curves and satiny skin and a tempting black bra.

"Please, Jarred," she begged, a little scared now. A little more the Maddie who kept fading into her sister's reality and needed saving because she was afraid she'd disappear forever. "Please…"

"I'm here." His thumb rubbed along her trembling lips. "You can let go here. You can have anything you want. What do you want, Maddie? Show me."

His challenge banished everything timid and unsure and weak from their dream.

"I want you." Her nails scratched down his shirt, biting deep.

She ripped at buttons. Tore the material back until she was scraping his bare skin. Fire from her touch streaked to every part of him that craved this hidden fierceness she allowed no one else to see. His own fantasies promised wicked retribution. She smiled at the images that filled his mind. The green of her eyes deepened, their dreamy softness beginning to smolder. The woman dragging his body closer was demanding. Wanton. Undeniable. Insatiable. An all-consuming passion Jarred craved.

In the dream he saw the grass beneath them become black satin sheets. The tree shading them from the sun's rays was now a velvet canopy of darkest ebony, shadowing them in a scorching realm of desire. The glide and heat of Maddie's body bewitched him. Every naughty wiggle challenged him to pin. To conquer until she screamed. Until the power of his need threatened to incinerate them both if it didn't release.

Jarred ripped away her bra. She laughed a sultry challenge. Her jeans went next, and—Jesus—the lacy thong beneath. She dug streaks down his back with her nails as he shoved his own clothes away. The pain and pleasure of it hardened the edge of violence riding him, until he slammed her hands to the sheets beneath her head.

"Is this what you want?" he growled. His thighs parted hers, his body poised at her core. It took every shred of restraint he still possessed to wait. He had to be sure. "Is it?"

"I want you to take me, Jarred." Her voice was soft and hard. Weak and powerful. Need and determination. "See me. All of me. Need me. Take what you need."

She rocked against the bedspread. In the dream they were wrapped in satin. She lifted her hips, and the soft, wet folds of her sex brushed the head of his cock. She moaned when he drove into her. Just an inch. Nowhere near far enough.

"Maddie." He should still be holding her hands instead of caressing her hips. He should be cherishing her gently, instead of guiding her closer. But reality was feeling further away as their dream demanded more. His fingers clenched the soft globes of her bottom.

"Don't stop." Her hips rotated, rimming him, stimulating flesh already painfully aroused.

He slid another inch into her tight, wet grip.

Pulled back.

"I…" This was their first time. Maddie was his soul mate. He'd never believed he had a soul before meeting her. He had to make this right.

Her hips surged. Took him deeper.

"Trust the dream, Jarred." She said his name like she could swallow him whole, milk him until he lost himself in her forever, and still she wouldn't have enough. "Don't stop. Show me how much you need me."

"God…" He closed his eyes.

Dream images of their intertwined bodies flashed through his mind. Slick with sweat and the summer rain now pouring down on them and the dream's satin bed. Then the sheets and canopy overhead were gone. And the dream world was growing still, as if waiting for him to decide between being afraid for Maddie and relinquishing control to their craving. To the certainty that he'd gladly die in this woman's arms, in her body, if it meant never being separated from her again.

Jarred's will surrendered to the erotic vortex of caring and loving and needing without restraint. Without limits.

"Yes," Maddie's sigh rang in his ears.

"God—" He drove into her, balls deep. "Yes!"

Their world exploded into driving, soul-shattering sex. Desire and ecstasy and a bottomless compulsion for more.

"Not enough…" Jarred bit out. He nipped her lips, her neck, her nipples, until her passion flared with his, flooding him, forcing them both higher. "Never enough…"

"More…" She rocked into him, her calves sliding up and down his thighs.

With each of his strokes, her nails pricked, then clawed at his body. A man could die from needing this way. Needing this much. Hearing a woman scream for him. Hearing her demand more. Feeling the need pour off her, savoring it until it ruled him. Until he became a slave to it. Until he'd do anything to keep it.

Until he was willing to—

"Stay with me forever," Maddie whispered, her skin misting with perspiration.

"Yes…" He pulled to his knees and sat back, still inside her. "Don't stop. Don't—"

"Never…" She straddled his hips, their lower bodies slapping together as her bottom rotated in an erotic dance.

She arched her back, thrusting her breasts toward him. Her pebble-hard nipple filled his mouth. Her nails raked his chest. He groaned and looked down at his body pistoning into hers. And all he could think was—

"More…"

Need consumed them, denied too long to require gentleness or care or nurturing. It had to bleed until it was dry. Until nothing remained but completion and the raw essence of a man and a woman who were made for each other. Until they were both screaming in release. Shaking in each other's arms. Throbbing and falling together. Neither letting go. Ever.

Jarred pulled Maddie closer. Tried to breathe. To absorb her softness. Her trust. Except…

Her body had grown suddenly rigid. Cold. And she was…

She was laughing.

A demented cackle that assaulted the testosterone-induced fog that had swamped him. A bawdy giggle taking over his mind, wiping out Maddie's whispers of completion. A laugh of hate-filled triumph. And that's when Jarred realized he couldn't fully wake up, no matter how wrong his and Maddie's dream had become.

The dream had taken control.

No. Something outside of it had.

It wasn't Maddie in his arms now, moving again and melting into his body and mind. Destroying his control. Taking his humanity.

"More…" the woman demanded in the altered voice he'd first heard in his office. The voice that kept coming back whenever Maddie lost herself.

"S…Sarah?" he gasped.

His mind rebelled against the wave of danger permeating the dream, but it wouldn't disengage. The dark creature in his arms snuggled closer, the cold bite of steel suddenly between them. In the dream. In reality.

In reality he held tight to Maddie's body, protecting her as Sarah's hate, her dark heart, grew even stronger.

"Maddie?" he called out. "Please…"

"Maddie's not here," the voice whispered.

She brushed a kiss across his eyes so he could see the dream clearly, and there she sat.

Controlling him with her mind.

Painting the deadly shadows shifting around them.

"Sarah," he gasped, fighting to pull back.

Back to the woman he loved.

But all he could manage was to gaze helplessly up at Death. And at the serrated edge of the knife clenched in her raised fist—in both the dream and reality—the knife Maddie had been holding at her mother's house.

CHAPTER TWENTY-SEVEN

A part of Sarah was horrified by the nightmare she was projecting. But the control, the power that came with her sister's dream... Sarah needed more. It had almost killed her, finding Maddie's mind again. Now Maddie's consciousness was feeding hers.

Sarah stared down at her sister's valiant doctor. He was mesmerized. Terrified. Dreaming beyond himself. Beyond Maddie. Lord, he was beautiful. Making Sarah feel what he made Maddie feel, and then some. Why the hell had her sister spent so much time avoiding the man, instead of strapping him on and taking him out for a test spin? His devotion to Maddie was unwavering. Infuriating.

Sarah had let herself believe in that kind of love with her Raven. It had led to nothing but being manipulated and used until she'd become the darkness he'd promised to protect her from. So, really, she was doing her sister a favor, ending this before Maddie was betrayed, too.

Besides, it was Maddie's turn to know real pain and loneliness.

Keith groaned while his mind battled for freedom. His gaze was pinned on the knife Sarah had made sure her sister swiped from their mother's house.

"Take the first weapon you find," she'd drilled into Maddie's mind during those few minutes they'd been joined at the center. "Be ready when I need you."

And now Sarah needed her sister to end her connection to the only person who could stop Maddie from coming to Sarah whenever Sarah needed her. Then Maddie would belong to Sarah. She would want whatever Sarah wanted—to end the Raven and the Wolf. As long as Jarred Keith no longer existed, Sarah would never be alone again.

She closed her eyes and absorbed the power of his and Maddie's feelings for each other. She ran the tip of the knife along Keith's chest, leaving thin trails of blood behind. And with each cut, his love for her sister fired higher than his fear. Sarah laughed at his stupidity. He knew she was Death. He knew it would be over soon. But he was enduring, believing he could stop her. Determined to save Maddie from her. While ravens circled above them in the dream.

Storm clouds swirled closer. A demented tree shifted in the wind. Cold steel cut into Jarred. But even in death, with anger and violence and evil haunting his unguarded mind, this man believed in the good in Sarah's twin. He'd love her forever. No matter what. Outside the dream, he was gazing into Maddie's eyes, the way the Raven had once gazed into Sarah's.

Maddie had to suffer for that look, the darkness growing inside Sarah insisted. Jarred's hateful promise of love had to go away. And then Maddie had to accept how much she needed Sarah, and only Sarah. Joining Sarah as Death was the only way. Then they'd be truly free. That's what the Wolf had promised when he'd turned Sarah loose on Maddie's mind.

Jarred's hands grasped Sarah, breaking free of her control. Drowning her with his desperate need to protect the woman he loved.

Sarah screamed, hating him. Because he was making her feel that love, and she'd promised herself as she sat huddled in an abandoned building and prayed that Maddie's mind would let her in, that she'd never feel anything again. But *now she was linked to her sister's mind, to the world she'd never been allowed to have. And Sarah's need for love was blooming back to life—even though she was still huddled and weak and alone, back where no one was fighting to save her. In that abandoned place, feelings meant only pain and loneliness until there was nothing left of her but death.*

Sarah wanted no more pain. No more love. No more need for anyone but Maddie. Until one day soon there would be no more them, either, once they made the Raven and the Wolf pay. No more demented legacy. She and Maddie were going to end this nightmare together.

"No!" Jarred screamed as Sarah wielded the knife, cutting into his chest in Maddie's reality. And still, his fear wasn't for himself—but for the woman his soul was bound to.

"No!" Maddie screamed, pushing through Sarah's control and clinging to the love she'd been too afraid to face before.

"This ends now," Sarah said, while she and her scared-little-mouse of a sister shuddered in unison, neither of them in control of the dream now.

They raised the knife together to deliver the deathblow.

Summer thunder rolled.

Raven wings spread.

A tree's ghastly limbs swayed . . .

CHAPTER TWENTY-EIGHT

"No!"

Outside the dream, Maddie saw the knife drop. She fought her twin's compulsion for control. She felt Jarred's shocked agony as cold steel pierced his chest again, ripping at his life and the love he'd given her...

"Die!" Maddie screamed in the dream. In Sarah's voice.

Ravens overhead dove through the branches of a haunted tree, eager for their next victim...

"No!" Maddie begged in reality, trying to force her body to move beyond Sarah's control. To throw the knife down and cover Jarred's bleeding body, as if just her touch could heal him.

But the knife stayed in her hand...

Thunder rolled within the dream, blending with the sounds of rustling wings and Jarred's cry of pain as she—Sarah—stabbed him again.

Sarah giggled in demented victory...

Jarred stared up at Maddie in the motel room, his love and acceptance and understanding still there, even in this. Even in death.

"Wake up!" she yelled at him. "I can't stop her. Please wake up!"

He had to wake up before—

"Please, God..." His voice was weak. His mind was

accepting the end. "Let Maddie be okay…Take care of her and let her be okay."

His prayer was her absolution, stunning both her and Sarah. Their father had said the same exact thing in Sarah's dream of the accident. Maddie grasped at the tiny crack that ripped through Sarah's control.

"Jarred?" she poured need into their link. Love.

"It's not your fault," he whispered. "But you can stop her, Maddie. I know you can."

Even while he was dying by her hand, he believed she could control this violent, brutal thing she and Sarah had become…

"Wake up!" she screamed in the dream. This time at her twin, who looked up in shock from her bleeding victim.

Maddie glared directly into Sarah's eyes for the first time in a decade. Both of them in the dream, but separate. Maddie could see the weakness and fear now behind her twin's drive for destruction. The jealous rage. The hate Sarah couldn't harness without Maddie.

A nauseating vortex of images transported Maddie to a vision of Sarah, curling in on herself, rocking side to side on the filthy floor of some awful building. And then Maddie saw herself, shaking her head and walking away from the heartbreaking scene, taking her strength with her, because control of the dream was hers now.

And there was Jarred, waiting at the door of what looked like a vacant storefront in the city. He was holding out his hand. His smile promised he'd always be there for Maddie, no matter what. And the wicked passion in his eyes promised much, much more. His warm embrace when she reached for him offered the understanding and acceptance and safety she'd always craved.

"Die!" Sarah hissed from her filthy, lonely corner.

Then the dream snatched Maddie back to the image of

Jarred, naked and bleeding, lying defenseless beneath an avenging Sarah. A Sarah determined to keep Maddie for herself, never once believing Maddie would find the nerve to stop her.

Sarah's ravens and the rain and the darkness were fading. But that didn't stop Sarah from drawing back her knife, staring her hatred at Maddie, and aiming the blade at Jarred once more.

"He has to die!" Sarah shrieked as her image continued to fade.

"No!" Maddie stopped the weapon's deadly plunge toward the man she loved.

Hers and Sarah's hands brushed in the dream. Their wills collided. And the walls of their nightmare world began to peel away, splintering their connection...

CHAPTER TWENTY-NINE

"Wake up!" Maddie shouted, her ears ringing with the sound of her voice outside the dream.

Her connection to Sarah broken, she sagged to the motel-room bed as her mind, her vision, her hearing shut down. Her awareness of anything or anywhere. Her ability to feel or remember.

What couldn't she remember?

There was something important. Something she'd been willing to die for rather than let Sarah destroy. But numbness spread throughout her body like a thousand tiny bees, their wings buzzing madly. She was shaking. Moaning. The air around her rumbled with fear.

Except the deep rumbling wasn't hers. It was close. Every agonizing breath was hers, but it was someone else, too. Someone in excruciating pain. Someone she could help if she could only remember before it was too late.

"Maddie?" The voice stroked her with love. "I…it's okay. I'm here."

A hand brushed across her hair. She wasn't alone in the darkness. Then the voice was coming from a chest wheezing in pain. A naked chest that she'd collapsed against after…

After…

"Sarah?" he asked. "Is she gone? The dream…" His next breath was a hopeless cough. "Is it gone?"

Sarah?

The dream?

The knife!

It was a horrible rush—everything crashing back in jagged waves that obliterated the last of Maddie's confusion.

"Jarred!" She tried to push away from his chest. But it took two tries, and she hurt him both times.

They were naked. They'd made love. Their minds had promised each other forever. Then her sister had destroyed everything.

"Hold on," Maddie sobbed, remembering the violence and the blood and the ravens circling in death. And Sarah laughing at it all. "Don't die. Please. Jarred…"

She was sitting somehow, her head throbbing until she couldn't see. But she stared down at Jarred, hard, until the very real carnage Sarah's nightmare had caused wavered into view. The ugly bedspread, soaked in blood. The knife that she still gripped in her hand. She threw it across the bed, her tears blurring everything once more.

"I'm…I'm sorry," she sobbed.

Sarah had won.

Maddie had fought her. She'd finally believed that she could. But it had been too late.

"It's okay." Jarred's voice vibrated with the promise of forever. "I'm here."

And he *was* there. Comforting Maddie, while his life bled away.

Move! her mind screamed when no words would come. *Don't just sit there, do something!*

Maddie wiped at her eyes so she could see him, really see him.

"Jarred…" she said in wonder at the brightness surrounding them.

Healing white, like the energy she'd felt when she

helped people at the hospital. It rolled off her. Reached for him. The kind of white that could fight the most brutal battles and never give up hope.

"You're beautiful." She reached a trembling, blood-streaked hand toward his face. But on its own accord, her palm covered one of the ugly wounds in his chest instead. A jolt of pain blasted through her from the gash, making her stomach churn. "I'm so sorry…"

"You…" Jarred's next cough shuddered inside her chest, too, as if they were one, just like in their dream. "You fought her, Maddie," he insisted. "And you won. You're stronger than Sarah's darkness. Don't ever forget that."

"Sarah won." Maddie clutched at his hand the second it fumbled into her grasp. "She—"

"She didn't win. I was there. I know what I saw. You fought her. You fought to protect me. And—"

"A lot of fucking good that did!" Maddie's curse beckoned closer the lingering traces of Sarah's broken mind. "I swear, next time, I'm going to kill—"

"No you're not." Jarred groaned as she pressed harder against the wound she had no chance of sealing. The blood didn't stop coming. It wouldn't stop until he was dead. "You'll fight her…You'll figure out how to keep Sarah from hurting anyone else. But you love your sister. You won't kill her."

Another groan followed, then a cough that made Maddie's tears feel like shards of glass clogging her throat.

Then Jarred smiled, and every whisper of pain disappeared from both of them.

"You're a healer, Dr. Madeline Temple. My healer. Not a killer."

"But I've killed you!" she sobbed.

"That was Sarah."

His voice was weaker, but his love filled more of her by

the second, promising that she'd never be empty, never be alone again. Or was it Maddie's ability to accept it, to feel that promise, that kept expanding?

"You got me out of the dream," he whispered. "You got us away from her."

"Your blood is on my hands." She stared at her palms.

He laced their fingers together.

"This was my choice…" His eyes fluttered closed. "There…there's no place else I'd rather be."

"Don't…" Maddie begged. "Don't leave me. I can't do this without you."

His free hand struggled to cover her heart. His touch was ice-cold against her bare skin.

"I'm here," he whispered. "Always. Sarah can't take that away. You're never alone, Maddie. Don't…don't be afraid…"

His hand would have slipped away, but Maddie caught it close. She battled to hold on to his mind, too. To keep Jarred with her, always, just like he'd promised. She kept her other fingers over his heart, covering the deepest of the gashes.

The scared little girl inside Maddie wanted to run, screaming, until she became what her sister had—lost and unaware of the damage she'd done. But Maddie wasn't leaving Jarred. She wouldn't do that to the man who'd risked everything to show her how to believe.

"You're not alone, either." She closed her eyes and quieted everything inside. Everything but the feelings she'd never thought could be real. Not like this. Like they would never go away. Like they'd never really be gone, no matter how much time passed or how long she was forced to live without Jarred.

Acceptance.

Belonging.

Understanding.

Love.

There was light inside Jarred still, deep down where he'd hidden so much of himself. It called to her touch. To the courage that facing deep truths demanded.

"I love you..." she whispered as she felt his heart falter.

His injuries were fatal. She could see them all now, feel them in her mind. It was only a matter of minutes, and he had to know before it was too late. He had to see.

Leaning closer so she could talk directly in his ear, she tried to speak, but her throat was too raw.

I love you. Her mind stroked his. *Always. You're never alone. I won't let you go. Ever. You were right. I am strong enough to stop Sarah, and I will. I promise. But I need you with me. Just like in the dream. You have to fight, Jarred. You have to try. Let me...help you...I can...Help me try. I love you, and that's a miracle. And if I can believe in something like love, anything is possible...Stay with me, and help me.*

She was babbling, and she was crying incoherently, and Jarred wasn't responding. There was almost no pulse in his body. No hint of life, except the weakest of flickers.

But inside Maddie, there was also no more hate for her sister. No more anger for her mother. No more fear of what Maddie couldn't remember or what the government or Sarah's Raven or his center had done to all of them. No weakness for Sarah to feed on. There was only peace. The peace Jarred had given her. The peace she could feel spreading from where her naked body touched his, helping her to believe.

Then the light and the truth surged to where her fingers covered his heart, becoming a force of their own. A connection, calling to Jarred and finding the final embers of his consciousness and refusing to let him go.

I love you, Maddie repeated, laying her head on his chest, her hand still covering his heart. *Stay with me. Help me...*

She let herself fall, all of her.

Into him, all of him.

She felt both their heartbeats. She felt the goodness of a man whose commitment to protect her had destroyed him. Now it was her turn to protect him. She was staying there, right there—her mind searching for him, her heart covering his and protecting him. Becoming him. Refusing to let him slip away.

"I love you, Jarred. I'll never stop loving you. I'll always be here . . ."

She didn't care if Sarah or her psycho doctor or a troop of center security officers burst into wherever Jarred had taken her. Maddie would die before letting go. This was where she belonged. This was where she was going to stay.

And there in the almost nothing that his consciousness had become, she saw Jarred's shadow shake his head. Then he was fighting, trying to shove her away. His shadow mouthed the word, "Run!" But Maddie wasn't running anymore. She'd touched real love for the first time in her life. She could still feel it, flowing through his fear for her. Love that didn't lie or hide or abandon you deep inside, where the real you fought to hide.

Maddie dove deeper into their connection. Into Jarred. She wrapped herself in the safety of his commitment and covered his shivering body in a blanket of pure white love. She caressed their link. She accepted where it would take her when he died.

And in their joined consciousness, she cradled Jarred's handsome face in her hands and kissed him until he stopped struggling and let her in. And then, with their foreheads touching, she gave herself fully to the light joining their hearts.

But instead of following him into the beckoning darkness, she felt her body jerk away from the sudden heat beneath her hand. She opened her eyes in the dream to find light shimmering from where her hand lay on Jarred's chest.

A chest that was breathing. Stronger. Faster. The pain of it vibrating through her as his body throbbed back to life and brought hers with it. He was telling her where he hurt and how to heal him. Showing her that she'd always been able to heal this way but she hadn't known how before sharing Sarah's dreams.

"Maddie!" *Jarred's body writhed beneath her, then jackknifed until he was sitting beside her . . .*

On the bed.

Outside their minds.

Both of them covered in his blood.

Maddie's hand lay over his chest, his wounds, healing light searing them in reality. From her fingers. Her palms.

The rest of Maddie struggled for balance as she straddled his lap. She was still naked, her body still open to him while renewal poured from her in blistering waves. Attacking his wounds as it healed them. Demanding that his struggling heart beat even stronger. Transferring life from Maddie to him.

Jarred's gaze jerked to hers in agony. His mouth opened but no sound escaped. He swallowed. Gritted his teeth. His breath seethed in and out, but he didn't fight her. He simply looked down at his chest. Her gaze followed, to see each wound circled with rings of gold.

Maddie's palms burned.

They both shuddered.

The largest gash in his chest began to close.

To seal.

"You're . . ." Jarred groaned as the next wave pulsed from her palm into his body. "You're . . ."

"No, I'm not!" Terrified, Maddie tried to pull away. The healing white began to fade. She couldn't do this. She couldn't be this. "No, I'm not like—"

"Yes." Jarred's hand trapped hers against his chest.

"You are, Maddie. You're just as powerful as Sarah. But the…opposite of her darkness. She hurts people with her mind, somehow. You're…healing me…" His gentle touch moved her hand below his rib cage, to where the knife had sliced into his diaphragm. "Metting said your abilities would continue to grow. You diagnosed that MVA victim with your mind. Now, you're—Ah! Holy shit, that hurts!"

"I'm killing you," she gasped.

"You're…healing…me…" Jarred sucked in a breath as her touch did its painful work. "Loving me…Don't stop, Maddie. Don't leave…"

"I'll never leave," she promised. "I'm here…"

But she was feeling weaker. Her eyes slid shut.

"Yes," Jarred rasped out, pleasure in the word. Strength.

Pain and death were losing.

They couldn't have him.

"I'm here." Maddie felt the lung the knife had pierced reexpand. His blood volume filled from some magical well that shouldn't exist. "I'm…"

Gray leaked into the world behind her eyes… "You're going to be okay," she said in their minds. Saying the words out loud would have cost too much. "You're going to be okay."

Her tears felt wonderful now. They were washing her clean. She'd been made to heal, not destroy. Jarred had given her that.

"Thank you," Maddie's heart whispered.

"You can let me go, sweetheart," he urged. "I—"

"No! I have to—"

"You saved me, now wake up. You have to wake up before—"

"I won't leave you!"

"I'm here. Right here beside you. In the motel. Open your eyes and see me. Let the dream go, before—"

"No!"

"Damn it!" His dream image reached for her. "You're fading . . ."

She inched away from his warmth, drowning in her tears now because this was the only way. Didn't he see? This way she'd always be a healer. He'd always love her, just the way he did now in this moment that was better than anything she'd dreamed she could be. Sarah would never come back and hurt him again. Maddie wouldn't be there anymore for her sister to use.

"You'll stop her next time." Jarred was far away. Then he was beside Maddie—moving too fast to avoid, the way things did in dreams. He shook her. Angry now. "Stop this. You have to let go. Sarah's not here."

"She's close . . ." Maddie was feeling more and more of her twin. The gray in her and Jarred's healing dream was fading to black, and Sarah would be waiting there, dangerous and destructive. Determined to take Jarred away so she could have Maddie all to herself. "I can't let her hurt you again."

"Stay with me." Jarred grabbed for Maddie's arm. Caught only her fingertips. "Fight, damn it! You're not going anywhere. Wake up. Come back to me."

But her twin had grabbed Maddie's other hand. She was there in the dream now.

"Damn it, Sarah!" Jarred spit out. "Get away from her!"

"She won't make it without me," Sarah hissed back. "She doesn't know how to wake up from projecting. Healing you is going to kill her, and she—"

"She needs me. She'll come back to me."

"Because you love her?"

"Because I won't let her hate—"

"Me? She hates herself, you idiot. Not me. And you've let

her. And now she's willing to die so that hate will finally go away. You're the one who's killing her, not me!"

"Get away from her."

"You can't take her from me." Sarah yanked Maddie closer. "I won't let you. I—"

Maddie felt her sister's attention jerk away, then back in a dizzying, panicked surge.

"Sarah?" Maddie asked.

"He's right, Maddie. You have to wake up . . ." Sarah was letting go. Casting a hate-filled stare over Maddie's shoulder. "You haven't won," she said to Jarred. "I won't let you win."

"Sarah?" Maddie was the one holding on now, terrified for her sister no matter how much damage Sarah's hate had done.

"She won't be able to move," Sarah warned Jarred. "But you have to get her out of there. Don't screw this up, asshole, or I'll finish the job the next time I try to kill you."

"What are you talking about?" Jarred demanded.

"They're coming." Sarah let go.

Maddie swayed at the lost connection.

Sarah slapped her across the face.

"Wake up!" she screamed. "Quit now, and it's all gone. Me. You. What we were born to be. Our mother. Even your precious doctor. We'll all die. Because you're too weak to accept reality."

"Maddie?" Jarred's hold was still there—both in the dream and in reality. He was stronger. He was going to live. "You have to—"

"Wake up!" Sarah screamed, her eyes full of loathing as she shoved Maddie into Jarred's arms . . .

CHAPTER THIRTY

Jarred held Maddie close. They were shivering against the room's bitter cold. And from the lingering power of Maddie's healing dream.

Maddie had healed him.

It was impossible for him to sort the reality of what had happened from fantasy. The love from the near-death. The loss from rebirth, and then loss again. All of it swirling through his mind until Jarred was certain of only two things. He and Maddie had loved each other with their minds and bodies. And—he looked down at the scars and blood left by the vicious slashes her sister had cut into him—healing him had damn near killed her.

Jarred clutched Maddie closer. He barely had the strength to move. He couldn't force his eyes open. But his hands were roaming Maddie's precious curves, reassuring him that she really was alive. His fingers clenched in the softness of her hair. His mind tentatively reached for hers, and he found overwhelming gratitude waiting for him. Maddie's relief that he was alive. That she'd been able to save him. Which meant he was right, and she'd been good after all.

Move! a voice screamed through the darkness.

Not his voice.

Not Maddie's.

Sarah?

You're in danger! Move your ass, and get my sister out of there.

There was no reason to believe the psychotic bitch. Except that Maddie was still alive instead of lost to him forever. And Sarah had been the one to shove her at Jarred before ending their dream link. But if Sarah was gone, how could he still be hearing her voice?

"Jarred?" Maddie shuddered and rolled off his body. She was pale as death. Covered in his blood. She stared down at his chest, at the roughly closed wounds that throbbed like a son of a bitch. "Sarah...she...she tried to kill you."

"But I'm alive." He ignored the pain and the fatigue and the motel room spinning around them and sat up, too. Focused on Maddie. "You wouldn't let me go, and I wouldn't let Sarah have you, and..." He swallowed. "And here we are."

"I..." Maddie was shaking. Like she had after saving her patient, only worse. She grabbed for Jarred's arm, every muscle in her body jittering out of control. "I... Sarah. She's saying it's not safe, and...I believe her."

"I do, too."

The irony wasn't lost on Jarred—his instinct to trust a woman he'd never met whose dreams were trying to kill him. He pulled the bedspread up and around Maddie, even though physical warmth wouldn't make a dent at this point. Her mind was shattering more with each touch of her insane twin's thoughts.

"Mmm-ove," she gasped in Sarah's voice, her muscles destabilizing into convulsions.

"Maddie!"

His hate grew for whatever evil was stalking her. For

the choice he had to make next. He couldn't protect her like this. Not on his own. He stroked Maddie's shaking body and willed her to hang on. Then he grappled for his jeans, where they'd been tossed aside when he and Maddie had ripped off each other's clothes.

He fished inside one of the pockets until he found the damned cell phone. Metting's trap had become Jarred's last chance, just as the other man had predicted.

CHAPTER THIRTY-ONE

"You don't have a choice," Richard insisted to Jarred Keith over the phone, squelching the hint of desperation in his voice. An impatient gesture silenced the questions of the man standing beside him. "You have to come in now. It's only a matter of time before the center finds you. They already have Phyllis Temp—"

"Or you do," Keith spat back. A moaning sound from his end of the call assured Richard that Madeline Temple was still alive, despite Keith's rushed explanation that the twins had had a "homicidal" nightmare. "Maybe you took the mother to get to the daughters. I'm not letting Maddie anywhere near you or this…organization of yours, until you tell me what's happening to Maddie and her sister. What just happened to me."

"I could have kept Maddie at the center, and you know it. All I had to do was give her to the center's directors, and they would have welcomed me back with open arms. But I didn't."

"Of course not. That wouldn't have gotten you Sarah back, and you've made it clear that she's who you really want."

"I could have had you both dragged in hours ago. A strike team is ready to bring you in at my command."

"And that's supposed to make me trust you?"

"We're a brotherhood of Watchers, Dr. Keith. We've been protecting the Temple twins' legacy for decades. I assure you, our objectives have never coincided with those of the Trinity Research Center."

"Except you worked with Sarah Temple there. And now you want Maddie after she leads you to her sister."

"Actually, all I want at the moment is for her not to completely lose her mind. That's why you need to bring her in."

Extended silence crackled over the line.

"The damage Sarah can do to her twin," Richard continued, "is nothing compared to what the center has in store for Madeline if they can get their hands on her. Calling me is the first right thing you've done. Don't backtrack now."

The data streaming across Richard's computer link gave him little more than ten minutes before he'd have to order an extraction. But he needed Jarred Keith on board. He needed the other doctor's cooperation and trust for Richard to have any chance of finding Sarah through Madeline.

"Maddie's getting worse," Keith finally said. "If you really want me to trust you, tell me how to help her."

"Is she getting worse?" Richard pressed. "Or stronger?"

"Well, she almost killed me during one of her sister's dreams," Keith snapped. "But then she saved my life once she finally accepted that she could control her abilities herself. Does that get you off, you freak? Knowing what you've done to these women. How about the seizure she just had? And how she keeps muttering—"

"Saved…She healed you?" Madeline would have had to immerse herself into Keith's subconscious body image to transform his physiology. Just like Richard had taught Sarah to release her consciousness into a host's dream, so she could control the dreamer's reality. "She's always been a gifted diagnostician. But has she ever done that before?"

No answer.

"If her abilities have progressed, Dr. Keith, it's important that I know how much and—"

"So you can exploit her healing dreams, the way you did her twin's nightmares?"

The mumbling on Keith's end of the call grew louder. "...coming...have to...before it's too..." a feminine voice rambled.

"What is she saying?" Richard told himself that it was Madeline he was listening to, not Sarah. But that voice... it was a dead-on match.

"Tell me how to help her," Keith insisted.

"Come in, and I'll help her any way I can." Richard covered the phone with his hand. "Get me a situation report from the strike team at the motel," he ordered. "I want an ETA to perimeter breach."

His assistant walked to the other side of the trailer Richard was using to monitor the motel and his team, an open com link to his ear.

"She's...Maddie's..." Keith's hatred for Richard was a living thing coming across the phone line. "She's a danger to herself, and I don't know why. And you do, you bastard, and I swear to God if you don't help her, I'll—"

"What is she saying, Doctor?" Metting strained to hear. Madeline's voice was getting stronger. She was speaking faster. "It's very important that you tell me—"

"You tell me what you've done to her, first." The other man dug in, steel in his voice. "Tell me how I can—"

"You can't help her." Richard heard snatches of,... closer...alert five...abort..."You need to get Madeline out of there, and meet me—"

"Not until you—"

"Perimeter breached," Richard's lieutenant confirmed, turning back from his conversation with the strike team. "Three minutes, max."

Richard gave the hand signal to bring them in.

"I'm afraid there is no *until*," he said to the man still ranting in his ear. "I'd hoped this would end another way, but you have only minutes before the center has you surrounded. And I can't let that happen."

"You can't…" Keith sputtered. "Who the fuck do you think you are!"

"I'm the man who's about to save your ass." Richard raised his own com link to his ear. His team's chatter would be minimal as they closed in, but he needed to hear every word.

"Abort!" Madeline shouted next. Richard had no doubt that it was Sarah warning Keith, not her twin. The fear in Sarah's voice seared through Richard. "Run!"

There was a crash, followed by Keith's curse and a woman's scream.

The line went dead.

"Contact made—" Richard's team lead reported. "Secondary target also engaged."

Then that line, too, shut down. Standard protocol until the scene was contained.

Richard cursed. The arrival of the team's secondary targets—a center squad that had been closing in but was only to be engaged if they interfered with Richard's plans—was a complication Richard's operatives didn't need while they neutralized Madeline Temple. It would be hard enough to safely bring her in without the center's hired guns adding to the woman's psychic confusion.

Richard should have signaled for extraction sooner, regardless of his plan to let Keith make the first move.

Earning the other doctor's trust bought Richard nothing if they lost Madeline to the center. Especially now that her latent abilities were strengthening.

He'd been doing his job, he reminded himself. His duty. For over a year. He couldn't reach Sarah now without Madeline, and he couldn't reach Madeline without Jarred Keith's willing participation. So Richard had done his job and waited, the same as he'd waited at the center until the Brotherhood knew everything it could about the government's Dream Weaver objectives. But tonight his duty may have destroyed their last chance to reach either Temple twin. To save their legacy from disintegrating into the kind of evil that only death could contain.

And if that happened, the center might as well hunt Richard down and kill him, too. He'd never survive knowing he'd failed Sarah so completely.

CHAPTER THIRTY-TWO

Jarred stood naked, a blood-soaked knife in his hand, between the woman he loved and the men wearing black on black who'd burst through the motel-room door.

"What the fuck do you want!" he snarled while Maddie babbled on in the altered state she'd slipped into.

"Alert five…abort…" she muttered while what looked like a black-ops team held Jarred at gunpoint and watched her warily.

In the next second, Maddie was fully conscious and springing off the bed, which shouldn't have been possible in her weakened condition. She grabbed the knife, naked herself without the bedspread covering her—She was facing the window rather than the armed men who'd just broken down their door. "They're here," she said with a shaky voice that wasn't her own. "Abort. Run!"

"Secure the package." The black shirt closest to Jarred reached for Maddie as the window shattered and a round cylinder flew inside.

Maddie grabbed black shirt's arm with her free hand, twisted it at an angle that wrenched the bone from the shoulder joint, then let him drop as the canister popped and began spewing thick smoke. She threw her body in front of Jarred, a warrior full-on, as two more men hurled into the tiny room, shattering the rest of the window and brandishing lethal automatic weapons. She picked up the smoke-spewing canister and threw it back outside before its fumes could fill the room.

All Jarred could do was stare as the exhausted and mentally drained woman he'd been determined to protect kicked ass. The first team killed the newest intruders with four efficient shots, then swept the dead men to the periphery of the room. Someone grabbed Jarred from behind, restraining his arms.

"Maddie?" he stuttered.

She stared down at the bloody knife in her hand, then at the man she'd maimed. She was shaking again, coming back to herself from Sarah or whomever else she'd just connected to, and whatever that connection had done to her.

"Secure the package," the black shirt at her feet growled though the pain from his injury.

The man made it to his feet as his cohorts surrounded Maddie. They took the knife away. A flinch was her only visible reaction.

"Don't touch her," Jarred warned.

The injured black shirt fingered a hands-free device wrapped around his ear. One of his team fished into his backpack, removing a rumpled pile of black clothing.

"Get them dressed," the injured one ordered. "Report," he said to God knew who on the other end of his communication.

Maddie whimpered.

"You're scaring her," Jarred said as he struggled into his clothes, hating the callousness of the hands stuffing Maddie into hers.

Then, suddenly, the shirts supporting a semiconscious Maddie raised their free hands to their throats. They began to choke.

"Oh, God," Jarred said.

"Roger, we've cleared the primary site. Package is in tow. We're underway for rendezvous in sixty." The wounded man's only response to his team's distress was to step directly in front of Jarred.

He was choking, too. Jarred could see the strain in his face as he calmly fought for air. But that didn't stop the man from lifting the lethal blade of his own knife to Jarred's throat. Meanwhile, Maddie's nightmarish visions of choking to death every black shirt in the room flooded Jarred's mind.

Help me... her mind whispered, begging for the same control Jarred had been for her as she'd reversed Sarah's damage to his body.

"Stop her, Doctor," black shirt bit out on a gasp. "Or I will by whatever means necessary. More center operatives are no doubt on their way. Ms. Temple is no longer safe without our protection. The Brotherhood's orders are to bring her in alive. The rest is at my discretion. I will make my rendezvous as ordered, even if it means damaging the package. You have thirty seconds to make up your mind."

"The package?" Jarred spat back, somehow knowing the man wouldn't slit his throat. Not if he needed Jarred to handle Maddie.

"Twenty seconds." The guy holstered the knife. He opened the chamber on the weapon slung across his good shoulder, revealing the same type of medicated dart Metting had used on them before.

"She doesn't know what she's doing," Jarred insisted.

"Understood. Fifteen seconds."

He snapped the chamber closed and aimed the weapon, one-handed, at Maddie. His face was turning blue, but he would fire. Jarred had no doubt.

"All right." As soon as Jarred said the word, the man stumbled out of his way. Jarred approached Maddie carefully. "Let her go."

The black shirts restraining her looked to their leader for confirmation. Then they sank to their knees, hands on their throats. Jarred caught Maddie to him, wrapping his arms around her shivering body.

"You're safe," he whispered over the sound of storming winds and rustling branches in their minds. "Let them go, Maddie. You don't want to hurt anyone."

She shook her head, tears filling her eyes.

"Let them go," Jarred said over the click of a weapon being primed to fire. "I love you. You have to trust me. I won't let them hurt you anymore…"

It was a lie. He could feel that she knew it, too. But then she was letting go, softening against him as the men choking on the ground collapsed to all fours and gulped in full breaths of air.

Jarred closed his eyes, wanting to believe he'd made the right decision. He turned with her to face the blackshirt leader—whose gun was trained on Jarred now.

"I did what you asked," Jarred raged.

"Is she unconscious?" the other man asked.

"Yes." Jarred positioned as much of his body as possible between Maddie and the gun.

The black shirts on either side of them rose to their feet, one taking Maddie's arm, the other taking Jarred's.

"Good," their leader said, dispassionately firing a dart into Jarred's neck. "That makes my job considerably easier."

We're death, and it's the Raven's fault. Never forget that. It's the Raven's fault…

Sarah's hate was the first thing Maddie became aware

of. Horrific images came next. Maddie choking security at Trinity Center, stabbing Jarred, attacking another man, facing down danger with combat skills she didn't possess because Sarah had been trained in them somehow. And what Sarah knew, Maddie did now, too.

Then came a new dream of using a bloody knife to attack the Raven. Except Maddie no longer had a knife, so she'd have to use her bare hands to get the job done.

No!

Maddie's mind clawed its way back to her own consciousness, rejecting Sarah's insanity. She forced her eyes to open and stay open, even though her body was still numb. She blinked into the dimness around her. The return of her hearing ushered in the sound of branches scratching and wind howling, just like in her dreams. In Sarah's dreams.

Except the nightmare around her now was very real.

He's there . . . Sarah whispered as she gathered the last of her energy for when the Raven showed himself. *He did this to me. To both of us!*

Wake up, Maddie, a gentler voice intruded. *Stay with me.*

Jarred.

He was there, too. He would always be there. Even after she'd stabbed him. After he'd watched her hurt that man back in their motel room.

That wasn't you, he insisted.

I . . . More of the world was coming into focus. The forest floor Maddie was sitting on. The very real tree she'd been propped against. Jarred's still body was sitting beside her. *I wanted to cut them, the same way I did you. Get away from me, Jarred. Run!*

Never. He didn't move. Not his body. Not his mind. *That wasn't you with the knife. Either time. I'm not even sure it was your sister. It was—*

The Raven, Maddie finished. He'd taught Sarah. Trained her mind. Turned her into this. And he was there, in the woods. Circling overhead. Waiting for the next dream. Maddie had to—

Wake up! Sarah screamed. *Move!*

Jarred's arm circled Maddie, pulling her closer.

Stay still, he warned. *Close your eyes and stay still.*

Jarred, on the other hand, was shaking his head, making an obvious show of waking. Attracting whatever attention was focused on them to himself alone. He felt responsible. He wasn't going to fail her again.

Don't you dare try to be a hero! her mind screamed at him, but she closed her eyes like he'd asked.

If Jarred did something stupid, or Sarah did something worse, before Maddie could—

Be still! both of them ranted at the same time.

Idiots in stereo, Maddie snapped at them. *Just the thing to keep a psychotic maniac from losing her shit!*

You're not psychotic, Jarred insisted.

Go ahead, lose your shit, was Sarah's response. *He's coming...*

Through Sarah, Maddie could feel the Raven moving closer. She sensed that he knew, somehow, that she was aware of his every step.

"Dr. Keith, it's good to see you again." the voice from Sarah's nightmares said.

Khaki-covered legs appeared in front of them. God! Maddie was...seeing through Jarred...while she felt the Raven approaching, through Sarah.

The man knelt.

Jarred spat in his face.

The Raven smiled as he wiped his cheek. He had them right where he wanted them.

Kill the Raven! Sarah screamed through Maddie's mind. *He has to—*

"Die!" Maddie launched herself into a deadly leap for the Raven's throat.

"No!" Jarred yelled.

Maddie toppled the man to the ground, consumed by Sarah's insanity and drive to hurt people as badly as she'd been hurt. Her hands clenched, crushing his windpipe. She was going to die tonight. Jarred was going to die, and it was all this man's fault.

"Maddie." Jarred tried to pull her away. "Stop!"

Maddie can't stop me anymore, Sarah chanted, as her visions of a long-ago accident, a hydroplaning truck, consumed Maddie's mind.

CHAPTER THIRTY-THREE

We're Death, and it's the Raven's fault! Sarah insisted, clinging to her fading link to Maddie's mind. *Kill him!*

"You're not Death," Maddie's weak-ass boyfriend said out loud.

"Get away from us, Doctor, or you're next," Sarah ranted through her twin. Maddie's hands squeezed tighter. "It's time to kill the Raven."

"You're not strong enough, Alpha." The Raven's body relaxed against Maddie's hold. "You're expending too much energy maintaining your link, and it's been too long since you've rested. Madeline's weak. She doesn't understand how to channel her emotions yet. The... hate, is it? Is that what your shadow control taught you to use? You should have known better. Your power here is dwindling. Disengage, Alpha, before you fry your sister's brain completely. Target—"

"Don't you dare!" Maddie screamed Sarah's threat. But she was fighting for her freedom, too, and starting to win.

Fuck that!

"I'll kill her," Sarah seethed in Maddie's voice. "I'll kill you all."

The Raven's men trained their weapons on Sarah's psychic hissy fit.

"No!" Dr. Useless tried to break Maddie's grip on the other man. "Turn him loose, before it's too late."

"It's already too late for Death!"

Sarah tried to make her twin squeeze harder. She was in control of Maddie's daydream, fuck what the Raven thought. She and Maddie had been here so many times in the Wolf's simulations. The storm, the wind and rain, and the truck driver taking aim for their family car. The loss. Anger. Hatred. Sarah feeding on Maddie's surging emotions. Funneling them into a drive to—

"Kill!" Sarah shrieked through her sister, pointing Maddie at the Raven like the lethal weapon the Wolf wanted them to be. "It's all his fault. He has to—"

"No!" her twin's companion insisted. "Don't do this. Listen to me, Maddie. You're a healer. Remember? You healed me."

The Raven smiled at Sarah—at Maddie, whose fingers had loosened around his neck.

"I'm…I'm a healer." Maddie shuddered, fighting Sarah's hold. "I'm not alone. I'm not Death. I don't want to—"

"No!" Sarah was losing. Slipping back into the lonely darkness she'd never escape.

"There's something powerful inside your twin, Sarah," the Raven said. "Something stronger than your hate. You have to let the hate go, or the…Wolf, is it? Don't let the Wolf win."

The Raven wasn't smiling now. He was concern and care and protection—everything he'd been at the very start. Everything Sarah had believed when she'd let him lead her out of the coma so the Wolf could drag her back into darkness.

"Can you remember, Sarah?" the Raven asked. "Can you remember what I taught you?"

"Ja…Jarred?" Maddie sputtered.

"I'm here." Jarred pulled one of Maddie's hands from the Raven's throat to cover the useless heart Maddie had kept beating. His love flooded Sarah along with her twin. He was making Sarah feel again. Making her believe there was another way. "I'm here with you, and I'm not going anywhere. I prom—"

"No!" Sarah forced Maddie to say. "The Raven has to die."

"Then kill the bastard yourself!" Jarred pulled Maddie's palm to his cheek, their link surging. "You're done using your sister to do your dirty work."

Sarah felt herself fading and the Raven watching. She'd seen him as a bird of prey for so long in the Wolf's dream. Blamed him for the evil the Wolf wanted her to become. But in her mind now, in her sister's mind, her Raven morphed back into the man Sarah had let herself believe in. The dream weaver who'd promised to be there for her no matter what, just like her twin's doctor. The protector who'd asked for her trust while he'd trained her gifts and taught her everything he'd said she'd need to keep her safe.

"Richard…" Maddie whispered in Sarah's voice.

He caught her—Maddie's—other wrist and pulled it from his throat, holding Sarah through Maddie's touch.

"I'm sorry, Sarah," he said. "I'm sorry I didn't protect you better. But this is your chance. Whether or not you're ready for it. Are you what this Wolf wants you to be? Will you and your sister lose everything to his darkness—everything your legacy could become? Or will you trust Maddie to help you? Stop using her like a blunt instrument of destruction. Stop trying to kill. Trust me, and I'll—"

"Never!" In her mind, Sarah was still strangling him.

Squeezing until the life drained from the Raven's eyes. "I'll never trust you again. I'll never give up. I'll find another way. And the next time I get my hands on you, I won't fail!"

"Target release, Alpha," the Raven said. Disappointment drained the warmth from his eyes until he was once again a soulless scientist putting his lab rat through its paces. "Reset to zero."

"I won't stop!" Sarah gathered herself. Shoved Maddie's consciousness aside. "I won't stop until you die!"

Maddie's hands snapped back to the Raven's neck. Squeezing, crushing, going for the kill…feeding Sarah the Raven's shock and pain…Jarred's fear…Maddie's disgust at what Sarah was capable of making her do.

"Help me," Maddie begged as her fingers dug deeper. Her nails pierced skin until blood ran down the Raven's neck. "I…I can't stop…Please, help me."

"It's…it's a dream," the Raven croaked. He was a flesh-and-blood man again as he reached toward Jarred.

"You have to…wake Madeline up," he said to the other man. "You're the only one who can. My men won't let her…kill…You have to…stop her, Dr. Keith. Madeline has to break her link with Sarah now!"

And Maddie could. Sarah could feel her twin's strength growing with these two men helping her. No one had helped Sarah. Maddie would win, and then she'd leave Sarah alone in the darkness forever.

"No!" Sarah ranted at her twin. "I'm not going to let you—"

"Come back to me." Jarred's finger drew Maddie's face toward his. Their connection became a healing light that Sarah couldn't fight. "I love you, Maddie. Come back to me."

"No!" Maddie screamed again. But her arms were

dropping. Her body, her heart, were falling into a place so safe, Sarah couldn't reach her.

"Damn it, do something!" Maddie's lover was yelling at the Raven. "Get up and help her, you bastard, or so help me God, I'll…"

Sarah was floating above them now, insanity returning in a welcome rush as she left Maddie's mind behind. She watched her twin's body shake. Maddie's doctor-love wiped at the blood running from her nose. From the corner of her mouth. He was frantic. Terrified. And there the Raven was, fighting to save Maddie, too.

The way he'd promised to save Sarah…

CHAPTER THIRTY-FOUR

Maddie was dreaming. She couldn't stop, but she didn't care.

She was running again, through the woods. But she was searching this time, not fleeing. She was herself in the gray of Sarah's dream world. And she wasn't just looking for her sister. She was digging for answers. The truth was there in the storm swirling around her. Maddie was going to finally understand what the hell her sister really wanted.

Jarred would be waiting for her when she woke. The Raven would be there, too. This time, she was going to have the answers she needed to deal with them. She'd know why her sister was so certain they were destined to be Death. She'd know how to stop her. Maddie was going to take her life back. Screw the curses and the government weapons programs and the mad scientists and demented dreams she couldn't stop.

Sarah was the one running blind now. And Maddie was locked into the madness with her. Again. It was time for the insanity to end, whatever Maddie had to face once she got her hands on her sister.

"If you don't take this fucking blindfold off me—" Jarred growled as he was led through yet another door, into yet another room in some mystery complex that might be the center. It might not be. No one was telling him a damn thing. "If I don't see Maddie in the next five minutes, *I'm* going to become a deranged killing machine!"

"Relax," Metting responded, speaking for the first time since giving orders in whatever forest the rendezvous had been in, to have Maddie sedated and Jarred blindfolded and carted along for the ride. "Your patient is safe, and my job is to keep her that way. Including making sure you can't tell anyone how to find this facility, if you were to escape and subsequently be captured."

The tightly wound cloth over Jarred's face was ripped away. Bright light assaulted his closed eyes. He held up a hand and blinked until he could see. The room was a sphere of white on white. Even the exam tables and cabinetry. The only relief was the color of his clothing and Metting's. Black.

"Your anger will make what Madeline is going through harder." Metting's tone was mild. Detached. "I'd recommend pulling yourself together."

In the woods, Jarred had seen the man's anxiety. Streaks of panic while he fought to regain Sarah's trust. Both were gone now. The only evidence that this was the same person who'd begged Sarah to believe him were the bruises on his neck. Metting turned his back while he studied something scrolling across the screen of a laptop docked on one of the high counters.

"Everything you're feeling," he said, "Maddie's feeling it, too. Interesting. She's—"

"She's dying," Jarred raged as Metting's men left the room. "Because of whatever you've done to her."

"On the contrary." Metting didn't look up as Jarred stalked closer. "I have nothing to do with what's happening to Madeline at the moment. It wasn't my programming that targeted her for dream projections. It's not my emotions ripping her apart through whatever connection you two have built."

"Programming?" Maddie's dissociative states and every nightmare Jarred had shared with her replayed in his mind. "What the hell are dream projections?"

"They're how Sarah's reached out to her sister." Metting dragged his laptop to the edge of the counter and beckoned Jarred closer. "They're the focus of the government's latest covert weapons testing."

"But…" Jarred started.

Then he realized he didn't know enough to even begin to know what to ask.

The laptop displayed something that looked like an EKG. But Jarred's familiarity with heart-monitoring technology told him that's not what he was watching.

"This is Maddie?" he guessed.

Metting nodded. "I tracked her sister's sleep states the same way, when—"

"Sleep states?"

"Brain activity is different, depending on the phase of sleep the mind is in. Maddie's mind will cycle in and out of the REM stage, six or seven times during an eight-hour period. She should be—"

Jarred grabbed the man by the shoulders and spun him around until Metting's back was pressed against the counter.

"Where is she? Stay the hell out of her brain and tell me where she is. Now!"

"That would be inadvisable, given your current emotional distress." The man sounded like a goddamned robot. "If Madeline's going to have any chance of surviving this, you need to pull yourself together."

"Surviving what?"

"What you came to me to protect her from—the center's plans. Which we know now means this Wolf's shadow programming, which he's had Sarah embed into Madeline's mind."

"The...what wolf?"

Richard studied him, then the laptop, before answering. "Does this mean you're ready to listen like a brilliant scientist, instead of a panicked lover?"

Jarred scowled at the wicked spikes on Richard's monitor.

"What wolf?" he asked with more control.

"A wolf is the dream symbol Sarah chose to represent the person controlling her shadow programming."

"Like you're a raven..." Jarred added this new bit of information to the rest.

"Except that I was never supposed to become an active participant in Sarah's dream projections. A control can't risk becoming the target of a simulation gone awry. He has to remain separate, so he can bring the dreamer back when needed. So she'll still trust him when everything in the dream is telling her not to. Given the fresh scars on your chest, Dr. Keith, I'd venture to say that you've already had some experience overidentifying with a dream projector. Now that you're immersed into Madeline's dreamscape, you can't afford to let your guard down. Not until her mind is trained well enough to tell the difference between dream and reality."

Jarred scowled. "You're talking like I'm—"

"A control? Yes. Madeline turned to you when Sarah's dream work began to split her from reality. Which makes you the only thing standing between your patient, and her absorbtion into the center's plans."

"*You* were with the center." Jarred glanced back at the laptop, at the ugly spikes and chaotic drops in Maddie's brainwaves—pain that this man had a part in causing.

He suddenly wanted to be the one throttling Sarah's Raven. "Because of you, Maddie's sister's out there alone, spiraling out of control, and she's taking Maddie's mind with her."

"Yes." Metting's clinical facade slipped, for no more than a second; then it fell back into place. "And no. I was there to protect Sarah, and I failed."

"Right. This government defense program you said you infiltrated. And you were there to do what, exactly?"

"To strengthen Sara's mind so she could resist the center's plans for Dream Weaver."

"And now you want me to believe that a wolf, not you, is the real threat to Maddie and her sister."

"The Wolf's simulations piggybacked my progress with Sarah, but they were kept secret from me. Which can only mean one thing."

It didn't take Jarred long to guess what. "The center suspected you weren't there to give them a weapon. So they hedged their bets with the Wolf."

"So it would seem." Richard nodded, as if to welcome Jarred on board his sinking ship.

"Okay," Jarred said into the silence that followed. "I'll grant that it's highly unlikely you're working with the center, if they're gunning for your operatives with tear gas and automatic weapons. So who's behind this mission of yours to stop them?" He gestured around the lab. "Who's so concerned about Sarah Temple they sent you on a suicide mission to stop what was being done to her?"

Jarred was battered and bruised and felt like he'd tangled with a freight train and lost. But Maddie's life depended on him seeing things as clearly as possible. He took his first close look at the man beside him. At Metting's rigid posture and the violent way his fingers snapped against the keyboard as he typed. Jarred saw controlled rage and a scientist's desperation to find answers. But there was no malice. No careless drive to hurt. This was a man on a mission to protect a patient who was now beyond his reach, the same as Maddie was beyond Jarred.

"We're a centuries-old secret society," Metting finally answered, his tone as ragged as Jarred felt. "Committed to watching psychically powerful family lines like the Temples'. We're charged with maintaining balance, tracking, and remaining uninvolved unless it becomes clear intervention is required."

"You're…" Jarred's first instinct was to laugh. But something in the solemnity of Metting's explanation stopped him. "So that makes you…"

"A Watcher." Metting pointed at the fluctuating patterns scrolling across the monitor. "A noninvolved protector. At least I was until a year ago. We'd known about the government's interest in Sarah for a while. Ever since she was transferred to the center. But a year ago, funding was approved for a black-ops testing program, with the ultimate goal of projecting Sarah's psychic abilities into other people's dreams. And through those dream hosts, into the world as untraceable daydreams."

"Daydreams?"

"Lucid dream states a host would have no control over, that a powerful psychic like Sarah could program, then trigger at will as—"

"Right. Daydreams." Jarred's head was going to explode. "You expect me to believe the government would bankroll something that—"

"Consider if the dreamer were to walk into an unsuspecting crowd with a bomb hidden in her purse. A bomb she doesn't remember building or testing, because each time she worked on it, she was dreaming. But she finally has access to a target the government needs eliminated. Maybe years after her programming was embedded. And since she's an everyday person with access to the mark, and she's on no agency's radar as a threat, she's become the perfect direct-strike weapon that can be remotely triggered from anywhere in the world.

"She's an innocent. She doesn't remember the dreams, or what they've trained her to do—because the mind is predisposed to forget troubling dream behavior. In her everyday life she wouldn't be able to build a bomb. But fueled by countless untraceable REM simulations, she can be trained to do anything. And the fuse for Dream Weaver? That's the kicker. It's simple human emotion—the conduit through which human dreams connect with real-world experiences. Heightened by the collective unconscious that exists all around us—a vast repository of the emotional, intellectual, and spiritual experiences of every living being, and those who lived before us. All a psychic projector like Sarah has to do is isolate the specific emotion that will trigger a desired action, and a walking time bomb has been created."

"How…close are they to getting this done?" Jarred asked.

"They're there, except for execution of a weapons-grade field test. For that, they needed a scientist with psychic abilities to complement Sarah's. The Brotherhood made sure they got exactly what they needed—me."

Jarred tried to speak. Then tried again. No luck. The image of Maddie holding a gun to her head kept replaying in his mind. Her slicing him open with her mother's paring knife.

"So…" He cleared his throat and glanced toward Metting's monitor. "When Maddie isn't in control of things she's doing?"

"It's most likely because Sarah has embedded programming directing her to—"

"To try to kill me? You? To kill herself? Why would Sarah do that if she really thought she needed her sister to break free of you and the center?"

"Most likely the shadow programming intended the command to kill to be for Sarah's other host. But once Sarah was linked with Maddie—"

"Most likely! You're the expert in all this. You're the center's go-to guy. And the best you can give me is *your guess is as good as mine?*"

"I'm Sarah's Watcher, not her shadow control. I wasn't involved in—"

"Well it doesn't sound like *watching* for a year has helped you figure out jack about what's going on!"

Metting actually smiled.

It wasn't reassuring.

"I'm learning more by the second, Dr. Keith. Such as how strongly you're linked, emotionally, with Madeline's dreams."

"And you know that, how?"

Metting nodded toward his laptop.

"Madeline's brain activity spikes each time your agitation increases. Her emotional state tracks yours, even though she's unconscious and two rooms away."

"So, I'm affecting her rest? What does that—"

"Her dreams, actually." Metting's gaze registered regret, then resignation. "It's clear after what happened in the motel and at the rendezvous that her shared dream states with her twin are out of control. She's been without the pharmacological cocktail I designed for Sarah, to sustain the nonactive sleep periods required to recover after dream simulations. And so is Sarah now. Which means both sisters are degenerating into continuous dream cycles."

"What are you telling me?"

"Sarah and Madeline Temple's psychic abilities originate in their emotions, more strongly than any other projectors I've studied. Watchers have tracked their family line for generations. Back to a distant aunt who was burned at the stake for supposedly holding half a village in thrall."

"Hence this curse Maddie's been trying to figure out?"

Metting's stare warmed with interest. "Their legacy, yes."

"Okay." Jarred stared, waiting for the rest.

"Absorbing her sister's emotions and Dream Weaver skills," Metting continued, "without the training and control I've given Sarah, means—"

"The twins' link is becoming more volatile every time their minds join."

"Which they're no doubt attempting to do at this very moment. They're feeding on each other's fear and psychosis, and it's unclear which twin, if either, is in control now."

Jarred's lungs wouldn't take in air. "But why would this Wolf want the sisters to damage each other this way?"

"He wouldn't have." Metting sighed. "I assume the intention was for Sarah to harvest Madeline's abilities, not the other way around."

"But…"

"The Wolf clearly didn't count on the extent of Madeline's gifts. More information got through than expected, and Sarah couldn't completely control their link.

f Madeline can heal now, if she could join her consciousness with yours and take on your body image, then she's absorbed her twin's ability to commandeer another consciousness. To direct another's reality at will. *And* she's found her own source of balance and control to draw on—from you."

Jarred swallowed, trying to understand. To believe. He studied the escalating peaks of brain activity on Metting's monitor.

"I thought you sedated her," he demanded.

"Madeline's dissociating, even under the influence of drugs I've found successful with her sister. There's no time for me to do more invasive work. She's beyond my reach. Until we have Sarah under control and I can stabilize Madeline's barriers, until we can prevent further Dream Weaver projections from damaging her mind, *your* presence will likely be the only thing that can get her back."

Jarred shook his head in denial, but he forced his mind's eye to see healing white. Maddie's white and blue—the restorative colors that had dominated her apartment.

"Good." Metting nodded without taking his eye off his monitor. "You're learning. And through you, Maddie will, too."

"And you?" Jarred demanded, his voice tight with the strain of not pummeling the jackass. "How are you going to fix this? How are you going to stop the Wolf that you've let set all this into motion? Or are you giving up on Sarah?"

Metting's attention snapped to Jarred.

"She's not just my patient, Dr. Keith, any more than Madeline is merely your medical charge. And I'll sacrifice whatever it takes to bring the real Sarah Temple back. Make no mistake. Sarah's gifts will not be further manipulated by this Wolf."

"You won't let her be manipulated by anyone but you, you mean?" Jarred would be damned if he understood what made this bastard tick.

Metting blinked before answering. "I won't allow her to continue suffering, even if that means doing the unthinkable."

The man was talking about having to kill Sarah. Contemplating the possibility was clearly ripping him apart. His hands were shaking as he resumed typing.

"Surely that's not an inevitability," Jarred reasoned with a hint of incredulous sympathy. "Not yet."

Metting turned away.

"My men outside will take you to Madeline," he said. "You have to reestablish your link with her. Pull her out of the fractured dream state she's locked into."

Jarred's surprise at being free to move about whatever complex they'd been taken to didn't last. He was beyond caring where he was or how he'd gotten there or what was going to happen next with Metting or his mysterious Brotherhood or Sarah's maniacal Wolf. He had to hold Maddie again. He had to reach her mind again—her soul.

"How much chance do you have of helping her if I fail?" he asked at the door, curbing the compulsion to run, not walk, to Maddie's side.

Metting looked up from his readings, regret consuming his features. "None at all, Dr. Keith. If I tried, with as little training as she's had and my limited understanding of the symbols and programming Sarah's embedded into her mind, I might irreparably damage your patient's consciousness. If you want the Madeline you know back, it's up to you to find her."

Chapter Thirty-five

Power surged through Maddie. The rage that she needed to keep going. Propelling her through the woods as she ran toward a cry of pain that had been seething for ten years.

A still-sane part of her realized the emotions weren't all hers. They weren't all Sarah's, either. Which meant neither one of them was in control of this. But Maddie couldn't stop. No more hiding from the truth. Even if the truth was that she was darkness. She was insanity. She was lost and afraid now, just like her sister. Destined to be alone. Forever.

Except she wasn't alone. He was there. Jarred. He was part of her light now, even in Sarah's dreams. Her mind clung to his healing calmness. Jarred would keep her from slipping away completely. He'd promised not to let her go.

So she kept running through the dream's dense forest. Underbrush crowded her, choking off any chance of escape. A flock of ravens circled, high above ghostly trees. Each shadow was a reminder of the accident from Sarah's memory. Of a rain-slick road and her father's car skidding in a deadly arc. Of Sarah's lie that the truck driver had taken malicious aim.

Maddie was sick and tired of the lies.

"It won't work, Sarah!"

She sprinted faster. Jarred's mind raced with hers, shock mixing with his growing concern. He could see it. The insanity that was inside Maddie, too. The lack of control. But he was helping her anyway. He understood that she had to do this. She was done being used. Done feeling guilty.

"You tried to make me kill Jarred," she screamed into the darkness. "You tried to make me kill your Raven. And you failed both times. Is that all you've got, Sarah? Really? Because I'm not afraid anymore. I'm pissed as hell. You're not getting away until you tell why you really came back to me. Tell me what these people want from us. Your Raven and your Wolf. What is it going to take to get you and these maniacs out of my life!"

Maddie was ranting. She was stumbling over fallen trees. Shoving through undergrowth. Wincing at the sting of briars and jagged twigs. Her mind reached for Jarred's, shamelessly using his energy so she could track Sarah farther. The same way Sarah had tracked Maddie, preying on her for months. Whatever Sarah could do, Maddie somehow could now, too. Their dream links had taught her that. The secret? All Maddie had to do was believe in her abilities—the gifts she'd been terrified of all her life.

And Maddie was starting to believe. It was the only way out of this dark place, she realized. Fighting to get the truth from her twin. Fighting to hold on to Jarred, who was still there, his mind clinging to hers. Maddie wasn't going to let him go. Ever. Not because of a sister who was—

"—too much of a coward to face me!" Maddie screamed. "What's wrong, Sarah? Too much of a sore loser to face the music? Who's the chickenshit now!"

"Fine!" a weak voice hissed. It was sandpaper thin, like the dry, dead leaves kicking up from the forest floor and blowing into Maddie's face. "Come and get me, you Goody Two-shoes bitch!"

The connection Maddie had been following suddenly grabbed hold of her. Hard. Brutal. Unrelenting. Maddie was spiraling downward, racing away from Jarred. Free-falling into her sister's demented mind...

Landing hard...

Stunned...

Maddie dragged herself back to her feet and tried to find her bearings in her sister's mind. A miniature house appeared through the trees, at the edge of a clearing. Maddie stumbled closer, realizing it was their childhood playhouse, from their home near the mountains on the other side of Massachusetts. It was painted bright white with blue shutters. Gone was the faded, peeling gray that had covered the structure by the time Maddie and Phyllis moved away.

The house had been Maddie and Sarah's sanctuary when they were little girls. A private world no one else was allowed to enter. They'd talked in secret there, about the things their mother had said weren't real. They'd supported each other. They'd fought when the strangeness of what they were got to be too much and the only way to deal with it had been to beat away at each other until they could handle the secrets again.

Maddie shoved against the closed door, banking on there being another grudge match tonight. The dimness of the woods hadn't prepared her eyes for the total lack of light within. She blinked the shadows into focus.

"Where are you!" she demanded, weaker now.

She couldn't feel Jarred anymore. She was alone in this place from her past. Pissed, she scanned the single room in jerky sweeps that revealed only emptiness and cobwebs and decay. The outside of the playhouse had looked as charming as the day their father had built it. But the interior was a broken-down, brittle mess.

"Sarah, I swear to God if you don't come out right now, I'm going to—"

A muffled whimper stalled Maddie's rant. It was a weak play for sympathy. A familiar combination of tears and self-pity coming from behind her. Spinning, Maddie found the door she'd just entered closed and secured with a wicked-looking padlock. A six-year-old version of her twin sat huddled on the floor in front of it. Sarah had wrapped her arms around her middle. Her head was buried against skinny knees that were bruised and bleeding. She looked as scraped up as Maddie felt, as if Sarah had just run through a vengeful, unforgiving forest.

"Don't start with the pity party." Maddie's warning emerged too soft and young to be her own voice.

She looked down to discover that she, too, was her childhood self. Complete with wearing a duplicate of her twin's pink and yellow sundress—one of the matching outfits their mother had hand sewn when they were six.

More sniffling filled the playhouse. Sarah's body shook, and then she began bawling. Maddie dropped to her knees beside her sister.

"Stop it!" she scolded in her little-girl voice. "It's not going to work. I won't feel sorry for you, no matter how far back you take us. It doesn't change what you've done. What you've destroyed. What you've let these people do to me. You've taken away my life. Again!"

Sarah's next hiccuping sob halted midwhimper. Her head jerked up, her expression a mixture of lost innocence and hatred.

"You?" little-girl Sarah screamed. She exploded into motion and tackled Maddie with an adult's rage. "It always has to be about you, doesn't it. This isn't my fault, you freak. You're the weak one. You're the cry baby who couldn't keep this to yourself. You just had to tell that doctor. You just had to fall in love and drag him into this. Why do you always ruin everything!"

"Get off me!" Six-year-old tactics returned in a rush.

Maddie grabbed hair and pulled. Her legs kicked for all she was worth, trying to dislodge her sneaky sister before Sarah could do any real damage.

"Perfect Maddie," Sarah mocked. She pushed Maddie to her back, sank a knee to the grimy ground on either side of Maddie's legs, and proceeded to pummel the shit out of her. "Maddie never messes up. Maddie always gets straight A's in school. And she's still perfect, while she whines all over the damn place because she got to have her make-believe life for ten years before it started to fall apart. Poor, pitiful, perfect baby . . ."

"I live a make-believe life?" Maddie ranted back. "Look at this place! Look around your spooky forest. At your bloodthirsty obsession with Daddy's death." Maddie yanked hard on Sarah's hair and rolled until she was on top. "What the hell are you doing, Sarah? You're the one who needs a swift kick back to reality. I know you hate me, but haunting me? Sending me perverted nightmares that make no sense? Throwing your dreams in my face, until my world is crap, just like yours? What's the point!"

"They're your stupid dreams, dumb ass. Haven't you learned anything?" Sarah was still fighting, but not as hard. And the tears in her eyes were less fake and more tragic by the second. "I just get to play with them once I'm inside you. You're the one who's repressed all your whacked-out memories about that night, so you can have your perfect life. You saw the accident. Through me. But you refused to accept that, didn't you? You forgot it all so you didn't have to know who you really are. But you felt everything I did then, just like you're feeling me now. Like you know everything I know now, even though your mind isn't supposed to be strong enough. Because you're just like me. Admit it!"

"You wound up in a loony bin, not me. You think you killed Daddy, not me."

"No. You just blame me!"

"*Because you wouldn't deal with your problems and that's why he was there that night, dragging your sorry ass out of jail. Again. You refused to deal with your shit, so Dad was putting everything on the line for you. If it wasn't for you—*"

"*—he wouldn't have had to die! Don't you think I know that? Of course I killed him. Of course you blamed me. For ten fucking years! That's where the stupid driver aiming for the car came from, Maddie. You have to blame Daddy's death on someone, and you've hated me for it since the accident. But my dreams won't let you make it my fault, no matter how many times you try, so that left the truck driver. But you won't accept that, either. You won't accept any of this, because that would mean you're as fucked up as I am. You're just going to keep hiding from the truth, and it's going to get you and your perfect doctor and everyone else killed, just like it killed Daddy!*"

With a soul-shattering bang, the door behind them crashed open and the ravens swarmed in, their wings and claws joining in Maddie and Sarah's screaming fight, as if they'd been there all along. Inside them. Around them. Always waiting. Always circling closer, until their weakest moment.

Now it was time for the kill.

Except Maddie could feel the light beckoning her again. From somewhere close. Through the darkness of the playhouse. Outside of it. Outside the haunted forest that had become the center of her and Sarah's hatred. A pool of pure white calm was begging her not to lose herself in the past. In the lies. In the fear she hadn't wanted to feel anymore, but still did. Because she was still hiding, just like her sister. She was still hating, just like Sarah. Which made what was happening, all that had happened, as much Maddie's fault as her twin's.

"Stop it, Sarah!" Maddie held on to her sister now. Protecting her from the ravens. Shaking her. Trying to see through the darkness to the truth beneath her sister's words.

"I'm Death. Say it!" Sarah sobbed. "Stop pretending that you ever loved me. Stop ignoring me like I don't exist, because you're ashamed of what I am and what that makes you. I make you want to kill and scream and rage, because all of that is in you, too. The gifts and the dark corners of your mind where you try to hide from them. You're just like me. Open your eyes, Maddie, and see what I am. What you are. Open your eyes and—"

"Die!" the ravens screamed, but they weren't screaming at Maddie and Sarah. They were screaming at the past. At the lies Maddie had drunk down until it was too late to stop this.

"No!" she cried as the demons clawed the skin from her body, pulling back every layer, every secret that had protected Maddie since Sarah's mind had been silenced. Since before then.

Until the hatred and the nightmares and the blame that had fueled their ten years apart were gone—and then the ravens were gone—and nothing was left but two sisters, lying broken on the filthy floor of a childhood sanctuary that was now in ruins. There were boards missing from the playhouse's walls and the roof. Light from a full moon set in a clear November sky pierced into their broken link. Except it wasn't really broken anymore. The dream had become the first real thing Maddie had felt, except with Jarred, since her father's death.

She could feel Sarah, really feel her. The Sarah she'd played with as a child. The little girl she'd promised never to abandon. The heart and the soul that had always beaten beneath the strange abilities that had taken everything else. And Maddie could feel them both letting go, falling backward in their minds to before the world and who they'd been had exploded.

Maddie could feel Sarah wanting to find her way back home. It's all she'd ever wanted. Deep beneath the anger and the killing fury, Sarah was craving the peace, the light, that a teenage Maddie had tried to help her keep. That was why Sarah had let the Raven coax her out of the nothing her mind had escaped to. But all she'd found once she woke was more darkness. More disappointment. Because her Raven had failed her just like Maddie had. After he'd promised to take care of her, just like Maddie had. And then Sarah had become Death. She'd become the darkness that the Raven had said he'd save her from. The murderous weapon that the Wolf had insisted was her and Maddie's legacy.

Now it was time to let go and—

Die!

"No!" Maddie crawled toward her twin. "You're not Death. We're not Death. Listen to me, Sarah. You don't have to dream anymore. You don't have to go back into the woods, to the accident, to find me. You're not alone. I'm here for you. I'll always be here for you . . ."

Little-girl Sarah wouldn't look at her. She shook her head and stared through the shattered door of their playhouse, into the forest that was growing darker by the second.

"I can't control it," she said. "It just keeps coming. The Wolf won't let me stop. And the Raven just circles overhead, doing nothing. And your light, it isn't strong enough . . . not for this. Not for what he wants me to do. You'll never be able to—"

"What who wants you to do? The Raven?"

Sarah shook her head. "The Wolf . . . You're right. It's not you. It's not the Raven. It's the Wolf I have to stop. I can feel him . . . hear him . . . He knows you're here. He'll make me dream again. He'll make you. I have to—"

"Then we'll find a way to stop him together. We're stronger, now that we've found each other. We've never been connected like this before. We'll—"

"No! No more together. Don't come back here, Maddie. Don't look for me again. That's what the Wolf wants. That's why he took Mom. Because he knew you'd protect her, even if you didn't care what happened to me."

"What does the Wolf want, Sarah?" Maddie hated the sadness in her sister's voice. The acceptance that she'd deserved to be abandoned all these years.

"I have to stop . . ." Sarah whispered.

She was trying to say more. To reveal the Wolf's plans. Maddie could feel the conflict within her twin. The light that was her sister's true soul railing against the darkness her mind had been taught to accept. Sarah's flickering instinct to trust Maddie, even now, after the Wolf had pitted them against each other.

"He wants another kill." Sarah was rocking. Forward and back. "I thought I was free. That I could leave. But I can't, Maddie. And I won't let him make me . . . Look at everything I've done. It has to stop. I won't be Death anymore. You have to go. I'll free Mom on my own. I'll deal with the Wolf and end this once and for all before—"

"No!" Maddie fought to see where her sister really was, beyond the battered playhouse and the hopelessness of the dream. She sank further into Sarah, ignoring Jarred's call— which was drawing closer. Almost as if he was in the forest, too. Running blindly toward her. "Don't you dare take that bastard on by yourself. They're using you, Sarah. They've been using you for who knows how long. To do God knows what. They've hurt you, and I didn't stop it, and now you're not thinking straight. I'm so sorry, Sarah. Tell me where you are. Let me find you, so I can—"

"They've hurt you, too, Maddie. Because of me. Through

me. Because I blamed you, and they knew it and they used me to get to you. You have to stay away, before all you are is darkness, too. Keep hating me. It's the only way you'll survive."

"I don't hate you!"

Maddie had been angry for a decade. She'd blamed her twin. She'd let fear talk her into believing the lies more than the truth. And she'd been terrified for months, thinking Sarah and her insanity were coming back, trying to drag Maddie under. But it had never really been hate, she realized. How could she hate a part of herself? The brave, outlandish, exuberant part Sarah would always be.

Sarah was right. This had to stop. Now. But not by shoving Sarah away and blocking her out of Maddie's mind. Not by fighting to go back to the lies, when Maddie felt safe and free from this thing they became whenever they were together. Not by hating what was real. What was honest. Instead, they had to fight. Together. Inside their dreams. Outside. Through the secrets and the lies, until Sarah was better and Maddie could deal with the world again, too. Until the darkness left them alone.

And Sarah knew how to fight. She always had. If Maddie could just convince her to hold on, Sarah's shattered mind held the answers and the power they needed.

"How will they hurt me?" Maddie asked. "This Wolf, he's been sending you to me. How? What's wrong with us. These... gifts. This curse that Mom wouldn't ever talk about. Tell me how we can be doing all this and why these people care. Tell me how to stop it. We can fix whatever the Wolf's done to you, Sarah. We can keep him from making you—"

"Kill?" Innocence and ageless wisdom swirled in Sarah's little-girl eyes. "I've killed for him, Maddie. I'm... Death. The Raven promised he wouldn't let them make me..."

A kaleidoscope of images flooded their dream link. The Raven gently coaxing Sarah's mind back to life. Teaching her to walk again, then filling her with combat knowledge, weapons training, survival skills. Getting her mind and body into shape, then showing her how to protect herself—the way Maddie had tried to protect Jarred against those soldiers.

"But the Wolf..." Sarah's eyes flashed with hatred. "He wants me to kill, and he thinks he controls Death. He thinks he can use Mom to make me..."

Their dream careened away, then spun back to the image of the clearing in the forest. The playhouse was gone. An adult Sarah stood in the clearing with their mother, surrounded by armed men, while the Wolf's order rang through her mind...

"You can't be there, Maddie. I'll have no choice if you're there. And I won't let him do this to you, too... I'll get Mom away from them, and then Death will kill them all! And you'll be free."

"What? No!" Maddie's blood chilled. "You're not confronting the Wolf like that alone. We'll get Mom out together."

The dream swirled back to the playhouse. They were little girls once more amid the ruins of their happy past. And Sarah was walking out the shattered door.

"Show me where you really are." Maddie tried to move, but she was frozen where she was.

She'd lost complete control of the dream. She was losing her connection to her twin for good. She was becoming nothing—what she realized she would always be without Sarah's soul to complete hers.

"None of this is your fault," Maddie pleaded. "Stop believing you caused it. Stop listening to what I thought when Daddy died. I was a child. We both were. And I was wrong. I don't hate you, Sarah. Whatever we've become, we're stronger together. We can figure the rest out. Let me come get you."

She felt her twin's consciousness take tentative steps closer, even though little-girl Sarah didn't move from the playhouse's open door. Next, the dream flickered to the scene of an abandoned warehouse. Or a storefront. Some forlorn place where Maddie had seen Sarah once before. Grown-up Sarah sat, freezing and huddled in a dark corner, her arms hugging her legs to her chest, her head buried in her knees.

Maddie was too weak to step closer. The image was already fading. She was too exhausted to hold on. She could feel Sarah doubting again. Letting go. The scene misted away before Maddie could see anything that would tell her where her sister was hiding. Then they were in the playhouse once more.

Sarah was leaving, her guilt for everything she'd done growing. Her acceptance that she had to end this the way she'd started it.

Alone.

"No," Maddie insisted. "Don't go."

"I can't fight him anymore. All I can do now is confront him and save Mom. Save you...Maybe that's our legacy. The good twin will survive because the bad saves her."

"You have to fight this." Maddie was weeping. Unable to do anything now but watch her sister give up, and crying for everything they'd lost. Everything their gifts might have been if they'd only understood them before it was too late. "I won't let you do this, Sarah."

"This is the way it has to be or the Wolf will have us both." Little-girl Sarah began to fade away. "Leave me alone."

Maddie grabbed for Sarah's near-transparent form. But her hands slid through the image, and she fell to the playhouse floor.

"No!" She fought to sink deeper into her twin's mind. She

reached out her hand. If she could just touch her sister, they'd be safe. "I won't leave you alone in the darkness."

"You have to."

Sarah looked beyond Maddie and rolled her eyes. Then she smiled. Just a little. "He's coming," she said. "If you want him, you'll have to make up your mind on your own. I'm not pushing you at him again."

Then Sarah's image faded to black.

"Let her go for now," another voice insisted.

Jarred's voice.

His light and his strength flooded the playhouse.

"Sarah's right," he said. "You can't help her. Not yet. You don't know what you're dealing with. You have to come back. You have to get stronger. Prepare. Or this . . . Wolf . . . will destroy you both."

"I have to save my sister!" Maddie hid in the shadows his light couldn't reach.

"I know." Jarred's love wrapped around her, finding its way to her no matter how hard she resisted.

Then he was beside her, inside the shattered playhouse that Sarah had abandoned. His arms pulled Maddie close. The ramshackle roof and the battered walls and the filthy floor shimmered away. Jarred and Maddie were beneath the base of an ancient tree that seemed familiar, but Maddie was too tired to care why. A lone raven circled high above, watching, waiting. The sound of an approaching storm rolled around them.

"I'll help you save her," Jarred promised. "But you can't handle that yet. You won't survive it. Neither of you will. Come back to me. Trust me to help you."

"But . . . Sarah . . . She's going to . . ." Maddie struggled against his hold. Struggled to keep him in focus. How could she let Sarah go now? She'd never find her again. "I can't—"

"You won't lose her. I won't let that happen."

"But..." Maddie blinked, but there was only darkness now. She could barely feel Jarred's touch. Hear his voice.

"You'll have to make up your mind on your own..." Sarah had said.

Maddie could trust Jarred, or she could slip away like her sister. Then she'd never have to face the damage she'd done. She could go on hiding, forever this time. Just let the darkness have her twin and her mother and the legacy that had taken everything and given nothing in return. Nothing, except a deeper connection to Sarah than she'd ever known. A common ground. A truth. A light Maddie and her twin could only save together.

And there was Jarred. All of this had given her Jarred, too. She'd never let herself think of forever before she'd loved him. She never would have believed she'd want her twin to be part of that forever. But she did. Because Jarred hadn't let her give up.

"Help..." she said into the darkness. "Please," she begged. She had to find Jarred. She had to wake up. "Help me..."

CHAPTER THIRTY-SIX

Richard monitored the video feed to Madeline Temple's observation suite. Jarred Keith had joined her twenty minutes ago.

Temple's dream environment was being controlled the best Richard could manage in the Watchers' underground bunker. Insulated from transient stimuli and fluctuations in light and sound. Madeline's headset was emitting a steady stream of white noise. Richard couldn't be sure which sounds would sustain her individual consciousness and which would plunge her further into Sarah's emotional chaos.

Keith had joined Madeline on the exam table—curling his body around hers. He'd cradled her. Gently kissed her. Whispered words too soft for Richard to pick up. Temple's restless movements had calmed for several minutes. Keith had closed his eyes, by all appearances doing his damnedest to fall into Temple's dream world. Madeline's eyes were still darting in REM sweeps behind their closed lids. Her arms and legs intermittently twitched, mirroring whatever dream she and Sarah were sharing.

Richard gritted his teeth. He was responsible for whatever this Wolf had done to retarget Sarah's dream conditioning. He was responsible for the casualties. Kayla Lawrence's life. Madeline Temple's mind. Whatever was happing to the twins' mother. Whatever the Brotherhood would do next, if Richard couldn't provide them a foolproof plan to resolve this disaster.

Movement on the video feed demanded his attention. Jarred's body jerked. His arms locked around Madeline. Her heart rate dropped.

Richard had a recovery drug prepared, but he couldn't risk dragging Keith away from the twins' link. If he pulled the man's mind out at the wrong time, he might lose each individual identity. Keith had to get Madeline out on his own. Then Temple had to remember the details of her links with Sarah. Enough to convince the Brotherhood that recovering the twins was preferable to terminating the threat they were becoming.

Help me here, Sarah.

Help Maddie save you.

Keith's body jerked again, this time as he tried to sit. Tried to pull Madeline up with him, their eyes still closed. They collapsed back to the table. Still asleep, Keith wrapped his body tighter around Madeline's, the same way Richard had wanted to hold Sarah every time he'd asked a little more from her mind.

"Prepare the injections," he said into the hands-free com device wrapped around his ear. "But no one enters the suite until I give the all clear."

He couldn't allow anyone to interfere with the fragile connection Keith had built with the twins.

"Come on, man…" Richard's fists clenched against a surge of powerlessness. "Break the link, damn it!"

Alarms drowned out his curse. The equipment monitoring Madeline's stats squealed in a symphony of death.

"Get her out!" he shouted.

Keith's body jerked again. The man's head pulled away

from Madeline. His eyes blinked open. Madeline's eyes were open, too. Tears were streaming down her face. Then her muscles began to seize. Blood trickled from her nose and mouth.

Her heart rate flatlined.

She collapsed.

Keith screamed her name.

Shit!

"Get in there now!" Richard ordered through his com link.

Not waiting to see how quickly his team administered the adrenaline cocktail that would either save Madeline Temple's life or finish ending it, he sprinted for the door. Keith's cry of denial haunted him as Richard left his calm, clinical laboratory behind.

Calm and clinical was his job. A Watcher was trained to be detached and remote.

But the center was closing in on Sarah and Madeline, using their mother as bait. The twins were taking lethal potshots at each other's minds. And the only chance Richard had to save the twins' legacy—and the life of the woman he'd fallen for the first time their minds had touched—was to push them all toward a confrontation with evil. A showdown the Brotherhood wouldn't let happen if he couldn't keep Madeline alive long enough to win her trust.

CHAPTER THIRTY-SEVEN

Maddie closed her eyes and leaned her head against Jarred's shoulder. He was sitting behind her on the exam table, still holding her close. His barely controlled anger was spiking her migraine higher. But his soothing touch was there, too. After everything, he'd still come looking for her, begging her to come back.

"I can't remember any more," she said to Sarah's Raven—Dr. Metting. Her throbbing head was the only reason she didn't scream the words.

The man's drugs had saved her life after she'd woken mindless, seizing, bleeding, and struggling to reconnect with Sarah and grieving when there was nothing left of her twin in her mind. But Maddie nearly dying clearly didn't rate the man's sympathy or a reprieve from his endless questions.

"You saw the playhouse," Metting pressed. "An abandoned storefront and a clearing in the woods where a lot of people surrounded Sarah. Tell me what other images she showed you."

They'd been through this two—three times. The man's experience managing the side effects of recovering from a dream link was remarkable. She felt more focused, more in control, than she had in months. Which might have earned him her respect. Except Maddie knew exactly how he'd gotten so good at what he was doing. She could imaging Metting driving her sister past her limits the same way.

"I saw Sarah suffering because she trusted you. Because you turned her mind into whatever she's become. And then you turned this Wolf character loose on her. Explain to me again why I would tell you anything, you sadistic bastard!"

Jarred hugged her body closer. His mind brushed hers in concern. So far he hadn't interfered with her and Metting. He'd explained about the dreams, about the research center and what this Dream Weaver program was supposed to be about. About Metting and some other secret scientist—Sarah's Wolf—and the damage the men had done to both Maddie's and Sarah's minds. Jarred was livid. Furious. Ready to beat Metting to a pulp if that's what Maddie wanted. But he was waiting. For her. With her.

We're going to get through this together, his thoughts promised. *We'll figure this out, and we'll fix it. You're not alone.*

Metting was studying the two of them. Almost smiling. As if he could hear everything going on in her head, which evidently he had the ability to do.

"You make me sick." Maddie remembered digging her nails into the man's skin, making the red slashes that streaked down his neck. She suddenly regretted resisting Sarah's instincts to get rid of the Raven that had betrayed them both.

"Obviously." Metting didn't so much as blink. "Think. Which of the things you saw in the last dream felt real to you, and which were mere projections of Sarah's dementia?"

"*Felt* real?"

"Use your intuition, Dr. Temple." Metting's tone was patient. Almost hypnotic. "Which parts of what you saw are about your twin's surroundings at this moment in time? Which were symbolic of other states of consciousness that she was remembering, or anticipation of what she'd see in the future? You'll know the difference by the strength of how what you shared made you feel. What actually took place is of less importance."

Maddie clenched her fingers into fists. Metting caught the hostile impulse to strangle him until he shut up, and he smiled in…approval?

"Your abilities are developing rapidly." He typed into his laptop. "No doubt because your psychic barriers have been breached so often by your sister's dream work. But the depth of the knowledge you've absorbed about projecting into others' minds won't surprise me again. I assure you, my defenses are formidable."

"Because you're…" She felt Jarred's arm snake around her. To protect her, or to keep her from launching herself at Metting?

"Psychic? Yes." Metting nodded. "Otherwise, I'd never have been able to reach Sarah's mind. She trusted me to—"

"To protect her?"

His eyes chilled to the demon black of Sarah's dreams. The rest of his expression stayed locked into the forced calm of damage control.

"Yes," he admitted, "the same as you're trusting Dr. Keith. And like him, I'm doing everything I can to salvage this—"

"Disaster?"

"Unexpected outcome. My mission was to keep Sarah's dreams from becoming—"

"Dreams you had no business picking apart, then manipulating!"

"Either I picked them apart, or the Watchers would have had no choice but to—"

"Kill my sister, even though she was no threat to anyone while she was lying in the coma you dragged her out of? If you think we're not going to have this conversation, *Doctor*, you're very much underestimating *me*."

Sarah couldn't remember which of the details about Metting she knew because Jarred had discussed them with her. And which she had absorbed—was still absorbing—from Jarred's mind, while he held and supported her and gave her the confidence to face the architect of her sister's nightmares.

I'm here, Jarred assured her.

"I'm not opposed to the conversation." Metting sure as hell sounded opposed. "We can talk all night long about how this is my fault, and how the Brotherhood is to blame for everything they've tried to stop the government and Trinity Center from doing. But the more time that passes after emerging from your sister's link, the harder it will become for you to connect with her emotions. And those feelings are the truth about everything you just experienced. I assure you, isolating each of them is the only way for you to save Sarah."

Maddie looked back to find Jarred's expression clouded with concern. He nodded reluctantly. As much as he clearly hated it, he believed Metting.

"You seemed…" Jarred said. "*Sarah* seemed the most upset when you two were watching your mother in the clearing, surrounded by men with guns. Is that where she is now?"

"You saw that?" Maddie turned back to Metting. "He…How is that even possible?"

"He surrendered his consciousness to yours. His reality, his body image, became subjugated, so he could be absorbed into your dreams." The Raven's raised eyebrow said he was impressed. "And he managed it instinctively, with no coaching or any real understanding of what he was doing. His trust in you allowed him to see and feel and travel with you, wherever Sarah took your mind."

His trust in you . . . The same trust that had almost gotten Jarred killed.

"The Wolf that Sarah keeps revealing," Metting insisted. "Was he there, with your sister and your mother?"

Maddie pressed fingers to the side of her head, feeling more scattered with each new question. She'd never trust Metting. But if he was the only thing standing between the darkness and Sarah and Maddie and Jarred, did she have any choice but to give him the answers he wanted?

"Sarah's emotions were…" Maddie searched for the words. Deeper inside, where a glimmer of her twin began to sputter. "…murderous at the clearing. I don't know if the Wolf was there, but I could feel her hate for him. I could hear his voice, and she wanted to rip his throat out. But…he had too much control for her to break free. And she'll be outnumbered…It…That was the future, I think." Maddie sifted through more of what she remembered. "She's not wherever that place is. It hasn't happened yet. But she knows it will, and she knows she'll die without me there, and she's determined not to let me come. She'll get our mom out without me. It… It feels like a trap, and she knows it is, but she'll go anyway, to—"

"Of course it's a trap." The übercontrolled Metting slammed a fist to the counter beside his laptop, then raked fingers through his black hair. "This whole thing's been a trap from the goddamned start!"

"You're…" Maddie didn't want to believe it. But it was right there, in the emotions rolling off Metting, and in her twin's feelings in their dream. With nauseating certainty, Maddie accepted the truth. "He's…"

She stole another glance at Jarred. He kissed the tip of her nose and nodded.

"Yeah. He's in love with Sarah."

"How could you be in love with her"—Maddie surged to the edge of the exam table, outrage overriding her exhaustion—"and make her do all those horrible things? Leave her to the whim of those horrible people, until she was so terrified she ran from you. You bastard…How could you!"

The light in Metting's eyes could have been madness. Or regret. A dying flicker of hope? "I did it to protect your sister and ultimately the gifts you were both born with."

"Our legacy. This family curse you're not going to talk with me about, because there's no time. Because there's no real point, is there? Not if my family and whatever we are has to end soon, because either you and your secret society or the government is going to destroy us because you can't control us!"

Metting was staring at his computer again, ignoring her outburst, his emotions shuttered away.

"I don't want to control you and Sarah," he finally said. "I need you two to learn how to control yourselves. I need you to work with your sister, so you can help me stop this situation before it's too late."

"And how, exactly, are the twins supposed to do that?" Jarred interrupted for the first time since Metting's interrogation had begun. "I almost didn't get Maddie back this time. You warned me that if I didn't, her mind would be lost forever. She's not going to work with Sarah anymore. She's not going back to the godforsaken place I found her. Not when you can't guarantee another dream won't finish shredding what's left of her sanity!"

***

Jarred had stayed out of it. He'd brought Maddie back and watched in horror as Metting and his assistants fought to get her heart started again. Then he'd held her as she came around, answering her questions and helping her piece together the last eight hours. Metting's drugs had calmed her mind and the worst of the dream's side effects. Then the bastard had insisted on this maddening debriefing of Maddie and Sarah's dreams. And Jarred had done his best to stay calm and supportive through all of it.

Enough was enough.

"You're not seriously expecting Maddie to search out her sister's mind again," he demanded.

Maddie shivered in his arms.

"We have to recover Sarah," Metting insisted, "before this meeting in the woods takes place."

"Bringing Sarah in is your problem. Maddie's already here, and—"

"And her mother is being held by the man her twin is planning to meet, so Sarah can kill him. I can persuade the Brotherhood to protect both Phyllis and Sarah, but only if I have the information we'll need to eliminate the Wolf and his men at the same time."

"Persuade?" Maddie was shivering from head to toe. Jarred could feel her fear and how hard she was trying to hide it while she gave Metting shit.

"If the center gains control of Sarah's mind, it won't matter that I erased the records of my Dream Weaver work from their systems. This Wolf has already used my techniques with some degree of success. He'll extrapolate the rest from Sarah, and the project will continue into full weapons testing. We can't allow that to happen, no matter the cost."

"We?" Maddie sputtered. "I don't work for you, Dr.

Metting. And I refuse to work with this brotherhood of yours that doesn't care about me or my family, except for how it can use us to get what it wants."

"So you're amenable to Sarah trying to free your mother on her own and getting herself killed or recaptured in the process? You really hate her that much?"

Maddie didn't answer. Jarred could feel the tears of frustration she refused to let Metting see.

"She's communicating with you about her plans," Metting continued, "no matter how volatile your relationship with her has become. On an unconscious level, Sarah still trusts you. She knows she needs your help."

"And she hates *you*." Maddie stopped rubbing the side of her head. Her hand slapped the exam table. "Why would I deliver Sarah to you people, after everything you've already put her through?"

"Because if you don't, you're signing her death warrant."

"And you don't care what this will do to Maddie?" Jarred held on tighter to the woman who'd claimed his soul. She'd almost died saving him from Sarah. Her heart had stopped, after she tracked her twin and almost failed to disengage from their link. How much more could her mind and body take?

"I care as deeply as you do, Dr. Keith." Metting sighed, and then Jarred could feel everything the man had been holding back. Guilt, shock, anger, grief, and…love for Sarah. The same way Jarred would love Maddie without end, no matter how impossibly they were separated. Then just as quickly, the door to Metting's mind slammed shut. "But my feelings are irrelevant unless we can save these women from being absorbed into an evil that can't be allowed to win."

"What exactly do you want?" Maddie demanded.

"I have to know everything you haven't told me about your dream," Metting said. "The information Sarah's not even aware that she sent you. Without that, your sister and my men won't have a chance to defeat this Wolf or the government's plans for Dream Weaver."

"Or to save my mother?" Maddie insisted. "You save my mother, or I don't tell you another damn thing. If Phyllis dies, there will be no hope for Sarah. She already blames herself for my father's death. She thinks I blame her. She's obsessed with trying to make what happened that night right. If this Wolf kills my mother because of Sarah, her mind will finish disintegrating."

"We'll do everything within our power to protect your family, Ms. Temple. That's the only promise I can give you. You're going to have to—"

"Trust you?" Jarred felt Maddie recoil at the words. "How can you expect her to trust you and an organization you've barely told us anything about?"

"I expect her to keep fighting for her and Sarah's lives, the way she has since she barged into Trinity Center. If Maddie stops fighting now, her sister and her mother die."

"What else do you need to know?" Maddie leaned deeper into Jarred's embrace, needing his presence to balance her hopeless fear for her family.

"You initiated the dream connection on your own this time," Metting said. "For the first time, you were in control of your and Sarah's dreams. You were seeing things Sarah never wanted you to see. Things she'd never have shown you on her own. What did you discover?"

Maddie hesitated. Sarah would see this as a betrayal, telling her Raven the secrets of their minds.

"His methods are twisted," Jarred reasoned with begrudging acceptance. "But I believe Metting's been fighting for Sarah all this time. And I believe he cares about her. I have some experience with what that can be like…" Jarred kissed the tip of Maddie's nose. "There's nothing I wouldn't do to put myself between you and whatever's trying to hurt you. If that's what he's been doing, then—"

"But he's the Raven!" Maddie confronted Metting. "Sarah wants to kill you."

"Does she?" His gaze pierced Maddie's certainty. "I've centered her mind, from the coma to waking to her very first dream projection and beyond. The Wolf would have encouraged Sarah to build on that connection, rather than trying to start over again with his own presence. He wouldn't have had time in the three months you say she's been involved in your dreams, to anchor Sarah with his own identity. Not and keep me in the dark about the dream projections he was doing while Sarah and I continued to work together."

"What are you saying?"

"The Wolf implanted a symbol of me into the dreams he had Sarah send you, as well as the ones he implanted into Kayla Lawrence. But Sarah took her connection to me further than he would have wanted."

"Sarah wanted you in the Wolf's homicidal dreams?"

"I think she wanted me to see what was happening."

"So you'd be proud of the little freak you'd made?"

"So the raven image would stop the projections somehow. Except I didn't. Now she's trying to get you to see. To stop her. There are messages in her simulations. In the recurring links you've shared with her. My dream image would have been close to whatever Sarah wanted most for us to know."

"You…" The Raven's cries. His wings rustling as he

flew overhead. Watching. Waiting. Maddie could hear them all over again. "You were there…"

"Where, Madeline?" he said in a hypnotically soft voice. Had he said it out loud? In her mind? She wanted to look back to Jarred to be sure, but she couldn't turn away from Metting's dark gaze. "Who did Sarah want to kill in your dreams? She's trying to tell us what the Wolf wants, so we can stop him before it's too late. Help me save your twin and your mother…"

Maddie felt the intensity of Metting's mind touch hers fully for the first time. His was a brutally honest consciousness. But there was a layer of concern. As if he knew how fragile her hold was on reality. He was being excruciatingly careful. Urgent, but careful. And honest. And he was doing nothing now to shield his own emotions—his commitment to protecting Maddie from as much of her memories of Sarah's nightmare as he could. And at all costs, to protect Sarah from the miscalculations he'd made.

"It…" Maddie grappled for Jarred's hand as she let Metting steer her back. Her stomach heaved at the sounds of a storm and of wind-torn trees…

The approach of rustling wings rushed along with her, returning her to the nightmare she and Sarah had shared for months. To Sarah's memory of the car accident—the memory Sarah had said was really Maddie's. Because Maddie had seen and felt it all that night, too. Their father's death. And Sarah's compulsion to die with him because she couldn't stop the horrifying scene from happening over and over. Maddie secretly blaming Sarah for surviving, when their father hadn't.

Then Maddie felt her sister's need to stop the car from sliding, and to keep the truck from aiming for …

The truck was aiming for …

Maddie was in the truck...
She was aiming for...

Maddie's eyes flew open. Her breath caught. The dream had frozen on the image of the eighteen-wheeler skidding toward her father's car.

"What?" Metting asked. He and Jarred were each holding one of her hands. "You're seeing your father's death. That's the shared memory the Wolf used to link you and Sarah, right? What was Sarah's trigger? What one thing did he program her to focus on, until she—"

"It...It wasn't Sarah," Maddie stuttered, following the Raven's voice. "It was me. I was the reason he died. It was all my fault..."

Metting's head shook side to side.

"Guilt is a strong emotional tie," he countered. "It's also the place our psyches are most vulnerable. You and Sarah share the guilt you feel for your father dying. So that's where the Wolf trained your sister to find you, no matter how damaging that place was to Sarah, too."

"I was the driver!" Maddie gasped. The dream fast-forwarded, then rewound, only to play again. "The nightmare keeps getting worse, every time. More bizarre. I...I thought it was just Sarah wanting to die with our father...But she wanted to kill, too...She was obsessed with it. She needed to stop him, I think. But she never could, and because she couldn't, the Wolf kept making her watch our father die...He kept making her responsible...Making her Death...so she'd keep trying to kill him...to save our father..."

"Who did Sarah have to kill?" Metting asked in that *you can trust me* voice. "Remember, it's just a dream. Whatever you're seeing now, whatever Sarah planted there, it's a carefully constructed simulation. Based in part on your memories. But precisely controlled with an explicit goal that the Wolf wanted Sarah to embed into your subconscious. You have to find that goal. The trigger the Wolf wanted you to react to. Who was Sarah killing in your dream? Who was your target supposed to be?"

"Stop it!" Jarred growled, pulling her closer. "She can't take any more right now."

"We can't afford to—" Metting insisted.

"We damn well can!" Jarred was wiping Maddie's nose. The corner of her mouth. "Remembering is tearing her up inside!"

"The…it…It was the driver of the truck…" Maddie grabbed her head, her hand brushing her ear.

When she looked down after pulling her palm away, blood coated her fingers. Her hold on reality shattered completely at the sight. The darkness swooped closer. Jarred and Metting kept arguing while she fell back into the dream.

"The man…driving the truck…Sarah was obsessed with him. And…It was me…Except it wasn't. I…maybe I was Sarah, and I was the one who wanted the driver to die…Ah!" Maddie's mind was exploding. Imploding. Ripping at the nightmare's images and refusing to let her see anything clearly. Refusing to let her see at all. Or to feel.

Except she could feel Jarred's strength as he curled her in his arms. The soft brush of his lips against her hair. The touch and smell and feel of him washing away the darkness and bringing her safely back to him. To the love that she clung to, while her sister's madness still raged inside.

Her body quieted.

Her mind stilled.

Her eyes fluttered open.

"Jarred?" She was staring into the endless blue of his eyes.

"You're going to get some sleep." His gaze turned ice-cold as he challenged Metting. "I'm putting her to bed for the night."

"And if we don't have until tomorrow to stop the Wolf's plans?" Metting asked. "How are you going to deal with *your* failure then, when your refusal to do what has to be done ends up destroying the woman you love?"

Jarred gave no answer, but Maddie could feel his acceptance take hold. The Raven was right. She either pushed her mind and her body now—gave Metting what he was demanding—or they lost everything.

"Just a few hours," she heard herself say. "Just let me rest a few hours, and then I want to try again."

"This is killing you, sweetheart." The pain of watching her suffer vibrated in Jarred's voice. In every beat of his heart. "I don't want you doing this anymore."

Sweetheart.

"You've gotten me this far. Don't ask me to quit now. I can't give up on my sister. I can't lose my mother to this, too. I just can't."

CHAPTER THIRTY-EIGHT

"You're going to rest, if I have to tie you to the bed." Jarred pushed Maddie gently back to the covers she was trying to struggle out of. "I don't care if you're feeling better. You're taking the full five hours Metting agreed to."

Meanwhile Jarred would be drinking in the sight of her. Watching her breathe. Counting every second he got to spend with her—before everything became about Sarah again and keeping the world safe from the Temples' legacy.

"I'm fine." Maddie lay back on the pillows and shoved his hand away. She curled her forearm up to cover her eyes. "Stop hovering like I'm going to break or something. Metting's meds are helping me recover faster from wherever my brain goes when I'm with Sarah. You're helping me, just by being here. If he thinks I'm ready to try again—"

"He and his brotherhood are after one thing at the moment," Jarred argued. "Getting to your sister through you as quickly as they can."

The brain bleeds and seizures and disorientation Maddie endured with each episode were ending more quickly, thanks to Metting's medication. Maddie had been able to pull away from her memories of Sarah's nightmares this time instead of completely dissociating. But Jarred didn't care. The situation was out of control.

"Metting's not the threat." Maddie frowned. "I can't believe I'm defending him, but—"

"He loves your sister, I know. But he's been manipulating her mind with his own agenda for over a year. Now he's doing the same with you. Are you telling me that's all right with you?"

"No." Maddie slapped her arm on the bed. "But do you see any other alternative than to work with the man? I need you both to keep me alive while I try to find a way to help Sarah. Metting said his men are on alert and ready to bring her in, all we need is a plan he can sell. He knows Sarah's mind a hell of a lot better than I do, but I'm the one with her memories. I may hate his methods, but he knows how to figure out what the Wolf wants. How to stop him. I don't."

Jarred picked up Maddie's hand and kissed her fingers. He felt on the brink of losing her before they'd had a chance to really know each other. Their psychic and physical connections had grown at lightning speed. They'd been violently intimate. They'd walked the same *dreamscape*, as Metting called it. She'd brought Jarred's heart back to life—both literally and figuratively. Now he had to help her put everything on the line for her sister. How did he do that?

"I don't begin to understand most of this," he tried to explain. He framed her face with his hands. Kissed her sweetly, then with more force as passion rose between them like lightning quickening before a strike. "Not how I found you this last dream. Not how you were able to reach Sarah's mind, after running from her all this time. Or how you're going to remember details from her maniac fantasies—enough for Metting to strike back against the center, or the government, or the Wolf or whoever these men of his end up going after…"

His voice wavered to nothing as the reality of the situation closed in.

"Jarred," Maddie whispered. Her soft, healing touch slid up his arms, pulling him closer until his body covered hers and she was kissing him as if she'd never stop. Her mind stroked his, needing to be closer, to feel closer, to feel whole again the way she only felt, he only felt, when they were together.

"All I know," he whispered back, "is that I'd kill anyone who tried to do to you what these people have done to Sarah. Thinking about you going back into Metting's lab and willingly subjecting yourself to what these shared dreams do to you makes me want to kill the man with my bare hands. Screw his noble intentions."

"You're the one who told me to trust him."

"Because—"

"Look at this place!" Maddie pushed herself up until she was sitting. "It's like some supersecret fortress. If this is what it takes to stay under the Wolf's radar, what kind of chance would I have to help Sarah and my mother on my own? I've accepted that. You accepted it before I did, when you called Metting and arranged for them to bring me here. And *now* you want me to stop? So I can what? Go it alone and hope for the best? Maybe…Maybe you should wait here when I go back to talk with Metting."

She was right. They couldn't stop now. There were still too many holes. Too much they didn't know. Except for one thing Jarred was certain of.

"You won't have to face anything on your own again," he promised. "Whether I agree with what you want to do or not, I'll be there. Always."

He cupped her shoulders and found her trembling. It

was still so hard for her to believe that she could be who she was and have someone accept her, love her, unconditionally. Jarred pulled her head to his chest. He pulled her closer in his mind, too, until there was no her. No him. Only them.

"I'm here," he said. "I won't ever leave you alone, no matter how bad this gets."

"I…" A silent sob shook Maddie. "I feel like this Wolf is stalking me, too, Jarred. Stalking us. He wants Sarah, and he wants me to bring her to him. He's going to kill my mother if I don't. I…I couldn't stand it if something happened to you because of me. Just like what happened to my father…All over again…"

Jarred stroked her cheek with the backs of his fingers. "You're not responsible for your father's death. That's Sarah's nightmare talking. Her emotions are still inside you." He could feel them. See them when he closed his own eyes. "Her mind's splintered into who knows how many realities. And through the dreams you've shared, she's altering you to a dangerous degree. You have to fight her feelings. You can't help Sarah until you do."

Maddie's smile trembled. Her touch traced his bottom lip. "I have to find a way out of this that won't get everyone I love killed. I can't do that without you."

"You won't ever have to." He'd have to watch her mind and her body shatter each time she reached for her twin. He didn't know how to let that happen without wanting to stop her. But he'd find a way. They'd find a way.

"Sarah will keep fighting me," Maddie said, "if I try to find her for Metting."

"Sarah's sick, and she's getting sicker without your mind to balance hers. She doesn't trust anyone."

"Not even me."

"I think she's shutting you out to protect you." Jarred

stroked Maddie's cheek again. His mind stroked the abandoned feelings dragging her back to the nightmare. "That's what she said in your last dream. Not to look for her, because it wasn't safe."

"She's running from her Raven," Maddie agreed. "She hates him because she loves him and he's left her alone for the darkness and the Wolf to take. I...I left her alone. For ten years. How will I ever make that up to her?"

"Love can be an awful thing when it's been betrayed. Sarah might never be able to trust Metting again. But she's already listening to you in your dreams. She's already letting you in. She protected you, even though it meant sending you back to me. She'll trust you when the time's right."

Just as Maddie finally trusted Jarred. His mind reached for the belonging she'd given him. A sense of safety with someone like he hadn't felt since he was a child. And it was there. Maddie's warmth and uncomplicated acceptance. And the passion they'd reveled in before Sarah destroyed it.

"She wanted to kill you." Maddie kissed him, following his memories back to that horrible moment when he'd realized it was no longer her in his arms.

"Sarah knew how much you love me." Jarred kissed Maddie back, feeling her physical response deepen, her body warming with his, to his, curling around him. "She thinks I'm going to take you away from her."

"And she keeps wanting to kill the Raven because..." Shadows from Sarah's dreams flowed through them. Maddie turned them and controlled them, analyzing now instead of being consumed. Separating the guilt from the images Metting said were the clues to understanding what Sarah was really after, and where she was going next.

"Because if she loves the Raven and trusts him again…" Jarred reasoned. "If she trusts him, and he turns out to be evil, like the Wolf, then—"

"—then she'll have no one left. Just like when my father was gone." Regret flooded Maddie's thoughts. "My mother would never be honest with us. She kept insisting that we hide what was happening. And then I did hide. I abandoned Sarah when my sister needed me most. She was totally alone, trapped in the dark, while I made a life without her. And then Metting came along and freed her and got her to trust him and promised her he'd be there to protect her. But he let the Wolf in, and more darkness, and—"

"Show me the Wolf, Maddie."

She was hurting, and Jarred hated it. But Metting had said there were clues in the nightmares. Key details Maddie had to find.

"In the clearing in the woods," Jarred pressed. "Not the accident with your father. You said you heard the Wolf in the clearing. The Wolf is who Sarah really hates. He's the darkness she's lost in. Show me what Sarah showed you. Show me what you need to know to save your family."

"He's…" Gray ringed Maddie's eyes. Her consciousness pulled away. But she was still holding tightly to Jarred's body. She was fighting to stay with him while she remembered.

"He's what, sweetheart?"

"He's…

…there, and he knows she's watching. He terrifies her… She hates him…"

"*Like she hates the Raven?*"

"No, the Raven's… *watching from overhead. Always circling overhead. No, from the trees this time, and she hates…*

*needing him there...But she does. She'll always need him
there. The Raven is...He's..."*

Maddie jerked, and her eyes cooled to their own spar-
kling green. "He's you."

"What?" Jarred was shaking from the rush of seeing
Sarah's dream along with Maddie. From sensing the
deadly purpose of the shadowy figures that represented
the Wolf's men.

"The Raven—Metting," Maddie whispered. "Sarah
won't survive without him, just like I wouldn't have survived any of this without you. That's why he's always
there, circling my father's accident in the nightmare.
Sarah needs him to stop the Wolf. She's wanted him
there from the start, to give her the control you give me.
But what if I can't get Metting there in time? What if
Sarah tries to face the Wolf on her own, and I—"

"We don't know that's what she's really planning."
Jarred gently shook Maddie, keeping her with him.
"You're not seeing it clearly enough yet. And even if you
were, you need Metting to help you figure out what the
scene in the clearing really means. Don't assume the
worst. Don't do that to yourself."

"He..." Maddie nodded. "Sarah's Raven will bring her
back..."

"Yes." Jarred agreed, praying he was right.

"He...He'd do anything for her..."

"Yes."

"Like...Like you'd do anything for me..."

"Yes. Even letting that bastard pry into your mind
again."

"You...You were willing to die for me—lie there and
let Sarah take you, rather than hurt me trying to stop
her." Maddie kissed him. "Don't ever do that again,
Jarred. Promise me."

"It's not going to happen again." He kissed her back, the heat of it taking over. "You saved my life. You proved to yourself that you're light. That you're a healer, not the Death Sarah thinks she's become." Their minds filled with Maddie's soothing whites and blues, and the sizzling sparks of her passion. "I'd do it a thousand times over, though, if that's what you needed."

"You'll stay safe." Maddie rolled until she was sprawling on top of his body. "Promise me you'll protect yourself and stay safe."

"I won't challenge anything you have to do with Metting," he promised. "And I'll be as careful as I can. But I'm going to be there with you, Maddie, safe or not. This legacy of yours, whatever it turns out to mean, I'm a part of it. Metting said we were drawn together because of it. I'll do whatever it takes to protect it and you. That, I promise."

She hesitated. The glimmer in her eyes told him she was considering slapping some sense into him. Instead, she straddled his hips. Dragged his shirt up and over his shoulders. He lifted his upper body to help her, then settled back to their pillows. Her hands roamed the wicked scars the knife had left on his chest. Her fingers spread as her consciousness wrapped around him. Her love for him, her acceptance of what they'd become, it felt as if it had always been there.

"What if I'm not strong enough to stop Sarah this time?" she finally asked, panic beating at the warmth between him. "What if you—"

"Shhh…" He gripped the hem of her midnight black shirt and slid it away.

Her glossy brown hair fell to her bare shoulders. Delicate shoulders. Beautiful shoulders. Just like the rest of her.

"No more *what ifs* until we talk to Metting again and tell him you know for sure that the Wolf was in the clearing with Sarah. Until then, no more danger and fear and death." Jarred sat with her still in his lap. His lips trailed up her neck, making her shiver and tip her head back to give him more. "For now, there's only this. Just you. Just me."

Maddie's answering moan did amazing things to his already-hardening body.

"No dreams at all?" Her mind fluttered against his, showering him with swirls of sexy, dark purples that smelled like autumn and tasted like the deepest brandy he'd ever sipped.

"How..." He rolled her onto her back. They were skin to skin from the waist up, their hearts beating against each other. "How are you feeling? Are you sure you're up for—"

"For loving you? Yes." But there were shadows in her eyes still. In her soul. "I need this. I need to know it's just us this time."

"Us?"

"Just you and me." She shivered again as his hands brushed up the backs of her thighs, finding the top of her Brotherhood-issue sweatpants so he could pull them down.

Which he did.

Damn! She had nothing on beneath, just like him. His cock jerked in response.

"I'm here." He shimmied out of the last of his clothes and resettled against her body. They were melting into each other, from ankles to waist. But he needed more. His hands rubbed up her spine, arching it. He couldn't stop himself from kissing her hip. Licking her belly. Then tracing each rib, until his lips had found a tight nipple.

Perfection.

She gasped, then groaned. And in her mind he found the vision of her perfect mouth drawing his dick into an aching vortex of wet satin. Swirling her tongue around him. Suckling him. He nearly came undone. Then all that passion, every shimmer of it, froze into a ball of fear. First in her mind, then in his.

He pushed up from her body, which brought their hips into tighter contact. His cock pounded for more. More pressure. More friction. More Maddie.

"What is it, sweetheart?" he made himself say.

"It…I…" She turned her head away. "Last time, it wasn't…me."

"Yes, it was," he insisted. "From the moment I touched your body in that motel, from the moment our minds first touched in the dream, it was perfect. And it was *you*. It was everything I love about you. It was everything I wanted. Everything we both needed. Just because it started as a dream doesn't make it not real."

"Oh, it was real." She glared up at him, while her hips rose to meet his, as if she couldn't stop herself. "It was so real, I pulled a knife and tried to slice you into little pieces!"

"*That* wasn't you."

"I tried to kill you."

"No, Sarah did. I can tell you exactly when she took over in the dream, and—"

"How do we know she won't be there now? What if I hurt you again?"

Silence resonated after her outburst. She'd finally said it—the lurking fear Jarred had sensed in her ever since they'd made love. He settled onto his elbows.

"I was there, Maddie. I remember all of it, with great clarity. I remember touching you and feeling like I was holding a miracle in my arms, just like I am now. You giving yourself to me, losing yourself in me until your release was washing over me and taking me with you."

"But then—"

"We're stronger now." He laid a finger across her lips, when she would have kept arguing. "Our link, our minds, are stronger. I knew when Sarah broke into our dream. I know the signs now. We won't let it happen again, even if she does come back. Which is a big *if*, given how weak she's becoming. Besides, Temple. You'll kick her ass if she gets another hankering for a three-way. And in a twin smack-down grudge match, my money's on you every time."

Maddie snorted, and even that was so damn enticing, Jarred had to kiss her again. And then again.

"She can't separate us," he promised. "No one can."

Tears could be beautiful when a woman's eyes filled with them and love and adoration all at the same time.

"Can you really accept me like this," Maddie asked, "no matter what happens next?"

"You and me, Maddie, no matter what happens. All I need is you and me. I'm not going anywhere."

Jarred held his breath as she blinked those misty green eyes, then slowly nodded. Then her lower body was doing that wiggling thing again—rotating her soft, warm entrance against him until he couldn't breathe at all.

"*You and me* feels really good." Her worry and fear eased as her smile bloomed.

Her fingers roamed his shoulders, then tangled in his hair. Then her thoughts were tangling with his again, promising things wicked and erotic enough to make him dizzy.

"Yes," he agreed before she crushed her mouth to his. He found her ass with his palms. They both groaned as he thrust home. "*You and me* feels damn good."

CHAPTER THIRTY-NINE

"Yes, sir, I understand," Richard Metting said into the phone he'd answered.

Maddie's head still ached. And no matter what she'd said to Jarred, she still hated being in the same room as the Raven. A state-of-the-art conference room this time.

"Try to relax." Jarred leaned closer from the seat beside her. He rubbed the base of her neck. "Focus on me, not him."

Jarred's touch, the memory of the perfect feel of him filling her mind and body, cooled Maddie's anger. Anger at Sarah. And at Metting, for playing God with her sister's mind and helping set the coming confrontation into motion.

"No, sir." Metting made eye contact from his seat across the table. His dark gaze always seemed to be looking too closely. Seeing too much. "We don't have a location yet. But the Wolf will definitely be there with Sarah Temple. Madeline is working with me to understand more. Intervening at Sarah's rendezvous is our best shot at reclaiming the Temple twins' legacy and crushing Dream Weaver once and for all."

Maddie glared at the man. *Reclaiming* them for whom? Exactly what did he and his Watchers think they were going do with Maddie and Sarah, once the Wolf was gone?

Metting's response to her silent rant was the smallest of smiles.

"Yes, sir," he said into the phone. "I'll be in touch when we have complete information for a strike."

He thumbed the cell off and folded his hands on top of the table. "You remind me of your sister."

"Psychotic and at the end of her rope?" Maddie shot back.

Jarred hugged her close and chuckled.

"Defiant and resilient," Metting countered. "You should have died twice over these last few days. Both you and Dr. Keith, actually. But here you are, spitting fury at me and contemplating which part of me to rip off, if I do anything else to hurt your family."

"Do I have to choose just one part?"

Metting didn't miss much. He certainly didn't miss the way she'd wilted against Jarred, needing to feel him alive and well beside her. Inside her mind.

"*Sir?*" she mocked. "I thought you were top dog in the mad scientist brigade. Who would you possibly have to say *sir* to?"

"You'd be surprised."

"Whoever it was, he sounds anxious." To save Sarah and Phyllis? Or to be done with the Temples once and for all? "What is this brotherhood's real priority?"

A supersecret society balancing the scales of good and evil…It was almost as hard to believe as Sarah and Maddie being the principal players in a secret government weapons program.

"My primary mission is to prevent your family from being manipulated by powers of darkness."

Maddie's laugh was as much a shock to her, as it clearly was to Metting. "Powers of darkness?"

"You can't possibly be that naive after everything you've seen and done. Evil exists, Ms. Temple. And even the best of us can be turned to its bidding under the right circumstances."

"So…" The man had a habit of being annoyingly right. Maddie realized she had no idea what to say next.

"Who was that on the phone?" Jarred asked. "Who decides whether you're meeting your primary objective, and when someone takes control of this fiasco away from you?"

Metting steepled his fingers in front of him. "The elders in our brotherhood make the final call."

"And those would be the Watchers' watchers?" Maddie snarked.

"This is all going to end before Sarah hurts someone else," Metting said. "The elders won't hesitate to levy a termination order the second it's clear you or your sister are falling back under center control. The only thing stalling them is my assurance that your link with Sarah is stable enough to extract her location, and if possible your mother's, before the Wolf makes his next move."

Maddie sat a little taller. "And what exactly was the bastard's *first* move?"

"Involving you. Impacting your life enough to draw you into the center. What was supposed to happen after that is unclear, since—"

"Since you chose that night to try to escape and keep Sarah for yourself?" Jarred didn't look up from where he'd clasped Maddie's hand beneath the table.

"I think the Wolf miscalculated Sarah's awareness of her dream work. He couldn't have known that I was reducing her meds. He'd have to have been administering the same protocol during his work, but he'd have no way of knowing that I'd modified mine."

"Which means?"

"It means that whatever alternate dream simulations he mapped for Sarah—"

"Stop it!" Maddie found herself out of her chair. Furious beyond her ability to hold it in. "You're talking about my sister, not a test subject the center and your *elders* had any right to study. And they have no right to be thinking about terminating her, now that your freaked-out plans have crashed and burned."

"Let him finish," Jarred cautioned. "Something this dickhead says might help you reach Sarah again."

Maddie kept glaring at the dickhead, but she settled back beside the man she loved.

"The Wolf's interference left Sarah increasingly distracted during our simulations," Metting continued, "generating unpredictable results with her hosts."

"What results?"

"Kayla tried to kill herself when we were nowhere near ready to execute lethal simulations in reality. Sarah pulled back the first time she dreamed it—a simulation I didn't program her to project, where Kayla held a gun she didn't remember buying to her head. The second time…"

"Sarah killed the woman." Maddie's entire body turned cold.

"Yes." Metting had the decency to sound repulsed.

"Just like the gun you had." Jarred waited for her to nod, then said to Metting, "Maddie had a similar…episode. She didn't remember buying it, but she pulled a gun from a drawer in her apartment and—"

"—wanted to blow my head off with it," Maddie finished. "But it wasn't me, it was Sarah, wanting to kill herself. Only, it wasn't her, it was you, making her kill someone else. Only maybe it wasn't you, it was this Wolf or whatever the bastard's name is, confusing my sister until she was so suicidal, so desperate to escape, she tried

to end her torture the only way she could, through me..."
Maddie's panic from that night, the horror of what she'd
almost done, roared back. She glanced down at the angry scratches on her wrists that were just now scabbing
over. "And here I am, trying to help you find her again?
I really must be insane!"

Metting typed several notes into his laptop.

"Good," was his infuriating response. "Images and
symbols from Sarah's Dream Weaver simulations bled
into her link with you. But the contact remained separate from the nightmare about your father's death—the
shadow simulation the Wolf designed for the two of you.
That's good."

"Good?"

"Sarah clearly wants to kill herself." Jarred's hold on
Maddie's hand tightened. "She almost drove Maddie to
suicide. How the fuck can you sit there and say that's
good."

"But she *didn't* kill herself, Dr. Keith." Metting finally
looked up from his computer. "And I suspect that's why
Sarah was reaching out to you, Ms. Temple, beyond the
Wolf's programming. I'm assuming there were other oc-
currences. Unexplained behaviors. Memory lapses. Confusion about why you were doing things that were out of
character—long before you turned that gun on yourself
and went after Jarred with a knife."

Maddie could only nod as she looked back at all the
strange things that had happened over the last three
months. All the reasons she'd been so sure she was losing
her mind.

"That's the nature of the dream work Sarah's been
trained to do. Part of it was the Wolf, targeting you so
Sarah could feed off your control. Part of it was Sarah,
crying for help, so—"

"So someone would stop her before it was too late,"

Maddie finished. "Before the Wolf forced her to do something she couldn't bear doing. She killed that woman, no matter how strong your hold was supposed to be on her training."

"Yes." Metting's expression settled into resigned acceptance. "She needed more than I could give her, once the Wolf subjugated my control of her psychic abilities. So she reached out to the only person who could save her."

"Me." The sister who'd walked away and hadn't looked back in ten years.

"Your psychic breakdown was your twin's cry for help. The incident with the gun is what pushed you into coming to the center, right?"

"Y…yes," Maddie responded.

"The incident with the knife pushed Jarred to bring you to the Brotherhood."

"Yes," Jarred agreed.

"Sarah wanted to be free. She knew she'd need Madeline's help. She knew Madeline would ultimately need mine. There are clues in everything Madeline's dreamed with her. They'll lead us to wherever the Wolf is holding Phyllis. Madeline may not know Sarah's plans to save their mother, but Sarah's shown her where she's going."

"The truck driver trying to kill my father—that's the Wolf's dream, right?" Maddie asked. "The tree and the raven circling every time. You say the Raven is you. Sarah wanting you to stop her. But the playhouse I saw this last time? The faceless men threatening my mother, waiting to kill her and Sarah? How can any of those vague images help you find her?"

"What were the ravens doing in the woods?" Metting asked.

"What?"

"In the playhouse," Jarred said. "You said the ravens flew into your childhood playhouse."

"They were trying to kill us…" Maddie cringed away from the memory. Jarred lifted her from her chair and sat her in his lap, her head nestled against his chest. His strong heart. Only then could she continue. "They were clawing our skin from our bodies…"

"And when they'd stripped away everything but the two of you, together in your safest hiding place, what happened next?" Metting's piercing gaze crawled inside Maddie, pushing her toward the answers they needed. "Ravens reveal truth, Ms. Temple. That's what makes Sarah picking that symbol to represent me so miraculous. That she'd trust me that much, even after I've failed her. What did you see after the ravens came? What did they show you? What did you feel?"

Jarred was stroking Maddie's hair, soothing her. His trust in this gruesome process, in her, quieted the panic boiling inside. Maddie took several breaths.

"It felt…" She struggled to see nothing but the memory. "It felt like we were young again. I didn't hate what Sarah's become anymore. I could see who she really was again. I…told her what we'd told each other as kids. That I wouldn't leave her. I told her none of this was her fault…"

It was all coming back. A hypnotic fantasy Maddie couldn't stop. Her sister's fantasy of a life before death and darkness.

"Where did Sarah take you next?" Metting asked. "Once you could see her clearly, what did her dream show you?"

Jarred's hug was an unspoken reminder that he had her back, whatever happened. That she could do anything as long as he was with her.

"She was in the abandoned building I told you about. She wasn't a little girl anymore, and she was terrified. Lost. Hiding from all of us. Then…she showed me the clearing in the woods…She was determined then. She was going to take care of Mom. She was going to keep Phyllis safe from the Wolf, even if it meant she had to…"

"Die?" Metting asked.

"Wh…What?"

"That's what Sarah's last host wrote beside her bed, right before she killed herself. One word—*Die*."

"So now Sarah's going to call the Wolf out, no matter the risk, because she's given up? Because she has a death wish after what you people turned her into!"

Metting's eyes narrowed. And in that moment, looking into his tortured gaze, Maddie began to believe that whatever his brotherhood's monstrous schemes were, Metting would put everything on the line to save her sister. She could feel the depth of his determination to make this nightmare end.

"Is it possible that this meeting is the Wolf's plan—" Metting's gaze remained shadowed, but his clinical tone was back. "—and the Wolf's unaware that Sarah knows about it? Are you sure Sarah's showing you her own plans? We need to know where this clearing is. Is it close to here? Is it near the building Sarah showed you, where she was hiding in Boston?"

"I have no idea…Stop! How am I supposed to know any of this?"

"Feel it." There was that mesmerizing tone again. The velvety softness that Sarah must have trusted when she'd first clawed her way back to reality. "Where did it feel like it is? Go back to the dream of the clearing, Madeline. Let yourself go back to your sister."

"I…" Maddie couldn't stop shivering. Her mind was sliding. The clearing was coming into focus. The faceless, soulless men threatening her mother. They were aiming their guns at Phyllis and Sarah. Threatening Maddie's family. "I…I can't…It feels…"

"She's had enough." Jarred was still stroking her hair, still supporting what she thought she had to do. But his anger was building. "That's—"

"Where is the meeting, Madeline?" Metting pushed. "What are you seeing? Has Sarah already contacted the Wolf, or has she—"

"I…I don't think so. Maybe…" The sound of a storm—of madness—joined the images of the deadly confrontation in the clearing. "I can't…"

"I said that's enough!" Jarred was wiping blood from her nose again. "You've got to give her more time."

"No!" Maddie pushed his hand away. "I want to keep trying…"

"There is no more time, Dr. Keith." Metting's words were coming from further and further away. "We have to know where that meeting is. When it is. My men have to be there. Madeline has to be there. Sarah's psychic break…Escalating…Won't be able to…on her own…back in the Wolf's clutches…no choice but to do what he asks…"

Further and further away.

Further from now.

Because Maddie was closer and closer to…

Dark.

Alone.

Maddie was dark and alone.

No. She was Sarah. Sarah was alone. Running through the night. Hitchhiking. Whatever it took.

The Wolf would be waiting. So would her mother. Sarah

had made sure of it. It was a trap. The Wolf would try to keep Sarah and Phyllis both. But Sarah had picked the perfect place. Easy to access. Easy to watch. In the woods. And she knew every inch of the path to get there. Just where to hide. She'd been there before. Many times. When hide-and-seek had been family fun. It was her favorite place. She'd wait through the darkness, then through the day for the next night. Death worked best at night.

The mountains loomed. Friendly. Welcome home. But not home anymore. Not welcome anywhere. The Raven was hunting. He had Maddie. Maddie would believe his lies. The way Sarah used to believe. Didn't matter. Sarah had to beat the Wolf. That's all she had to do now. And if she didn't survive? All the better. It would be over. Death would finally be silenced.

But the Wolf would go first. Then the demons he brought with him. Sarah would watch. Listen. Feel. Each of them. Their greatest fears. Their nightmares. They'd all be hers. She'd make each one reality. Phyllis would finally see the monster she'd let the Raven create.

Sarah would tell Phyllis to run for the car. The one Sarah would steal. Give her the keys. Watch her run away, as one last nightmare consumed Sarah. Sarah would be good enough for the flames then. They would take the Wolf. Then they'd take her. She'd finally be free. Just like her father.

A raven's wings would spread.

Ghostly tree limbs would sway, while mountains watched over their shoulders.

The explosion of her father's car would rip through the night. Only this time Death would be with him. This time, Sarah would—

"No!" Maddie jerked awake, to find herself held safely in Jarred's arms.

He was shaking as badly as she was.

"Sarah!" Maddie muttered. "She's running…after my mother…She's made some kind of deal with the Wolf, and she's going after him herself. She won't survive it… She's seen that, and she doesn't care…I don't even think she wants to live."

"Shhh." Jarred brushed his forehead against hers. His fingers tangled in her hair. "We'll find her. Metting will help you figure out where the hell you just went. What everything you saw means. We'll find Sarah before it's too late."

"But…" Maddie's head was spinning. Too many images. Too much of Sarah. Pounding. Her stomach was churning. She swallowed the reflex to vomit. "Sarah… She's so alone…In the dark…She's out there all alone…"

"Shhh." Jarred rocked her, his anger and fear colored by something far stronger—love and determination to support whatever Maddie had to do. "Just let me hold you, sweetheart, until you're ready to talk. You found her. Metting won't let Sarah face the Wolf alone."

CHAPTER FORTY

"What does *home* mean?" Metting asked Maddie for the third time.

"How am I supposed to know! It was Sarah's messed-up mind. I don't know what any of it means."

"You're her twin," Jarred reasoned, still beside her. "You must have some feel for what *home* means."

He winced when her next glared blasted him, but he didn't back down. He and Metting were still with her in the conference room. A Watcher team somewhere in the bunker was preparing to leave. But no one could do anything *but* prepare, until Maddie figured out where the hell they were going.

"In her dream, she's traveling." Metting's manner remained calm and patient. "Could she really be returning to your childhood home?"

"To Lenox?" Their small mountain hometown in the Berkshires, not far from the Massachusetts-New York border.

Everything Maddie knew about her sister now felt like Sarah despised looking back. Everything but—

"Our playhouse... It seemed so real..."

"Maybe because she was already fixated on returning to the area." Metting typed into his laptop. "Then when you connected with her just now, her mind was on the move. Maddie, think. Was she traveling for real?"

"The mountains were there, outside the windshield of whatever she was riding in. But—" Sarah had been falling apart, emotionally and physically. Sick with her grandiose plans for proving to Phyllis that she was the good twin after all. "—nothing she was thinking was making sense…"

"Forget about sense," Metting pressed. "Did it feel real?"

"I…" Maddie allowed the memories closer, while she tried to hold on to the present. To Jarred. "It was like she'd contacted the Wolf, somehow. He'd be waiting for her, except she'd get there first."

"And then what will she do?" Metting stopped typing.

"She'll…wait…all day. She wants it to happen at night. *Death works best at night* . . . She has to be the good daughter now…"

"By getting herself killed?" Jarred held Maddie tighter.

"She wants it to happen where?" Metting was beside Maddie now. He took her hand. "Stay with the memory, Madeline. Believe what your feelings are telling you. Tell us where she's forcing the Wolf to meet her, before she destroys herself in a single act of stupidity!"

"She's as smart as I am!" Maddie slapped her sister's Raven across the cheek. "Smarter. She just can't handle the feelings…the constant barrage of everyone and everything, closing in on her until…"

"Until she's let it destroy her mind," Jarred reminded her. "Don't let these bastards do the same thing to you."

"Sarah never said where they were meeting," Maddie insisted.

Jarred kissed the top of her head and curled her closer in his lap. "Try, sweetheart. She's left her mind open to yours because she needs you there. She needs you to figure this out and stop her."

But what if *Maddie* didn't want to figure it out? She stared at the imprint of her fingers on Metting's face. What if she couldn't face what her sister had become—what she herself might very well become? Alone. Cold. Insane, with no hope of escape. Craving a violent death she was determined to control, when she could no longer control anything else.

But Maddie closed her eyes anyway. She held tight to Jarred. She wasn't abandoning her sister again.

You'll never be alone, Jarred's mind whispered. *We'll take care of Sarah and your mother together.*

And on the heels of his promise, came the images from Sarah's last vision. A disjointed rush…

The mountains and the Wolf. The car and the road. Symbols that Metting had said could mean almost anything. Symbols of a place and a trip to the place, but none of them necessarily representative of what Sarah was really doing. Except that Sarah was also thinking about…

"Hiding," Maddie said out loud. "She's thinking about hide-and-seek. Maybe that's where the mountains came from, because she and my dad and I used to…"

The images swirled again, drawing Maddie back in, beguiling her to really look. To dig. Because there was something Sarah had said. Something she'd thought about that had felt so real, because part of it was Maddie's memory, too…

"Hide-and-seek," she repeated, her eyes closed tight. "Sarah's playing hide-and-seek. Waiting for them. She's good at hiding. Our father always said she was the best. I always got caught. We'd go play in the park near our house, in one of the open fields people used for picnics. Sarah had the best hiding places. She'd sit forever and wait for us to give up, and she'd never tell us where she'd been. She'd come running into the field, laughing and smiling and squealing when our father scooped her up and told her how smart she was, and…"

Maddie could see the past now, the way Sarah was remembering it. The feeling of it was so real, there were tears in Maddie's eyes. Running down her cheeks. It had been so long since she'd been able to see her father this clearly, as if he were right there. Close enough to touch and hold on to, so he'd never leave again.

She didn't dare open her eyes, because then the memory would be gone. She could almost smell his aftershave. Hear the way he used to chuckle while he watched them play. See Sarah smile as he swung her around in that sunny field they'd always gone to…

"Our field!" Reality yanked Maddie back with a jerk. No warning. No chance to say good-bye. Her eyes snapped open. Her heart thundered to a halt. She scrubbed tears away with the back of her hand. "She's meeting the Wolf in our field. It's real. It really is real."

"What's real?" Metting urged. "What were you feeling?"

"Home…It feels like home. Like I was really there, except Sarah wanted to be there alone. She's desperate to do this alone. She's not just drawing the Wolf out. She's taking our mother home, so Phyllis can see Sarah the way our father did—the good little girl he was so proud of in the park. She's not going to let me win. I never win when we play hide–and–seek, and this time I'm not even going to get to play."

"But why go all the way across the state?" Jarred rubbed a soothing hand down Maddie's arm.

But comfort no longer came with his touch. The reality of what Maddie had felt in Sarah's mind wouldn't allow it. The depth of her twin's insanity was the legacy waiting for them both. Even if they stopped this showdown with the Wolf, the darkness would still be waiting for Maddie.

She eased away and stood. She couldn't look at either man now. Metting, because she might finally kill him for ripping away her blinders and showing her what she really was. What she couldn't have. And Jarred, because his love and concern wanted her to believe in happy endings. In the future and things like always being there for each other. But her future was a demented place. A place she wouldn't drag him into, only to hurt him and lose him and learn to hate him the way Sarah had her Raven.

"In the dream," she explained, because saying it out loud might finally make her accept just how hopelessly fucked up she and Sarah were. "The nightmare the Wolf made her send me. Our father's accident, over and over again. Sarah kept trying to reach our father. To prove that she was still good, by saving him. But every dream she'd fail. In her mind she thinks she killed him, because she couldn't save him. She's Death. But if she saves our mother, she finally wins. She gets to be the good twin before she dies."

"What are you saying?" Metting asked.

"Sarah's not bravely confronting the chance of losing her life, she's running toward it. She's drawing the Wolf across the state because I'm here and she'll be there, and she thinks there's no way I can stop her. She doesn't want my help. She's playing into that maniac's hands. Because in her twisted version of the dream, dying is the way out of what we are. She's going to fix this legacy of ours—by dying while she saves our mother!"

Maddie turned toward the Raven, careful not to look at Jarred. The love shining in his eyes would only make the truth harder to face.

"My sister's going to get herself and my mother killed tomorrow night, in the place where we played games with our father as children. Because Sarah's insane need to get rid of these *gifts* everyone wants to get their hands on is telling her this is the only way she'll be free. And I'm suddenly very afraid she's right."

Jarred paced across his and Maddie's bedroom at the bunker, ready to rip his way through the locked door and the security outside.

"Get away from me," Maddie had said, when he'd reached for her after their meeting with Metting. "My entire family is poison. This is going to end bloody, and you can't stop it. And if you're there, I'll have your death on my conscience for real this time. I don't want you involved when this blows up. And if I can't stop what this is turning into, you don't want me, period."

Stay away from her?

Maddie hadn't looked at him when they'd left the conference room. Or when Metting had led her in a different direction while one of his men dragged Jarred away. Jarred had fought every step, until he'd been ushered into the bedroom and told to cool off. Four hours ago.

He couldn't feel Maddie now. He had no idea where she was or what she was planning to do. The lock cleared on the door. He stepped beside it. Metting was the first person to come inside.

Excellent.

Jarred went for the jaw. Metting went down. Two of his men yanked Jarred's hands behind his back and pulled him away, while Metting got to his feet and swiped at his bruised lip.

"Where's Maddie?" Jarred demanded.

"She'll be on her way momentarily." It was the Raven looking back at Jarred now. Deathly serious. Totally unimpressed with Jarred's explosion.

"To catch her sister?" Jarred asked.

"Yes."

"Alone."

"With a dozen of the Brotherhood's best snipers. And myself."

"But without me!" Jarred surged against the arms restraining him.

"You were a distraction, Dr. Keith. Madeline has one chance to stop her sister. One chance to stop the Wolf's plans for her family. We had to map the quickest route to this Kennedy Park she remembered. And I needed her listening to me when I explained my men's tactical plans for when we get there. Distraction, because she's convinced that her legacy is a death sentence for you, wasn't an option."

Jarred actually bared his teeth. "There's no way you're keeping me from following her. If I have to tear this place down, I'll be at Lenox by tonight."

"Of course you will." Metting motioned for Jarred to be released. "You'll ride in a second van, leaving ten minutes behind me, Ms. Temple, and my lead strike team."

Jarred rubbed circulation back into his forearms instead of attacking. For now. "What the hell is going on? Why the cloak-and-dagger? Why lock me up in here and hide me in a chase car, if you want me at the clearing when everything goes down?"

"I *need* you at that clearing. Madeline needs you there. I suspect that when it's all said and done, you'll be our best hope of saving the Temple legacy from whatever the Wolf has planned. And, trust me, he has a plan of his own. This is all happening too easily, otherwise.

"The Wolf was strong enough to damage Sarah's link with me, but he hasn't located her now that she's on the run? *Sarah's* the mastermind behind this showdown? He's not going to just hand over her mother and expect the woman he's turned into a psychotic mess to passively follow him back to his lab."

"But Maddie and Sarah's safety are your only priority, not getting them both back into *your* lab?" Jarred pressed. "Is that what you want me to believe?"

"Yes," Metting answered without hesitation.

And the man couldn't succeed without Jarred playing along.

"The only way I'll help is if the sole objective is stopping the Wolf's manipulation of the Temples' minds. Period. You get their mother out. You make sure this bastard never comes after Maddie and her sister again. Then you and your secret society will leave them the hell alone."

"That I can't promise." Metting didn't waste time feigning an apology. "If Madeline and Sarah's gifts fall back under the center's control, I won't be able to stop the termination order. Our only chance of avoiding that is if you and Madeline do this together, live or die."

"Live or die?"

"Madeline is convinced she and her sister will die fighting the darker side of their psychic gifts. She thinks that's their legacy. If you're not willing to fight to the death with them, you'll never secure her trust at the rendezvous."

This is going to end bloody, and you can't stop it...If I can't stop...You don't want me, period.

It wasn't Jarred Maddie didn't trust still. It was the light within her, the healing power she'd finally embraced, that she was certain would fail her.

"I'm going to be there with her, Dr. Metting, whatever happens." He knew Maddie's light was stronger than Sarah's insanity or this Wolf's depraved plans. And he would fight beside Maddie until she could believe it, too. "Tell me how to help her. Or get out of my way, and I'll figure it out myself."

Metting stared for several seconds. Then he nodded

at one of his men to open the door. He led the way into the hall.

"Sarah's joined with you once before," he said without waiting to see if Jarred followed. "The two of you have already fought together to protect Madeline. You have a shot at being a bridge between the two of them again. But once they're together at the rendezvous, no one can predict the effect it will have on their psyches. You will be their only tie to the world outside their legacy. You have to fight to keep their minds from slipping into the darker side of their gifts—the side of Sarah that the Wolf now controls."

"But you're Sarah's Raven." Jarred hustled to keep up. "You know what her mind is capable of. How her dream links work. Why can't you—"

"Neither of the twins trust me. My mental presence would damage their ability to defeat the Wolf, not improve it. My men and I will cover them tactically. Shield them psychically as best we can until they're in place. Your connection with Madeline will become key then. She'll either accept you into whatever psychic connection they forge, and have a chance of defeating the Wolf, or she'll very likely lose herself to the same darkness that's taken her sister."

Metting began to run toward wherever their transportation was waiting. Jarred raced beside him.

CHAPTER FORTY-ONE

Maddie hadn't been back to Lenox since she and her mother moved away. Leave it to her maniac sister to finally drag her home. Kennedy Park was only a few miles from their old house. Not that far from where their father had died.

Maddie looked up at the winter sky and shivered. Cold seeped through the insulated gear Metting's people had provided. The bare oak trees looming above the familiar bike trail she was following were the trees from Sarah's nightmares. It was dark, but a harvest moon laced everything with ghostly beams of light. Its illumination shifted with the howling wind blowing around Maddie. The sound of the storm overhead and of ever-moving branches, of her boots kicking dead leaves off the frozen ground, hinted of rustling feathers looming closer with every step she took.

And with every step, she could feel Sarah more, as if her twin was reaching for Maddie somehow, even though Sarah's plan had been to do this alone. Their link had grown stronger, the closer Maddie got to the park. She'd first noticed it when the Watchers' van crossed into Berkshire County. Now, with Metting and his men following her at an undetectable distance, all she could feel was the darkness of the night. Sarah's fear, closing in. Her sister's confusion and exhaustion and determination to end this.

Sarah was hiding. Watching. Trying to find Phyllis with her mind. To sense the Wolf before he could draw Sarah into the open.

Maddie stopped, panicked that she'd do something to expose her twin to danger. The confusion of Sarah's chaotic emotions was spiraling higher. Taking over. Blurring everything but the impulse to be good, finally, or die trying. What was the plan—that Maddie should wait for Sarah to make her move? Or was she to wait for the Wolf to show himself? Or should she avoid a confrontation, grab her twin before Sarah could reveal herself, and restrain her until Metting's men could recover their mother?

Maddie couldn't remember.

She couldn't think.

She had to hide.

She grabbed her pounding head and ducked behind a tree. She slid down its trunk until she was squatting on the forest floor, her mind exploding with streaks of red and black…Sounds of death circling ever closer. Flashes of her father's accident. The explosion. The fire that she needed to get to, because this time she had to—

Die!

"No!" Maddie whispered. "It's only a dream. The Wolf's dream…"

She had to keep it together. She was the Raven's decoy. She was Sarah's sanity. Her light.

"Get your hands on Sarah," Metting had said. "Hold her down if you have to. Control her emotions. The Watchers will take care of the Wolf."

Maddie could do this. She could make this right for Sarah. For herself. They were getting Phyllis out. They were ending Dream Weaver. It was the only way Sarah could be free of the darkness. The only way Maddie could go back to Jarred, assuming he'd want her after the way she'd left him.

No more death.

No more insanity.

No more lies.

White. Healing white. Maddie was born to be a healer. Jarred had helped her see that. This time, she'd heal the other half of her soul. Her twin. It was the only chance either of them would have to start over.

After several cleansing breaths, Maddie opened her eyes to the darkness surrounding her. She opened her mind even more—letting Sarah's turmoil flow through her. Letting it lead her. No more fear. No more hiding. She stepped back onto the narrow trail that wound through the dense forest of their childhood.

"Find your sister," Metting had reminded her just before she'd left the Watchers' van. A full day of strategy and travel, armed warriors that had her back for when things got ugly, but ultimately it was all up to her. "Don't contact Sarah. Try not to alert her that you're there, or that we're behind you. Focus on her emotions. Let them lead you. Secure her. Don't let Sarah engage. The Wolf will be waiting. He'll be overconfident and careless. My men and I will take things from there. Just keep Sarah out of it. Remember… You've reached her twice now. Inside your dream link, you're stronger than the Wolf. You can control Sarah regardless of his plans. You have to believe that, so Sarah can, too."

Closing her eyes, Maddie pictured her twin, crouching and still, the way Sarah had looked hiding in that abandoned building. Only there were trees and underbrush around her now, and wind and fear and hate…

…*hate for the loss and the death and the lies and the center and the Wolf—even for her Raven. But not for Maddie. Not anymore. Maddie would take care of their mother. She'd take Phyllis somewhere the center would never find them. And Sarah would finally get to be the good sister.*

All she had to do was free Phyllis. Maddie would figure out the rest. Both of them would finally see that Sarah wasn't Death—not in the end.

Sarah knew she could do this. She was feeling better. Focused, now that the moment was finally here. Ready to end this. It would be okay. Once Sarah took out—

The Wolf...

He was in the clearing.

Clutching Phyllis to his side.

"You can't hide from me," *said the man who'd painted himself as a gray wolf in her dreams. The night was storming around him, blurring the scene into more dream than reality.* "Stop hiding, Sarah. Your life for your mother's, that's our deal. You dragged me here. She's fine, just like I promised. Live up to your end of the bargain, and I'll let her go."

In Sarah's mind, a raven circled overhead. Drawing closer by the second. Fitting. He'd get to see her victory. But he'd be too late to stop her. Sarah would beat the Wolf while the Raven watched and finally knew she didn't need him. He'd started this. She'd end it.

"Come out now," *the Wolf demanded.* "I'm losing patience."

But Sarah couldn't leave her hiding place.

A buzzing was tickling her mind. An alarm. Something telling her not to move. Someone. Or was it just the wind and the trees and the shadows and the Raven and how much it all reminded her of what the Wolf wanted? What he'd wanted from the start...

No! Her mother. Sarah had to remember her mother, not the Wolf's shadow dream. She had to stay focused. Save Phyllis. Beat the Wolf. Make her mother and the Raven watch.

"Let her go," *Sarah called from her perch beneath the grandfather oak—Maddie's name for the ugly, looming tree her* sister had never guessed was Sarah's secret hiding place.

It was the same tree the Wolf had painted into each of their shared dreams.

"If you want me," Sarah called out, "let my mother go first."

Then Sarah would walk up to the Wolf, pretending to cooperate. She'd walk right to him and slit his throat. His men, hidden at the edge of the clearing, would try to open fire. But they'd be dead, too, before her mind was gone completely. Because they'd turn their guns on each other, not her. Sarah could see it in her mind—all of them, shooting one another. Killing. Dying because they were too weak to fight the daydreams she'd plant inside them while she hid.

She'd take care of them after the Wolf was down.

After Phyllis was free.

"Let her go!" Sarah projected whispers into the Wolf's men's imaginations. Distracting them, so they wouldn't detect where she was hiding. "Let my mother walk across the clearing. I won't come out until you do."

"Oh, I think you'll do exactly what I say." The Wolf pushed her mother to the ground. "Come out, Sarah, or I'll kill her."

He raised his gun. The raven circled closer. So did the buzzing in Sarah's mind.

"Leave my mother alone!" Sarah stumbled away from the tree's cover. "Let her go."

The Wolf's smile lit up his gray face. Phyllis stared at her. The Wolf flicked the safety off his weapon.

The raven's wings spread. Bare tree limbs swayed.

The gun in his hand fired.

A scream ripped through the night. Sarah's scream, as she sprinted for her mother . . .

"No!" Maddie's mind broke from their psychic link as

she bolted into the clearing, too. She was too late. Always too late. "Damn it, Sarah! Stop. Stay away from him!"

Sarah raced from the grandfather oak. Her head was splitting. Her heart was breaking. Flames of defeat consumed everything. She was too late. Always too late.

The Wolf's thin laughter reached her. Engulfed her. Destroyed her absolution.

"God, please don't let her be dead…" Sarah prayed for her mother. The way she prayed for her father in every dream the Wolf had forced her and Maddie to have.

"She's not dead," the Wolf chided. "Not yet."

The flames cleared from Sarah's vision, enough for her to see Phyllis sobbing uncontrollably but unharmed at the Wolf's feet. For her to sense the very real nightmare approaching from behind. Running toward the Wolf, exactly the way he'd planned all those times he'd made Sarah reach for her sister's mind. Torture it with memories of their father dying. Implanting the shadow-dream simulation that was about to unfold, no matter how hard Sarah had fought to keep Maddie out of this.

She spun around.

"You bitch!" she shrieked in her twin's face. "You just couldn't stay away, could you? You couldn't stand it— letting me win. Letting me be good for once. Now look what you've done!"

"Sarah." Maddie reached out her hand, the way she had in the playhouse. "Back away from the clearing with me. It's going to be okay, I promise. But—"

"Okay?" Sarah felt the Raven drawing closer for real.

For a fleeting moment Sarah let herself hope she could stop this. But the Wolf's men were closing in, too. She couldn't stop once the Wolf's simulation took over. No one could, not even the Raven.

"You have to take my hand," her sister insisted.

"No!" Sarah shouted over the Wolf's laugh. "Run away, Maddie. Now!"

"Not without you." Maddie stepped to her side, her eyes already going vague with the shadow dream Sarah had no choice but to project. "We're in this together, and—"

Maddie flinched.

So did Sarah.

Their gazes met.

Their minds.

Their dreams.

One dream...

The one Sarah had been forced to project into Maddie's mind every night, while Sarah worked with the Raven's host. Over and over again. All of it building to this awful moment.

It's too late...Sarah's mind whispered across the buzzing link that the Wolf had somehow kept her from recognizing was Maddie.

Too late...Maddie's mind repeated back, as the raven's wings spread overhead and bare tree limbs swayed.

The Wolf stepped closer.

"Lucid field simulation," he commanded. "Engage."

Sarah watched Maddie's eyes glaze as they both fell into the nightmare. They were awake. But the Wolf's dream was all they could see...

"Holy shit!" Their father's attention jerked to the rain-soaked country road.

His panic sliced into them.

Their car skidded across the center line. Sarah and Maddie screamed, just like a hundred times before. Held their breaths. Prayed the tires would grab. But the car's wheels spun faster instead. Death raced toward them, more precious by the second. Because like an addict, they were reaching for it now. For the grace that came only in this moment.

Their absolution.

Because a split second before the tanker truck pulverized the driver's side of their family's Chevy, their father's anger evaporated.

Please God, let my girls be okay.

Make them okay again.

Take care of my little girls.

The truth was agony, when it no longer mattered. But Sarah's and Maddie's minds clung to their father's thoughts of unconditional love.

Then they were ripped away . . .

The agonizing jumble of what followed swallowed them. Psychic energy beating at them, splitting them, until the racket of the crash drowned out every other sound.

Just like every other time . . .

Except the Wolf was in the dream this time, dragging Maddie toward the crumpled truck that had ground to a halt near the car.

"No!" she and Sarah cried in unison.

"Look who killed your father." He forced Maddie to gaze into the driver's window. "Look who has to—"

"Die!" she and Sarah screamed, as the truck driver from the earlier nightmare, the one with the Raven's black eyes, disappeared.

In this final simulation, it was Phyllis Temple in the driver's seat.

Their mother had done this. All of it. She'd lied about the legacy since they were little. When their father was gone, she'd hidden Sarah away and lied again. She'd let the Raven and then the Wolf turn Sarah into Death, so Maddie would never know the truth.

And the truth was, that Phyllis Temple had to—
"Die!"

Richard and his men arrived at the Wolf's rendezvous less than a minute behind Madeline. But everything had already gone to shit.

Madeline stood in the clearing, facing her sister, their mother sprawled on the ground. And behind Sarah, forcing her to direct whatever psychic confrontation she and Madeline were locked into, was the man who'd made himself Sarah's Wolf.

"Ruebens," Richard said.

"Sir?" Jefferson, his second-in-command, was tracking the line of armed men ringing the far edge of the clearing.

"Alpha's wolf. Her shadow-dream control. The man who drew the Temple twins back together." The gray-haired, gray-bearded bastard had always seemed more cruel and unforgiving than the center's other scientists. But he'd never appeared as evil as he did now, smiling while the twins squared off. "Dr. Thomas Ruebens is the Wolf."

But it was only when Madeline reached for the man's gun, only when he stepped aside so she had a clear shot at her cringing mother, that Richard fully understood what was unfolding. Why the man had allowed Sarah to contact her sister *undetected*. Why Sarah had been *allowed* to run free, after escaping the center, so her psychosis would pull herself and her twin together.

It had all been planned. Every move. Even Richard equipping Madeline and Jarred with just enough information to motivate them to play along. The Wolf had seen it all. Planned every move.

"Oh, my God. The Beta field simulation the center was pushing for. The shadow dream about the Temples' car accident, that the Wolf used to link the twins...The center directors never expected me to complete full lucid dream testing. Ruebens had his own design in the works. He knew exactly which dream host would most impress the DOD, when the host was forced to kill against character...to kill her mother in a lucid daydream that made Phyllis Temple responsible for her husband's death."

Jefferson stared at Richard, then at the nightmare unfolding before them.

"Prepare to take all targets," he said into his com link.

"No!" Richard ordered into his own. "Belay that. Stand by, but stand down."

"If the legacy evolves fully into darkness while the Wolf controls the twins," Jefferson argued, "then—"

"There's still time. I'm not giving up on Sarah yet." Even though Richard had promised himself he'd end her suffering before he'd let the center have her back.

He'd promised not to let Sarah kill again, and there she was, aiming Dream Weaver's Beta prototype—her twin—at her own mother. Both women were primed to blow Phyllis away. Dream Weaver was about to become a very deadly reality.

"Sarah won't go through with it," he insisted. "I don't care what programming the Wolf's embedded. Madeline won't let her. Together they're—"

"An unstoppable evil, if the Wolf can get them to do this! You took an oath," Jefferson insisted. "We all did. The elders want this contained tonight. I'm not going to sit here and watch—"

Richard yanked the other man up by his Kevlar vest.

"You'll damn well watch whatever I tell you to watch until I'm removed as lead. Is that clear!"

Jefferson shoved him away. They'd been through too

much together, on too many suicide missions they'd somehow survived, to be intimidated by each other.

"The twins will take us all out," Jefferson said. "They'll do whatever the Wolf's programming tells them to do."

"Or they'll kill him," Richard countered, "and with him our worries about the center and Dream Weaver."

Jefferson glanced back at the frozen scene in the clearing. Madeline still held the automatic weapon, while Sarah and Ruebens and Phyllis and all of the center's men watched in either awe or terror.

Disengage, Alpha, Richard demanded, dropping his psychic shields and blowing his team's location. *Target release.*

Ruebens's head came up to find Richard and his men on the other side of the clearing. Sarah and Madeline jerked in unison. But instead of dropping the rifle, Madeline raised it higher.

"Die!" Madeline's voice carried over the sound of an approaching storm.

"Prepare to—" Jefferson started to say on his com.

"No!" Richard grabbed his friend's arm. "Just a little more time. Give them just a few more seconds."

Please, Sarah. Disengage. See your mother. See your sister. See what's really happening. Trust me just one more time . . .

Jarred shouldered his way to the front of the armed men he'd followed through the frigid park. He'd heard someone give the kill order over the com system.

He skidded to a halt beside Metting and another man, and looked out into the nightmare scenario that Maddie was never supposed to have walked into.

"What happened?" he demanded.

"Talk to her," Metting insisted without preamble.

"What?"

Jarred stared at the moonlit clearing. At the positioning of the people grouped in its center. At Maddie as she—

"What the hell is she doing?"

"She's trapped in a lucid dream," Metting said. "She's trying to—"

"—kill her mother?"

"Stop her, Dr. Keith. However you've reached her before—"

"—in dreams. It's mostly been in dreams!"

"Screw the dreams. Reach her with your mind. Now. Or I won't be able to hold my men off."

Maddie aimed the gun at her father's killer—at the bastard who'd shattered it all.

Her sister's hold on her sanity. Her father's life. Her mother's love for her daughters—forcing her to choose one over the other, and ultimately to lose them both. And Maddie's life. Her family. Her future. Her dreams of having something that wasn't tainted by darkness and death and destruction. Of loving a man who could accept what she was, and never having to let him go. This bastard had taken it all.

The killer of everything she'd ever had cowered before her, beside the burning carcass of the truck that had hit her family car. In her hand was the gun that would finally end the destruction. It was armed. The safety off. Killing him was the right thing. It would make the nightmare finally go away.

"Die!" she screamed into the night.

But the coward in Maddie couldn't fire. Or was it the healer she'd once thought she could be?

"Kill him!" commanded the gray Wolf standing beside her.

"Sarah?" Maddie needed her sister. Sarah was there in the dream's darkness. Was this really what they wanted? Did Sarah really believe killing would fix their legacy? Was that really who they'd been born to be?

"End him, you stupid bitch," the Wolf screamed.

"Sarah?"

Maddie's finger twitched on the trigger, but a surge of caution reached her from somewhere nearby. Concern. Worry. Love. She turned to find her twin staring off into the woods.

"Who's out there?" Maddie asked.

A beam of light was shining behind the clearing, encompassing everything in its path. Warmth and love rolling toward Maddie, eating up the dream's darkness.

"Don't do this," the light said in a familiar voice. "This isn't you."

The gun suddenly felt heavier.

Colder.

"Come back to me," the light tempted. "Come away from the Wolf."

The killer on the ground was crying now.

Soft, feminine sobs.

Familiar crying that sounded like—

"Kill him!" The Wolf's demand ripped Maddie's attention away from the light.

"Don't." The other voice was closer. "I'm here. You're not alone in the darkness. You're not a killer."

"J...Jarred?" Maddie turned to find him right where he'd promised to be—by her side. Forever. And for a second, it was just her and Jarred and the light they'd made together. "How...Where..."

"It's the shadow dream, Maddie. The Wolf's nightmare. It's the Wolf who's evil, not your mother. You have to see that."

"My mother?" Jarred was too far away to touch, and Maddie couldn't move. "But she...Phyllis was in the car with my dad that night. The truck driver tried to kill them both. He killed my father. He has to—"

"Turn around Maddie. See her. See who the Wolf's dream wants you to kill."

"I have to...The driver has to...Where's Sarah?" Maddie stared down at the ugly weapon in her hand.

"Turn around." Jarred's mind stroked hers. "You can stop this. You and Sarah can stop this together. It's just a dream."

Maddie wanted to hold him until her confusion evaporated. But the Wolf wouldn't let her. This was the Wolf's warped reality, she realized. Not hers and Sarah's. The Wolf wanted her to kill, not her sister. Maddie turned and blinked the dream into sharper focus...

An old man, not a predatory animal, loomed over Phyllis, not the driver of the truck. And there Sarah stood beside Maddie—little-girl Sarah from the playhouse, looking bedraggled and terrified as she wrung her hands in guilt because it was their mother the old man's dream wanted Maddie to kill.

"You psychotic bastard." Maddie threw the gun to the ground. She tried to break away from the daydream, but his control held. "What the hell is this?"

"This is your legacy, Ms. Temple." His smile was as demented as the dead gray of his eyes. "This is what you were born to be—what your mother made both of you into."

"No..." Phyllis whimpered. "I loved you girls."

"You loved them so much, you left them with no control over their powers." The old man picked up the gun and raised a hand to stall the armed men heading down the slope behind him. "You did nothing to prepare them for their destinies. You loved your daughters so much, you abandoned *them to flounder in weakness and fear. Luckily, I'm here to guide them for you."*

Maddie could feel the light behind her still. Jarred belonged in the Wolf's dream, too, because he and Maddie were one. But his wasn't the only light she'd need to defeat the nightmare's darkness. Maddie smiled at the little girl cringing beside her.

"Our mother gave us everything." Maddie reached her hand toward her twin. Little-girl Sarah hesitated. Then she reached, too. "When she gave us this."

"No!" The old man raised the gun as Maddie's and Sarah's fingers found each other . . .

The light of their legacy roared to life through their touch. Surrounding Sarah and Maddie and pushing outward. The power of it shoved the old man and Phyllis away. The light was inside Sarah and Maddie, too. It was them, as the little girl's dark eyes glowed. Her hair shone, flowing around her porcelain complexion like silky rain.

"Sarah?" Maddie had forgotten that her frail, damaged sister had once been this beautiful.

"Wake up, Maddie," Jarred's voice whispered urgently. "Wake up and stop the Wolf before it's too late!"

"He's right," Sarah said. "We have to stop this. Now."

Maddie stared in awe as Sarah shifted back to her adult self. Their hands still clinging to each other, they turned to find the Wolf's gun aimed at them.

"Stop this?" he jeered. "Are you really that deranged? You can't stop me." He raised the gun higher. "Dream Weaver doesn't succeed or fail with your shadow simulation alone. And since you're clearly of no more use to my plans, I'm happy to say that it's time for you both to—"

"Die!"

The command echoed. A raven's wings spread. Bare tree limbs swayed.

"No!" Their mother's scream ripped through the night.

She threw herself in front of Maddie and Sarah as the Wolf's gun fired.

"No!" Sarah and Maddie yelled in unison.

Then their horror at what was happening, their determination to stop it combined. Built. Ripped the Wolf's dreams to shreds . . .

With her next blink, Maddie opened her eyes to a real-world nightmare. The old man was still there. Sarah was still there. Their mother was, too. But Phyllis was bleeding. Shot. Dying on the ground between all of them.

"You bastard!" Maddie and Sarah screamed in unison.

Summer thunder rolled across a turbulent winter sky. Lightning snaked down, blasting the earth between Sarah and Maddie and sending them flying.

"It was a dream. It was still part of the nightmare . . ." Maddie tried to assure herself as she sat up. "It wasn't real. The Wolf didn't shoot—"

"Mom!" Sarah stumbled to her feet and ran to where Phyllis lay. Maddie raced with her. They dropped to their knees beside Phyllis, their tears flowing at the sight of her crimson-soaked blouse.

It had been real. Their mother had protected them with her own body, and now she was dying. And it was Maddie's fault. She'd tried to stop it and failed, because—

"Because you're Death." The man who'd made himself Sarah's Wolf dragged himself to their side from where the lightning had thrown him. His left arm hung at an extreme angle. A compound fracture had shattered the femur of one leg. "Just like Sarah, you were born for darkness. My work will help you focus that power. Death is your legacy. It's what both of you were meant to be. It's not too late. Come with me and there's nothing we can't do together. Or you can die a coward just like your mother."

"No!" Jarred stepped closer. He was really there. He would always be there. "You're a healer, Maddie. You both can be. You and Sarah. You can be light together, just like the Raven promised."

"The Raven?" The old man lifted the gun he'd dragged back with him. He aimed it in a shaking arc at Jarred. "Would that be Richard Metting? The idiot Watcher who let all this happen under his nose?"

A red dot appeared on the old man's forehead, a split second before a neat hole sliced straight through his brain.

"That would be him," Jarred said as the man's lifeless body sank to the cold ground.

Then all hell broke lose. Guns firing and the Wolf's soldiers racing forward, only to drop in their tracks one by one as the Watchers' snipers proved themselves as skilled as promised. Jarred hit the ground and tried to drag Maddie beneath him. But she pulled herself and Sarah to their feet instead.

United outside their dreams for the first time since they were children, she and Sarah stood between the approaching danger and their mother.

CHAPTER FORTY-TWO

Maddie gripped Sarah's hand. Phyllis's blood coated their fingers. Blood that held the potential for bottomless darkness. But for light, too. Never-ending light.

Jarred stood beside Maddie, his love washing away her doubt and fear. Sarah's Raven had joined them, the velvet touch of Metting's mind calling to the light Maddie felt flickering within her sister. Sarah's fragile hope that she was no longer alone.

Only a few of the Wolf's men still advanced, and they were locked into battle with the Brotherhood's snipers. Sarah was reading their minds. And through her, Maddie was, too.

"Let them build," Sarah whispered.

"What?" Maddie was transfixed by the sound of her adult sister's voice. "Let what build?"

"The feelings. Yours. Mine. The Wolf's men. Let the feelings build. Hold them until the last possible second."

Maddie's and Sarah's fingers clenched around each other. Phyllis moaned softly.

"Now, push," Sarah instructed.

And with what felt like no effort at all, they used the Wolf's men's fears against them. The men stalled, paralyzed by dark fantasies. Whatever most haunted their souls. Their mission to reclaim the Temple legacy was forgotten. Their fight for survival against the Brotherhood suddenly meant nothing. Each man's horrifying daydream became his only reality.

In mere seconds, the snipers had downed the last of them.

"Mom!" Sarah dragged Maddie back to the ground where Jarred had already knelt to attend to Phyllis.

"Let your feelings for her build," Maddie instructed.

She was shaking and weak, but Sarah would help her. Love had been the key to saving Jarred. Now her and Sarah's love would heal their mother.

"I'm so sorry…" Sarah shoved Jarred aside and hugged Phyllis. "It's all my fault. It's my fault you're here, just like when Daddy—"

"It…" Phyllis's voice crackled with pain. "No. Your father's death wasn't your fault, honey."

Sarah cried harder. Maddie could feel her sister's heart breaking at the sound of Phyllis calling her *honey*. At the forgiveness filling their mother's words.

"He wouldn't have been in that car," Sarah argued, "driving in the rain and distracted, if it wasn't for me."

"He was in the car because he loved you." Maddie took her mother's hand and pulled Sarah close with her free arm.

"Loving me got him killed." Sarah stiffened. "Now look what it's done to Mom. I'm Death!"

"No! You—" Phyllis's breath caught. Jarred lifted her head into his lap. "You're not Death, Sarah. None of this is your fault. I never…should have left you…You've had to battle this alone…Not fair…Not your fault…"

"Rest, Mom." Maddie could feel her mother's heart slowing and Jarred's silent warning that there was little time left. "Don't talk."

"No…The legacy…That center…" Phyllis dragged Sarah's and Maddie's hands together, then clung to them with her own. "You have to—"

"It's over," Maddie insisted. *Let the feelings build,* Maddie repeated to Sarah through their link. Then to her mom she said, "You have to—"

"No!" Phyllis's hazel eyes flashed with determination. "Listen to me…The legacy—I wouldn't let myself believe it. I refused to believe that paper. That picture. I threw them away, but it's still here. The prophecy. It's still inside both of you. You have to remember…"

"Light and dark," Maddie offered, needing her mother calm so she and Sarah could concentrate. "Twins and a chance for good and evil. And Sarah's chosen good, Mom. The Wolf didn't win. It's going to be okay."

"There's…" Phyllis wheezed. "I heard those men talking after they took me. His people won't stop. There's more—"

"You can tell us later." Maddie clutched Sarah's hand. *She's fading. We have to try now!* "Just lie still, until after we—"

"No!" Phyllis struggled to sit up.

Jarred settled her against his chest. His concerned expression locked with Maddie's.

"I'm not important now," Phyllis insisted. "You two are. You two together, like this…Making sure the darkness never wins. You have to—"

"We won, Mom." Maddie glanced toward the Wolf's lifeless body, just to be sure. "The government won't have us as weapons. I'll help Sarah. Dr. Metting will, too. And I'll stay with her until she's better. You'll see."

"Metting…" Phyllis's nails dug into their hands. "He knew…He said he knew…about the legacy. To—" A bone-shattering cough racked her body. "—to call him, if anything happened. He'll make this right. Find him. He'll…know what to do…*Another will be born,* the legend said. I heard that old man talking to his people."

"I'm here, Ms. Temple." Metting knelt beside them.

"Tell her it's over," Maddie demanded. "Calm her the hell down so Sarah and I can help her."

"No—" Phyllis let go of their hands and pointed a shaking finger at Metting. "You tell them…*Another will come.* It's not over. These people…won't stop. I heard them. Look at what they've done to Sarah. What I let them do…Don't let them…not again. Don't let them do it again. You promised me…"

Phyllis's crazy-scared memories bombarded Maddie with images of greed and hate. The Wolf and his men— smug that even if they lost Sarah and Maddie, they still had another chance. Sarah was seeing it, too. Their mother's memories of her captors. Their evil plans swirling around an innocent life locked into a centuries-old battle of good versus evil. Phyllis's panicked need to save that life. To not fail her, too…

The memories faltered, along with Phyllis's heartbeat.

"Mom?"

Maddie pressed her and Sarah's palms to her mother's chest—to the gaping wound the Wolf's gunshot had made. She tried to breathe through her panic. Her mother's eyes drifted shut.

Focus! Maddie screamed in her twin's mind. *Focus on the light.*

"Sarah's right here, Mom," she said out loud. "She's here with us, and you helped save her. She's safe now. The Wolf can't hurt her anymore."

"No…" Phyllis slumped against Jarred. "Not Sarah… *another will be born…*"

And then there was nothing where her mother's presence had been.

"No!" Maddie screamed, forcing healing light into Phyllis.

She struggled to become one with her mother, the way she had when she'd healed Jarred. She fought to bring Sarah with her, to reclaim the power they'd shared just a few minutes ago.

"Mom? Stay with us!"

But it was too late. Maddie and Sarah's link was too bruised and battered. There was too much blood.

"It's…" Maddie sank to the ground, grappling for Jarred. "I can't…"

"No!" Sarah dragged Maddie's hands back to their mother's chest. "We're not giving up! Fix her, Maddie. Heal her!"

The Raven placed a palm on Sarah's shoulder. And then his mind was there, too. Pushing her and Maddie's link deeper, until there was a spark, and then a flicker, and then a flash of healing white. Maddie ignored her exhaustion and searched for the center of Phyllis's injuries. She dug for the miracle that would save her mother's life. A weak, terrified woman who'd finally found the courage to fight for the legacy she'd given her girls…

The gray that Phyllis's consciousness had become pushed back. The absence of light cloaked everything in mist. Until finally, all Maddie could see was the memory of their mother's smiling face, years ago, as she'd held her infant twins in her arms. And their father was there, too. So young and proud. He curled a strong arm around Phyllis—his whole family safe by his side.

"I'll be okay," Phyllis assured them, healthy and happy and no longer afraid. "He's waiting for me. Stay together, my

brave girls, just as you are now. Fight together. Don't ever let each other go . . ."

And with one last near-transparent smile, Phyllis faded away, the gray ebbing until empty mist was all that remained . . .

"No!" Sarah screamed. "Bring her back!"

"She . . . She's gone." Maddie clung to Sarah's hand. She'd never needed her sister more. "She was injured too badly. I couldn't . . . There was no way to—"

"But your jackass boyfriend—you could heal him? Fix this, Maddie. Bring her back. She can't . . . I can't . . . I can't be Death anymore. You have to fix this!"

"I can't," Maddie cried. "We're both too weak. She was hurt too badly. I . . . We can't." What Sarah had said finally registered. "But that doesn't make you—"

"Death? That's what I am. I'm exactly what the Raven made me, so the Wolf could kill my mother. I'm Death, and it's all the Raven's fault!"

Sarah ripped away from Maddie and launched herself at Metting. Maddie collapsed onto the ground, too numb to do anything but stare.

"Let them work it out." Jarred laid Phyllis's body aside and pulled Maddie into his arms. He drew her head to his shoulder and rocked her. Rocked them both. "Just let me hold you, sweetheart."

He felt so good. Maddie wanted his arms around her forever, while she grieved and tried to find a way not to follow her mother into the mist. She wanted to drown in the reality of her and Jarred and never feel fear or pain again.

"It's going to be okay," he promised. "Metting will get through to Sarah. We'll get you both the help you need. We'll fight whatever your mother thought was coming after you next. It doesn't matter. As long as we're together, sweetheart, it's going to be okay."

Together.

Every step of the way, Jarred had refused to let Maddie give up. Until she'd grown strong enough to fight on her own. And even then, he'd raced to be with her. Her soul mate, in both darkness and light. Her hope and her faith. Her center.

She placed her palm over his scarred heart and softly kissed him.

"I'll always be here," she said through tears of acceptance and love. Whatever her legacy was, it wasn't to be alone any more than Sarah's was to be Death. "No matter what, Jarred. I promise I'll never leave you again."

"I'm going to hold you to that." He kissed her back, his mind stroking hers with the calm, soothing peace that had first drawn her to him.

"You bastard!" Sarah shrieked, still slapping at Metting. She raked at his face with her nails. "Look what you did! Look what you made me into. What you made me do!"

"I won't fight you, Sarah." Metting made no move to defend himself. "I won't ever hurt you again. But you have to listen to me. Your mother—"

"Don't talk about her!" Sarah's fist slammed into his nose, but she was too weak to do much damage. "She was just another pawn in your sick plans. You used me, and you used her."

"The Wolf was your puppet master." Metting caught her arm, the next time she swung. "He used us all. And yes, I let it happen. I was blind. But I was trying to protect—"

"Shut up!" Sarah tried to wrestle free and failed.

She drove her knee into his side, but Metting took advantage of her wobbly balance to roll her onto her back.

"Get off me!" Sarah pummeled him with her fists.

Metting caught her hands, immobilizing her with his body.

"Leave her alone." Maddie struggled free of Jarred's hold.

A part of Maddie was still joined with Sarah. She could feel her twin's madness flaring. The blind anger. The guilt. Sara's hatred for the Raven, but for herself most of all.

"Let me go!" Sarah screamed.

"Not until you listen to me." Metting's tone was grim. "You and your sister, you both have to listen. Your mother's right. I saw it in the Wolf's mind when he decided to kill you."

"You saw yourself in his mind." Sarah's knee came up, barely missing Metting's crotch. "And you liked it. Admit it, you deranged bastard. You liked hurting me as much as the Wolf!"

"It killed me, every time you woke another day in the center, in that cage I built for you." Dark emotions seethed beneath Metting's admissions. "And I let my feelings cloud my judgment. I didn't see Ruebens for what he was. I'm begging you, don't do the same thing now. Hate me if you need to, but listen to what your mother tried to tell you. There's more to the Temple legacy than you and your sister know."

Jarred helped Maddie stumble closer, dread leaching the warmth from his touch. Sarah had gone limp beneath her Raven. She was staring into his eyes now.

"That's it, Sarah. Listen to me. Me—the man you once trusted, not the specter you made me into in your dreams. I'm trying to protect you and your sister. I'm fighting to keep your legacy alive and out of the clutches of men like Ruebens."

"The..." Sarah shook her head. "The Wolf is dead. It's over. You killed him. You killed the Wolf and all of his men. It's over..."

"No." Metting's head dropped. His dark hair brushed Sarah's cheek before he sank back on his knees.

Only then did Maddie notice that Metting's soldiers had surrounded them. The clearing was silent and still, except for the storm still rumbling overhead.

"No?" Sarah's mind reached for Maddie. So did her hand.

Their fingers found each other.

"What do you remember about your legacy?" Metting asked.

"Nothing," Maddie said. "We found some old piece of paper, and our mother took it away. Secret powers and twins and good battling evil...I don't remember any more. What did my mother overhear the Wolf's men talking about?"

"It didn't seem to matter," Metting said instead of answering. "Neither of you had ever had any serious relationships. There was no reason to suspect..."

"Suspect what?" Maddie demanded. "What did you see in the Wolf's mind?"

"A little girl, with dark eyes and dark hair and an innocent smile. A child who has no defense against the darkness, because she's alone."

Sarah shivered at his description.

"I saw her, too." Maddie didn't get it. "In the playhouse dream and here in the clearing when the Wolf was controlling our nightmare. But that was Sarah when she was a little girl."

"No, it wasn't Sarah the Wolf was projecting." Metting sounded so sure. "It wasn't Sarah that Ruebens was thinking about when he lost control of your minds and decided to cut his losses. Your mother wasn't talking about Sarah, when she tried to tell you what she'd overheard. When she said, *another will be born.*"

"She's…" Sarah's voice was distant, looking inward. "The little girl…She's part of our legacy."

"What legacy!" Maddie demanded.

"*Twins will be born to the line,*" Sarah recited in the dead Wolf's voice. "*And with them, great good to commence. Or great evil, should darkness descend. Through them, another will come, to spread light far and wide. Or to cast the ultimate shadow on a lost mankind.*"

Maddie shivered, as the words she'd read as a child crawled over her skin.

"She's…" Sarah said in her own voice. She was rocking, just like the little girl had been in their playhouse. Her head dropped to her raised knees. Her hair covered her face. "She's…"

"She's what?" Jarred curled an arm around Maddie as his alarm grew.

No matter what this is, his mind assured her. *I'm here. It will be okay. We'll make sure of it.*

"The Temple legacy speaks of another child." Metting pushed to his feet. His men fell in line behind him. "The Brotherhood have monitored you both since you were born. Watching for any chance that this child might come to be."

"But neither of us have children," Maddie insisted. "There is no child!"

Except there was.

The child whose image had been there, over and over, in her links with Sarah. Links poisoned by the dream programming the Wolf had planted in Sarah's mind.

Maddie could see the little girl now, in Sarah's mind.

Rocking back and forth. But not in their childhood play-house. She was in a laboratory of some kind, surrounded by cold steel and bright lights and no one to love her. There were only dark creatures training her to kill. Forcing her to become what Sarah had barely escaped.

"Oh, my God…" Maddie confronted Sarah's Raven. "How could your brotherhood let this happen!"

"I can only surmise—" Metting began.

"*Surmise?*" Jarred demanded.

The memory of Phyllis's final words returned. *Another will come. It's not over. These people . . . Don't let them do it again . . .*

"Oh, my God," Maddie repeated. There was another little girl out there with special gifts she didn't understand and couldn't possible control. "Trinity?" she asked, the pieces of the puzzle she'd been racing to solve finally clicking into place. "The name of the research center is Trinity…"

A nod seemed to be the only response Metting could manage.

Dream Weaver wasn't dead. The center wasn't through with the Temple legacy. Not even close.

Maddie knelt in front of Sarah. She brushed her sister's bangs aside. Tears were streaming down both their faces. Jarred was there, too. Laying a supportive hand on Sarah's shoulder. His unspoken promise to protect Sarah, no matter what had happened between them. Because she was part of Maddie.

"Trinity," Sarah was repeating, over and over as she continued to rock. "Trinity… Trinity…" Her gaze tracked to Maddie's. "Three… There are three of us… All this time, and I didn't know. What did they do to me? To her? We have to find her," Sarah pleaded. "We can't let her go through what I did."

Jarred tightened his grip on Sarah's shoulder as Metting knelt, too.

"We will find her." Maddie had never meant anything more. "Together." She looked to Jarred and felt the healing light of his love reaching for her, warming her. "From now on, we're not in this alone.

✂ ☐ **YES!**

Sign me up for the Love Spell Book Club and send my
FREE BOOKS! If I choose to stay in the club, I will pay
only $8.50* each month, a savings of $6.48!

NAME: _____

ADDRESS: _____

TELEPHONE: _____

EMAIL: _____

☐ I want to pay by credit card.

☐ **VISA**   ☐ **MasterCard**   ☐ **DISCOVER**

ACCOUNT #: _____

EXPIRATION DATE: _____

SIGNATURE: _____

Mail this page along with $2.00 shipping and handling to:
Love Spell Book Club
PO Box 6640
Wayne, PA 19087
Or fax (must include credit card information) to:
610-995-9274
You can also sign up online at **www.dorchesterpub.com**.
*Plus $2.00 for shipping. Offer open to residents of the U.S. and Canada only.
Canadian residents please call 1-800-481-9191 for pricing information.
If under 18, a parent or guardian must sign. Terms, prices and conditions subject to
change. Subscription subject to acceptance. Dorchester Publishing reserves the right
to reject any order or cancel any subscription.